Rober

Robert Muller, born in Hamburg in 1925, worked as European Manager of *Magnum* in Paris, then for *Picture Post* and other magazines in London, Paris and Munich. He became an interviewer and later Chief Drama Critic for the *Daily Mail*. He has written seven novels, six in English and one in German. He is the author of many original television plays and adaptations (*Man of Straw, Nana, Bel Ami, Vienna 1900*, etc.) and three stage plays. He has twice been the winner of the Grimme Prize in Germany. In the US he has won the Peabody and Christopher Awards. He is married to Billie Whitelaw. They live in Suffolk. He has two daughters and one son.

THE WORLD THAT SUMMER

'A remarkably cool and compelling book which underplays its horrors, and imagines brilliantly the climate of fear which breeds monsters'

Observer

'Robert Muller has written a deeply compassionate, moving and haunting book'

New Statesman

'This is a convincing, moving and at times horrifying novel on a subject about which we still know all too little'
The Times Literary Supplement

'What makes this novel something more than a fictionalised indictment of Nazism is the emphasis Mr Muller has chosen to give it. It is the boys who walk away with the story and the cruel baiting conversations of adolescence are caught to the life; the politics of it all exist only through their warping effects. It is a book the more powerful for its restraint.'

Guardian

'Mr Muller unfolds this grim story with skill and power. This is a novel which pulsates with the drama of real life and will not readily be forgotten'

Irish Independent

Robert Muller

The World that Summer

sceptre

First published in Great Britain in Sceptre Paperbacks in 1994

Sceptre is an imprint of Hodder and Stoughton Paperbacks, a division of Hodder Headline plc.

A John Curtis Book

An earlier version of this novel was published in Great Britain in 1959

British Library C.I.P.

Muller, Robert
  World That Summer
  I. Title
  823.914 [F]

ISBN 0-340-60966-4

Printed and bound in Great Britain for Hodder and Stoughton Ltd a division of Hodder Headline plc by Cox and Wyman Ltd, Reading, Berks. Typeset by Hewer Text Composition Services, Edinburgh.

In memory of my grandmother
Elsa Schickler
(1877–1941)

CHAPTER ONE

The afternoon loitered. The tenements threw blocks of shade into the dusty yard of the tram depot. Hannes and his friends preferred to squat in the sun.

It wasn't all that hot, anyway. It had to be 27 degrees before Hamburg schools were allowed to close. Very soon now the holidays would start.

'Jesse Owens won't win the long-jump,' Rolf Sandmann announced, roughly thumbing his bicycle bell. 'Tell you that for a start. Nor the two hundred neither.'

Hannes knew that nobody would contradict Rolf. From his usual commanding position astride his bicycle, one foot kicking the pedal, the other scraping the ground, Rolf looked up into the sky, crinkling his eyes against the sun in imitation of Fähnleinführer Hinrichs.

'My dad says winning the 100 metres was a swizz,' Rolf continued. 'He'll live to regret that, the black bastard.'

'He's got long legs,' Uwe Schmitt ventured, spitting on one of his grubby knees and washing it with his fingertips. Schmitt had a small cropped head, a cold sore at the corner of his mouth. Hannes did not like to stand too close to him. As he had once told his mother, Schmitt smelled of mice.

'He's a nigger, so he sweats a lot,' Rolf informed the others. 'Everybody knows that.'

'Means they get exhausted quickly, don't it, Rolfie?' Werner Schemel asked obsequiously. 'Bet we can lick the niggers at everything. We'll smash them other countries and all. We'll win the Olympics by miles. Won't we, Rolfie?'

'That's right, cripple,' Rolf approved. 'You stick up for your fatherland.'

Absently throwing out his arm, he caught Werner Schemel by
the sleeve of his shirt and dragged him towards the bicycle. The
metal supports round the polio victim's left leg chimed against
Rolf's back wheel.

'Don't,' Werner Schemel squealed, excited that Rolf showed
him so much attention. 'You'll twist my bleedin' arm off.'

'Match your funny legs then, won't it?'

Whistling the Badenweiler March, Rolf squeezed the peaky
face into the crook of his arm.

Hannes had noticed it before: Rolf made a ceremony of
whistling, fluting his lips into a snout and puffing his cheeks
out as if blowing down a tuba. The indentation between his
short, straight nose and his top lip became a crater, pearled
with sweat. Rolf had a round, cheerful face, his straight
blond hair and innocent blue eyes often reminding Hannes of
early Jungvolk recruiting posters, which had now disappeared
from the hoardings. There was no longer any need for such
publicity.

'We'll win,' Schemel simpered, grinning up at his tormentor.
'We'll win, won't we, Rolfie?'

'Mind his leg, Rolf,' Kloth protested mildly, 'it's getting caught
between your spokes.'

Jürgen Kloth was leaning uncomfortably against the wall. He
was small and dark, with a waxy complexion, and large, startled
brown eyes. His fine black hair fell across his forehead. Though
the same age as the others at the depot, twelve or thirteen,
he looked younger. He was well spoken and neatly dressed;
his parents reputedly owned a café in Eppendorf. Worse, he
also went to the Eppendorfer Realgymnasium, which Hannes
Hacker also attended. The overlap was dangerous. The worlds
of the depot and school had to be kept apart. If Hannes' secret
were discovered at school, it would be all over for him at the
depot as well. Hannes wished Jürgen Kloth would keep away
from the tram-yard where he wasn't wanted.

'What's it to you, Asthma?' Rolf snarled. 'Werner ain't
complaining, are you, boy?'

'Lemmego,' Schemel gurgled, 'please, Rolfie.'

'Please, Rolfie,' Schmitt echoed.

Schemel extricated himself, taking care not to hurt his torturer. Then he lifted his arms like Eimsbüttel's inside-left Rohwedder did whenever he scored a goal.

'Goal!' he yelled.

'Arsehole,' Schmidt grumbled.

'I'll go in goal,' Hannes said, walking towards that part of the wall on which someone had scrawled goalposts. An improvised game of football might distract Rolfie from further persecuting the unfortunate Schemel.

'Too hot,' Rolf decided, watching a tram clank through the yard. 'Besides, a bunch of zeros don't make a team.'

He had a point there. Watching him grunting and puffing his way through the Badenweiler March again, this time accompanying himself with a rhythmic jangle on his bicycle bell, Hannes asked himself why Rolf Sandmann, undoubtedly a leader of men, surrounded himself with such conspicuously feeble friends. Schmidt smelled of mice and had running sores, Schemel was a cripple, Kloth suffered from asthma. Some gang.

Why, Hannes pondered, does he tolerate me? Did he know more than he admitted? Was he perhaps only waiting to pounce?

Kloth pulled a paper bag out of his pocket and proffered it to Rolf.

'Keeps toffees in his pocket and says nothing,' Rolf complained, helping himself. 'Liquorice ones as well.'

Kloth was about to offer the sweets to the others, but Rolf put his hand over the bag.

'Don't give 'em all away,' he advised. 'They're yours, aren't they?'

A portly, red-faced tram-driver, wearing his heavy black uniform with red piping, sweated his way across the yard.

'Old Herrings in Tomatoes,' Rolf jeered.

'That's a good one,' Schemel laughed. 'Old Herrings in Tomatoes.' He cupped his hands over his mouth and clumsily hopped about, his weakened leg scraping over the asphalt. 'Herrings in Tomatoes,' he yelled after the retreating figure. 'Dirty old Herrings in Tomatoes.'

'Who's got the ball?' Hannes asked impatiently.

'We're going to beat them hollow in the riding events,' Rolf prophesied, returning to his favourite topic, the Olympic Games, which had just begun in Berlin. 'My dad saw it in the papers. We'll lick the lot.'

'What about the Swedes?' Kloth asked politely. 'They're good on horses.'

'What about the Swedes?' Rolf mimicked the other's posh accent. 'They're good on horses.'

'Well, they are, aren't they?'

'Well, they are, aren't they?'

Schemel and Schmitt were sprawled on the ground, convulsed with laughter.

'All right then, if you can't talk properly,' Kloth said.

'All right then,' Rolf echoed, 'if you can't talk properly.'

Uwe Schmitt held his stomach with grimy fingers. His gym shoes, with their frayed holes, kicked the air. None of them had ever been to Schmitt's home; nobody knew exactly where it was. Quick and cunning, spurting across the yard like a cat, Schmitt appeared and disappeared, carrying with him the fetid air of the slums. His mother, they said, did filthy things with her lodgers. His father was on the dole and went on long, tearful binges at Sandmann's pub. When confronted, Schmitt denied these things. How could his old man be on the dole? Unemployment didn't exist any more, did it? It said so in the *Hamburger Tageblatt*.

'Well, better be off,' Kloth said despondently, hands deep in his pockets. Something seemed to root him to the spot, preventing him from setting off on the long walk across the asphalt yard.

'Well, better be off,' the others shouted in unison. Hannes turned quickly away. He sometimes felt a bit sorry for Jürgen Kloth.

Rolf Sandmann dismounted from his bicycle, gave it to Schemel to hold, began to box his shadow on the wall. He was fighting, Hannes realised, his boredom.

'We'll win the bleeding boxing gold medals as well,' Rolf sang out as he shadow-boxed. 'We're just as good as Maxie Schmeling.'

'Just as good as Maxie Schmeling,' Kloth parodied his leader, pulling a face to underline his revolt.

'You wait, Kloth.' Rolf narrowed his eyes, continuing to box. 'You wait!'

What for? Wait for what? Hannes leant back against the warm wall, watching his best friend dispensing left hooks. What was so special about Rolf? It wasn't as if he had brains. He often boasted that book-learning was a waste of time. He'd leave school when he was fourteen to take over his old man's pub. No, the only reason they all venerated him was that he, and nobody else at the depot, possessed the Jungvolk knife. The knife made him what he was. He had won it fairly and squarely, too, passing his test with flying colours. Rolfie was entitled to wear the polished knife with the inscription 'Blood and Honour', and wear it he did, in a sheath suspended from the leather belt of his uniform, a razor-sharp hunting knife, with an inlaid mother-of-pearl swastika on the wooden handle. Rolf never allowed anybody at the depot to forget The Knife. He even cleaned his fingernails with it.

'Wish they'd let us go to Berlin to watch the Games,' Schmitt said, scratching his cold sore. 'Our Fähnlein never goes any bloody where interesting.'

'We might go, our lot,' Rolf said grimly. 'Old Hinrichs mentioned it only the other day. He might take us.'

Hannes allowed the lie to pass, as Rolf knew he would.

'Breaking up tomorrow,' Schemel brooded. 'Wish we was going somewhere.'

'I'm going to the seaside,' Kloth volunteered. 'Travemünde.'

'You would,' was Rolf's comment. 'We're not all bleeding profiteers around here.'

'We aren't going anywhere,' Schmitt informed Rolf with pride.

'Week-end in camp is good enough for me,' Rolf stated sternly.

'Me as well,' Schmitt agreed.

'What about you, Hacker?' Kloth looked at Hannes.

'Same as Rolf. We're in the same Fähnlein.'

'Wish they'd take me in the Jungvolk,' Jürgen Kloth grumbled. 'I've tried. They won't take me.'

'I've got asthma,' Schmitt and Schemel chorused.

Hannes felt embarrassed. If only Kloth wouldn't keep irritating Rolfie with that posh accent of his.

Rolf suppressed a yawn. 'We're sick and tired of your asthma, mate. Talk about feeling sorry for yourself. Werner here, he's a cripple. He don't bang the bloody drum about it all the time. Anyone want to play Traitors?'

'Traitors?' Schmitt asked alertly. 'Never played that before, Rolfie.'

'Just need the right people,' Rolf mused.

Hannes watched Rolf uneasily. Rolf was good at inventing new games on the spur of the moment. His games came in various guises but usually turned out to be variations on one theme: an enemy or informer or traitor was arrested and interrogated, then exposed with the aid of secret information to which only Rolf had access.

Once Rolf and Hannes had collaborated on a secret code designed to catch and destroy an invisible enemy. Another time Rolf had devised a game of observing local girls and keeping a dossier about suspicious associations and meetings. The dossier was never written. Then, for a whole week last spring, the depot gang had been encouraged to report to Rolf all owners of beards. The 'beavers' had to be sorted into their agents and ours. The operation never advanced to this stage; Rolf tired of his games almost as quickly as he invented them. After a villain had been caught, questioned and punished, he lost interest.

To Hannes' relief, the potentially dangerous 'Traitors' never got under way.

'Here they come,' Rolf groaned, shading his eyes, 'the Hoheluft gang.'

'Dorn's in charge,' Schmitt confirmed, in evident awe of the three lads strolling into the tram yard. 'Quick, through the archway.'

'Coward,' Rolf jeered. 'You bugger off if you want. We're staying. We're not afraid of those Jews!'

'Jews?' Hannes asked. 'How do you know?'

'You don't know they're not,' Rolf snapped. 'We're staying put. Let me handle this.'

The three newcomers approached slowly. Dorn, their blond, ferret-faced leader wore full Hitler Youth uniform. His two minions were in mufti, except for their black Jungvolk caps. They wore them rakishly back to front.

Dorn was widely feared, estimated to be sixteen and reputed to go with girls.

'I've heard he takes them down the Isebek in a rowing boat,' Rolf had told Hannes. 'Cuddles them and that. Dirty sod.'

'What are you tram dwarfs up to?' Dorn asked Rolf, acknowledging him as the leader of the depot regulars. He jingled some money in his pocket and chortled without apparent enjoyment. Dorn was noted for his sinister and mirthless chuckle. He liked to show off his teeth. They were bright yellow which turned to a slimy green where the teeth joined the gums. Dorn must be suffering from bad toothache. Hannes couldn't imagine teeth like that not hurting horribly. To show his indifference to Dorn, he took out his mouth-organ and began to suck it pensively.

'We don't need your lot around here,' Schmitt said militantly. 'Sod off to Hoheluft.'

'That's right,' Rolf wheeled round the hostile gang in ever-widening circles. 'You sod off back where you came from.'

Suddenly he had pedalled out of the yard, whistling aggressively. Dorn chortled.

'Abandoned by your leader.' He often attempted a clipped military accent. 'You're all under arrest.'

'What for? We done nothing.'

It wouldn't have surprised Schmitt had the Hoheluft gang marched them off there and then.

'Bleeding little hero,' Dorn chuckled. 'Don't teach you much in the Jungvolk, do they?'

'His father's Blockwarden,' Schemel informed Dorn. 'He ain't afraid of you.'

'That's it!' Dorn yelled. ''tention!'

Without another murmur, the four boys fell in.

'Put that thing away, Hacker!'

Hannes hastily slipped the mouth-organ into his pocket.

'At ease,' Dorn said. 'Saw your sister out last night.'

'She's too old for you,' Hannes grinned proudly; one of Dorn's lieutenants had failed to suppress a guffaw.

'Not so much lip, midget,' Dorn commanded. 'And another thing. Tell her to stay away from Georg Koch. If I catch them at it again, I'll deliver the message personally. Tell her that, OK?'

'I'll tell her,' Hannes looked flushed.

'Know all about it, don't you?' Dorn needled him. Know what "intercourse" means, Hacker?'

Hannes nodded.

'Well, what?'

Hannes could hear Schmitt tittering.

'Means people eating together.'

'People eating together, is it?' Dorn repeated sardonically. 'Well, Hacker, see your sister don't come home with a fat belly one day – from eating together too much . . .'

They were all laughing now. Schemel was whinnying with delight. Hannes felt sure the cripple didn't know any more about these things than he did.

'You tell her, Hacker,' Dorn said. 'Erika, isn't it? We know all about her friend. So watch it.' He showed his teeth again. 'Now then, you bunch of Shirley Temples, let's hear you salute.'

Unanchored by the absence of their leader, the members of the gang looked dubious.

'Don't you recognise a member of the Hitler Youth?' Dorn barked. 'Don't they teach you anything in the Jungvolk?'

He clicked his heels together. His right arm shot out, his left clutched the buckle of his belt.

'Heil Hitler!' he shouted.

'Heil Hitler!' the boys shouted back obediently.

'Louder,' Dorn commanded.

'Heil Hitler!'

'Can't hear them, can you, Karl-Heinz?' Blood had shot up into his quivering face, as he consulted one of his lieutenants.

'Heil Hitler!' the youngsters roared.

This time Dorn seemed almost satisfied.

'They'll never send you bleedin' lot to Nuremberg,' he told them bleakly. 'Can't even make yourself heard. Pathetic.'

Herrings in Tomatoes, the red-faced tram conductor, was padding through the asphalt yard, on his way to the trams.

'Drilling 'em, Sergeant?' he asked the boy in uniform and grinned understandingly. 'That's the style.'

'Shirley Temple brigade, dismiss!' Dorn turned and began to walk away casually. 'Come along, men!'

The two minions followed at a discreet distance.

'Dorn's going to be a big shot in the Hitler Youth,' Schmitt whispered ardently, once they were out of earshot.

'What did Rolf want to run away for?' Jürgen Kloth asked quietly.

'Rolfie had his reasons,' Schemel told him.

'Leave Rolfie alone,' Schmitt added. 'What's it got to do with you?'

'I'll tell Rolfie what you said, Kloth!'

Schemel limped off purposefully.

'You wouldn't do that, Werner!'

'Can't you ever keep your stupid mouth shut,' Hannes told him. 'You know what Schemel's like about Rolf.'

'All I said . . .'

'I heard you. We all heard you.'

Trudging slowly across the yard, Hannes kicked a big stone into one of the tram lines. He stopped, hesitated for a moment, then went back to the rail to pick up the stone. He looked over his shoulder and met Schmitt's gaze. The boy who smelled of mice had caught him in the act. He was sure to tell Rolfie. It was sabotage.

CHAPTER TWO

Walking home, Hannes lingered in the draughty arched passage that connected Falkenried with the tenement's inner courtyard. The walls were scrawled over with faded demands for 'action' and 'national awakening' and with chalk drawings which Rolf said were filthy, though he couldn't, or wouldn't, say why.

Hannes lived with his parents and sister on the fourth floor of one of the bleak slabs of concrete that towered like guards over the depot. The side of the tenement facing the tram-yard was windowless and painted over with huge coloured advertisements for Persil and Imi, mottled and faded with time. Hannes was glad the windows looked out on the street: his mother couldn't see him when he was down in the depot with the gang. Fortunately, she was not as nosey as Frau Schemel, who liked to lurk in the yard, pretending to be on her way to the wash-house or beating carpets. In reality she was only spying on her Werner.

Their flat was small and dingy, like all the flats in the block. Unlike the others, though, it didn't smell of vegetable soup. The Hackers had two rooms, a bedroom for his parents, and a sitting room, now never used during the day. Here his father kept his old books, and he and Erika had their beds. Erika, seventeen and a shorthand-typist, often complained about this arrangement, but she refused to follow her father's suggestion that she sleep in the kitchen. It was in the kitchen that the family lived.

Hannes remembered the many other flats they had inhabited, but could no longer distinguish between them. In the composite 'old' flat preserved in his memory all the rooms were large and flooded with sunlight in the mornings. He and Erika had a room each, and his mother didn't spend all day in the kitchen. He had an image of her, sitting on a sofa in a white, waistless dress, with strings of pearls hanging down her front and some sort of ribbon tied around her head, giving tea to his father's office friends. Her hands, he recalled, had been very white. She had worn rings and talked very animatedly.

Nowadays it hurt Hannes to look at his mother. She had become a part of the tenement flat, an animal adopting the colours of its surroundings. Hannes often had an urge to protect and console her, but she did not seem to want his sympathy, and because of this he did not like to ask for hers. Whenever he wanted to talk she was either scrubbing the kitchen floor, or wanting to lie down and sleep off the effects of her headache tablets. Or so it seemed to Hannes.

Perhaps they were all asking too much of her. Yet when anybody offered help she resisted. Was she trying to punish herself for something she had done? Hannes no longer bothered to help. As for Erika, she was usually at her office or out for the evening with her friend. Papa, when not drinking at Sandmann's, liked to boast that he had never boiled an egg or washed up a plate.

His father was never more pleased than when his mother called him a Bohemian. Hannes associated this with the opera his grandmother had once taken him to hear. It wasn't difficult for him to imagine his father stalking about in velvet jacket and beret, or idling in cafés, singing with girls.

In the days when he still worked for the *Hamburger Anzeiger*, his father had been a bit of a dandy, sporting a cane and, whenever he took them boating on the Alster on Sundays, wearing a straw hat pressed on top of unruly red hair.

As he gazed at his parents across the supper table now, Hannes was reminded that the alchemy that had changed his mother was also at work on his father. He sat wrapped in a shabby mauve bathrobe, the towelled collar turned up as if part of a smart dressing-gown. He wore it, Hannes knew, to protect his only remaining good suit. This he needed to keep his badly paid job at the glove-counter of Tietz, the department store on the Jungfernstieg. His ginger moustache, upturned ends once elegantly waxed, now drooped. He fingered the ends incessantly, as if to reassure himself they were still there.

Briefly, Hannes warmed to the thought that his father had begun to age more quickly than his mother, but glancing across at her, he felt familiar pangs of rage and shame. The skin under Mama's eyes was puffy and grey; blackheads were accumulating around her nostrils and near the roots of her dark hair. She would always be five years older than Papa. Over the years the gap could only widen.

'They've arrested a tailor in Lüneburg.' Erika didn't look up from her magazine. 'Racial defilement.'

There was nothing wrong with his sister. No wonder Dorn had noticed her. There wasn't a better looking girl in the block. She had Papa's restless green eyes, the delicate, bird-like features of her mother. Her skin was without blemish, she wore her wavy auburn hair long. It fell over her eyes when she bent down to read.

Nobody reacted to Erika's statement. Mama turned to Hannes to ask where he had spent the afternoon.

'Nowhere,' he told her, munching his cheese sandwich.

'I know where he goes,' Erika's face remained hidden behind *Die Koralle*.

'Oh?' Hannes asked innocently. 'Where's that, then?'

'Plays in that tram depot with Rolf Sandmann and his louts.'

'At least I keep to my own sex.'

'What's that supposed to mean?'

The two vertical lines that appeared between Erika's eyebrows whenever she frowned made her look like a Teddy-bear.

'You got a rotten reputation with the kids down there.'

'That's quite enough, boy,' his father said, stuffing a cigarette into a horn holder, trophy of his days as a *feuilleton* journalist. He never addressed either Erika or Hannes by name. It was always 'girl' or 'boy'. Did he avoid calling them by their proper names because he did not want to be reminded that he was responsible for a daughter of seventeen and a son of twelve? It had been different when they were small, when he could rock them on his knee to show them his name in the paper. Now he obviously thought of them, 'the children', as a burden.

'An illiterate,' his father exclaimed, throwing down his paper. 'Horvath! The office boy! Brought me my morning coffee! Bad coffee! Asked me once if *Wilhelm Tell* was by Goethe or Schiller.'

'And you said "Rossini".'

'Don't be cheeky to your father,' Mama said.

Papa folded his paper meticulously and puffed through his holder. He had decided to ignore his son's impertinence.

'They could have let me go on writing my stuff under another name. Still. Little Horvath is a party member, so anything goes.'

'Dorn's got a message for you, Erika,' Hannes said.

'Who's Dorn? Don't know any Dorn.'

'One of the boys.'

'What boys?'

'Down at the tram depot. Says they know all about you and Georg.'

'Who's "they"?'

'Search me.'

'It might be important.' Erika frowned. 'What did they mean by "know"?'

'You look like an old Teddy again,' Hannes chortled. He lifted the sports' page from his father's newspaper, started to concentrate on the latest results from the Olympic Games. It looked bad. Germany was winning everything, as usual.

Erika shook her head in exasperation. 'Can't you get Hannes to stop playing with those tykes down there, Meta?'

Erika thought it modern to call her mother by her first name.

'He's got to try and make the best of it, Erika,' Mama said. 'Who do you want him to play with?'

'I don't *play*,' Hannes said. 'For God's sake.'

'He doesn't have to be like them.' Erika turned to Hannes. 'Just remember what you are,' she said. 'Don't think you're one of them, 'cause you're not.'

'No good taking that attitude,' Papa told her. 'He's got to try to make the best of things. They can't go on forever. They've had three years. I'll give them another two.'

All very well, Hannes thought, they can't get at you. You're an Aryan. You're clean.

'He oughtn't to be in the Jungvolk at all,' Erika brushed a strand of hair from her eye. 'It's all wrong.'

'Youth organisations are all much of a muchness,' Papa said. 'Wanderbirds, Boy Scouts, Jungvolk – keeps kids off the streets. A bit of discipline is a good thing for a lad.'

'Not if the lad's got a Jewish mother,' Erika said.

'Dorn and his bunch don't scare me.' Hannes surveyed the line-up for the 5,000-metre race and pencilled in the likely winner. 'They'll never find out about us. Not from me, they won't.'

'Just be careful, Hannes.' His mother touched his arm. He noticed that her fingers were swollen and red. 'Never take chances. Always think before you speak. Don't forget how cunning they are. Never tell them anything you hear at home. Never get close to anybody. In our position we can't afford friends.'

'You're giving the boy an anxiety complex.' Papa blew out a perfect smoke-ring and watched it disintegrate. 'He goes to the Eppendorfer Realgymnasium, doesn't he? He's in no trouble there, is he? They can come and examine my family tree any time they like. The Hackers go back to the Hundred Years' War. My grandfather's grandfather fought with Frederick the Great at Leuthen. You still don't understand these people, Meta. They're impressed by that sort of thing. They're all snobs with mountainous inferiority complexes. Upstarts all.'

'You make them sound human,' Erika said. 'They chucked you off the *Anzeiger* quick enough.'

Ludwig Hacker ran his tongue over his lips.

'You don't appreciate the subtleties of behaviour involved in a situation like that, my girl. There are subterranean networks of jealousy and envy operating on a newspaper. A lot of people on the *Anzeiger* thought I was too much of an intellectual. The fact that my mother-in-law's name is Rosenteich was just an excuse. In any case, my dismissal was utterly illegal . . .' He waved his holder about, his eyes darted nervously around the kitchen walls. 'They'll come crawling to me before long. You'll see. A few more weeks of Horvath's rubbish and I'll have them on their knees . . .'

He turned to switch on the radio. After he fiddled with the knobs, there came, through crackling and whistling, the strains of the Internationale.

'Moscow!' Ludwig Hacker announced with a compere's flourish, and turned up the volume.

'Not so loud, Ludwig,' Hannes' mother begged. 'The Rohdes next door . . .'

'Don't know why you bother,' Erika demanded. 'You never believe a word they say.'

'Of course I don't. They're as bad as the Nazis. Worse.'

Erika shot out of her chair. Before Papa could stop her, she had pulled out the electric plug.

'Don't you be brave at somebody else's expense!'

Hannes recoiled a little, certain his father would slap Erika's face.

'The house is crawling with spies. They'd denounce their own mothers for a free drink at Sandmann's. You should know. You're down there often enough.'

Papa did not slap Erika's face. He just got up and slipped off his bathrobe. Then he picked up the jacket that hung over the back of his chair, brushed it meticulously and walked out of the kitchen. He might have been walking through the foyer of a luxury hotel, dispensing tips.

After the front door had closed behind him, Mama turned to Erika:

'How *can* you talk to your father like that?'

'He only wanted an excuse to go down to Sandmann's,' Erika was frowning again. 'It's not *he* who'd get it in the neck if somebody heard us listening to Radio Moscow.'

'You're too impulsive, Erika.'

Hannes watched his mother rise heavily, her hands supporting her weight as she prised herself up from her chair.

Just like an old woman, he thought. Once again he felt rage boiling up inside him.

*   *   *

He was still wide awake in his bed when Erika came home just
before midnight.

'Where you been?' He fell into the hushed tones they
automatically adopted in the darkness of their bedroom.

'Why aren't you asleep?'

'You been out with Georg?'

'Yes.'

'Where did you go?'

'Out.'

'What do you do when you go out with Georg?'

'None of your business. High time you were asleep.' He could
hear her undressing at the far end of the room, then slipping
on her nightgown. She opened the sideboard to take out her
eiderdown.

'You hurt Papa's feelings,' he said. 'Again.'

'Can't help that. He's a fool.'

'How would you feel if none of your friends wanted to see
you any more?'

'I wouldn't stand up for *them* for a start.'

'He doesn't really. And, you've got to admit, he's not strict
like some fathers. He doesn't mind you going out with Georg.'

'Doesn't care, you mean.'

Hannes heard his sister walk barefoot over the lino, then
crawl into bed, drawing the eiderdown up to her face.

'Does he kiss you and that? Georg, I mean?'

'Nothing to do with you. Think of something nice and go
to sleep.'

The bed groaned as she turned round. He heard her breathing
in emulation of sleep; it meant he was to keep quiet. He thought
of the shadows he had often seen enlaced in the darkness of the
arched passage late at night, double-headed shadows . . .

'Erika?'

'What now?'

'Go to the pictures?'

'Yes.'

'Capitol?'

'Oh, *please*. I've got to go to work tomorrow. Just because
your holidays start tomorrow . . .'

'What was showing?'

'*Queen Christina*. Greta Garbo.'

'Love picture?'

'Not really. Historical.'

'Full Supporting Programme? Donald Duck? Laurel and Hardy?'

'Just the Newsreel.'

'Jesse Owens? Olympics?'

'We got in too late.'

In the street below some drunks were bellowing a popular song. According to his father's paper, Germany had beaten Hungary 23 to 0 at handball. You couldn't be sure, though. They lied about everything. If Rolf Sandmann had read that score he'd never stop crowing. Hannes closed his eyes. It was no good, sleep wouldn't come.

'Erika . . . about Georg . . . Is he . . . is he working, you know, *underground*?'

He heard her move and sigh.

'Don't ask.'

'I wish I could do something as well.'

'It's not a kid's game.'

'You hold meetings in a cellar?'

'Don't talk rubbish.' Erika sat up in bed. 'Listen, Hannes. What did that what's-his-name say about Georg?'

'Dorn? Just said they knew all about him.'

'Who're *they*?'

'I don't know. Hoheluft gang, I expect.'

'Can't you tell me more?'

'Don't know any more. Forget it. He's a bit too keen on you, that Dorn. Wants to – you know.' He giggled. 'Got a bad reputation, Dorn. And vampire teeth.'

She sighed with exasperation.

'You're no better than that scum you hang around with. Next thing you'll be helping them to smash Jewish shop windows.'

He turned his face to the wall. Why did she always lose her temper? He hadn't done anything wrong . . .

I hope we lose at everything, he thought, wrapping his bedding around him. I hope the niggers win the lot.

CHAPTER THREE

'Think of it as a pyramid,' Professor Helmut Waldmeister spoke
at dictation speed. 'The unalterable natural law of racial hier-
archy: at the summit of evolution the German and Scandinavian
races, Siegfried's heirs. Descending from this peak, we come
step by step upon successively poorer stock, until, right at the
end, at the bottom, among the primeval slime . . .'

'Pardon, sir?' a high voice piped up.

'Primeval slime,' Professor Waldmeister repeated patiently,
while the boys' pens scratched over the pages of their exercise
books. 'P-R-I-M-E-V-A-L . . .' He cleared his throat and went on:
'. . . among the primeval slime we find the collective muck of
gipsies, Jews, negroes and their like . . .'

'Negroes and their like,' Hannes scribbled. He thought
of Jesse Owens running the one hundred metres at 10.3
seconds.

The sun poured through the arched windows of the class-
room, forming white shafts of dancing dust. Next to Hannes
sat a fat-faced boy named Hanff, who surreptitiously rolled small
olive-coloured bread pellets. Professor Waldmeister glanced at
his wrist-watch. His elongated top lip quivered in anticipation
of some unknown pleasure; behind thick, rimless glasses, his
eyes glittered.

'Before I continue,' the Professor said, 'I had better make
sure that we have no gipsies, Jews or negroes here to whom
my remarks might give offence. Hands up all gipsies, Jews and
negroes.'

While the laughing subsided, Hannes guessed that the
Realgymnasium's Professor of History had come to the end

of his notes and was now aiming to amuse rather than inform. Professor Waldmeister relied on a pleasing compound of racial theory, lavatory jokes and contemporary asides, to achieve popularity and discipline. Such was the success of this formula that many of the school's older masters had begun to copy it. The Professor pretended to be genuinely astonished when no hand was raised.

'Excellent. Then we need not mince words, need we? Anybody read this morning's leader in the *Fremdenblatt* by any chance?'

Without waiting for answers to his questions, Professor Waldmeister began to comment enthusiastically on new laws concerning the transfer of certain Jewish businesses to Aryan owners.

'Not all Jews are wealthy, of course,' he explained. 'Some are poor and addicted to ghettoes of quite indescribable squalor. Indeed, indifference to all basic standards of hygiene makes this gentry detectable from one side of the Alster to the other.'

The local reference reaped the Professor renewed laughter.

'We mustn't forget though, that rich, or poor, Jews are guests of the fatherland, uninvited guests moreover, and one cannot allow house-guests to walk away with the silver, can one? *Can one, Hacker?*'

Professor Waldmeister had a notoriously quick eye for absconding attentions.

'No, sir,' Hannes said, rising.

'No, sir, what?'

'One can't allow house-guests to walk off with the silver.'

'I'd like you to tell the class what you find so fascinating out there, Hacker. Are you a student of cloud formations?'

'No, sir.'

Hannes' face coloured. All around him he heard derisive laughter.

'You look a bit sleepy to me, Hacker,' Professor Waldmeister said, glasses flashing. 'You shouldn't go to so many operas. Sit.'

Numbed, Hannes sat down. He could hear Professor Waldmeister's voice droning on; the teacher had become an indistinct blob by the window. That he should ask him to repeat his remarks about the silver could be explained away. His attention had been concentrated on Jesse Owens and the hundred metres. But that reprimand about the opera was deeply sinister. He had let his grandmother take him to the opera because it was so unlikely she would ever meet any of his school or depot friends there. And now this! Abandoning all pretence of listening, Hannes let his mind cast around for some harmless interpretation of the reprimand. His eyes focused on his desk, at the deep gashes filled in with blue ink, the neat row of pellets Hanff had assembled in the groove intended for pens. His panic mounted. *No harmless interpretation was possible.* Professor Waldmeister had seen him at the opera! He wished to indicate that for some reason he did not approve. Perhaps he had already made discreet enquiries . . .

The curtain rose on a vivid nightmare. Professor Waldmeister was interrogating him to amuse the class:

Who were you with at the opera, Hacker? *I was there with my grandmother, sir.* Your what? *My grandmother, sir.* (*Laughter.*) Who is your grandmother, Hacker? *Pardon, sir?* What's her name? *Her name, sir?* Yes, Hacker, your grandmother's name. *Oh, her name. Her name's Rosa Rosenteich, sir.* Rosa Rosenteich? *Rosa Rosenteich* . . .

While the two words indicating both crime and confession echoed in his mind, Hannes recalled his interview two years ago with Dr Gilbrecht, the headmaster. Dr Gilbrecht had a worried, desiccated face; thin strands of hair were carefully combed across the flecked dome of his head. He sat behind a big desk in a panelled study and ground his fingertips together. Though his watery eyes were upon Hannes, his attention seemed to be centred elsewhere. He spoke in a dry, brittle voice, only just audible above the shrieks and shouts that wafted up from the playground.

'I see from your father's letter that he appreciates our little difficulty,' he was saying. 'I expect he told you that we have known each other for some time. His newspaper and the school have organised many a . . .' His voice trailed away and he began anew. 'The fact that he is – er – Aryan, and that you have passed

all your examinations for a secondary education mitigate, shall
we say, in the matter's favour. Now then . . .' He leant across
his desk, compressed pallid lips and batted his eyelids rapidly in
what could have been interpreted as a wink. 'We look like a fine,
upstanding German boy. Let's always remember that's what we
are and be proud of it. Eh? You follow?' He sat back and began
grinding his finger-tips again. 'You can start here next term, but
it's an experiment; any trouble or misdemeanour and — ' The
headmaster also left that sentence unfinished. 'I shall write to
your father. You may stand down.'

Hannes considered Dr Gilbrecht to be the guardian of his
secret; a bargain had been struck. He had done his best to
honour that bargain. He knew himself to be a better than
average pupil, but strove for no distinction. He worked hard in
subjects he disliked, biology and history, made no effort to excel
in those that came to him easily – arithmetic, sports, music. As
his mother often reminded him: what mattered was never to be
conspicuous or provocative, never to let other people know what
you were thinking. To exercise self-restraint was the secret of
staying undetected.

Only once had he become involved in an 'incident'. He had
dawdled one winter morning on the way to school, flinging
snowballs at passing lorries. He arrived eight minutes late.
He had been 'sent in' to report to Dr Gilbrecht who personally
punished offenders against school discipline.

Hannes listened, head bowed, as Dr Gilbrecht lectured him
and another late-comer on the virtue of punctuality and the
traditions of a school that had sent many great names out into the
world. Suddenly Dr Gilbrecht had pointed to Hannes' shoes.

'Don't you clean your shoes every morning, Hacker?'

'They got wet in the slush, sir.'

'Answer my question.'

'Yes, sir.'

'Look at my shoes, Hacker.'

Hannes had glanced down at the headmaster's shoes – narrow, pointed leather shapes, their orange surfaces polished so
brilliantly that not only the light from the windows was reflected
in them, but the square frames.

The offenders promised their sins would not be repeated. Hannes' hand touched the door-handle, but Dr Gilbrecht called him back.

'I do not ever want to see you in here again, Hacker,' Hannes heard him intone. 'Is that absolutely clear?'

For a long time afterwards, Hannes had been haunted by that voice. He had betrayed Dr Gilbrecht's trust. Whenever the headmaster subsequently passed him in the corridors and pretended not to see him, Hannes felt relief and gratitude.

A bell rang out shrilly. Hannes was brought back into the present. The period was over. He rose to his feet with the others. The Professor of History brought his heels smartly together. Like an orchestra conductor at the start of a performance, he looked around imperiously to make sure no eye was distracted. Then he rapped out the customary salute to the Führer. The boys roared back at him. Hannes had already learnt that if you felt scared it helped to shout louder than anybody else.

At the end-of-term show, Hannes found himself sitting next to Hanff again. In the assembly hall's cleft darkness, the other boy pulled a catapult out of his pocket. From time to time, he projected pellets at selected targets.

The film, the famous documentary of a Nuremberg Party Rally, began mysteriously, with revolving cloud masses which finally revealed an aeroplane in flight. Like some hero of legend, the Führer was riding through the sky. *Why had Professor Waldmeister asked him about cloud formations? Why had he gone out of his way to mention opera?* Hannes knew that if he failed to find out before school broke up, his holiday would be ruined.

The Führer was standing in an open car, driving in triumph through festive streets. Hannes recognised the latest Mercedes-Benz model, not a bad job, though he preferred the low-slung new Auto-Union racers. To drive through Europe winning big races like Rosemeyer or Caracciola – that was the life he wanted after leaving school. Professor Waldmeister couldn't stop him from becoming a racing-driver, not even if he *had* seen him at the opera. For that you didn't have to matriculate at the Eppendorfer Realgymnasium.

The car passed cheering women and children, their heads thrust forward to catch a glimpse of their Führer. Little girls threw bouquets of flowers in his path.

Beside Hannes, Hanff was concentrating his bombardment on a small bespectacled boy named Grötchen, whom everybody called Brötchen – sandwich. Grötchen was a safe target. If he protested, someone in the row behind would simply clout him over the head. After a while Grötchen ignored both bombardment and clouts. Complaints were of no avail. No master would place himself in a position of appearing to protect the weak against the strong. A really progressive master like Professor Waldmeister claimed that mild baiting of weaklings provided a healthy temporary outlet for emotions the new society was learning to harness and deploy.

It was night. The Führer had arrived at his hotel. People thronged through the street below, flinging out their arms, shouting in chorus that they wanted to see their Führer. He finally did appear. Then a number of politicians made speeches.

Hanff's supply of pellets was exhausted. He squirmed in his chair, stretching out his legs under the seat in front of him. Hannes sympathised with his boredom. If it had to be a propaganda film, they might have selected an exciting one, like the previous term's offering, *Hitlerjunge Quex*. It had a thrilling chase at the end with the young hero ending up in a pool of blood, stabbed in the back by a Communist. He was dying so that the fatherland could live. Comrades marched on into a sunny future, singing:

> *Our flag flies in the van*
> *Our flag is the new era.*
> *We are marching for Hitler*
> *Through night and dread*
> *Carrying the flag of youth*
> *For freedom and bread.*

Hannes had seen a lot of his class-mates cry that time, though they denied it afterwards. As Fähnleinführer Hinrichs always told his charges: a German boy never cries.

Now it was daylight again. The rally began, the Führer's car travelled along endless columns of Jungvolk faces, all reminding him of Rolf Sandmann. Hannes stretched himself. If the film went on for much longer, he would be late for his weekly lunch with his grandmother. Veal stew with lemon cream for dessert she'd promised him . . . Could it have been *after* the opera that he had been detected? His grandmother had taken him to the Automat restaurant that adjoined the opera house for some layer-cake and lemonade.

His attention returned to the screen. The projectionist had turned up the sound. *Triumph of the Will* was finally moving towards its climax. The Führer ended his final speech amid a storm of cheers.

That was it. At last the lights came on. The boys rubbed their eyes, slapped each other across bare thighs, then lined up to troop out into the dazzling sunshine of the playground.

'First rate, I thought,' said Jürgen Kloth as they waited for Dr Gilbrecht to dismiss school for the summer holidays. 'Wish they'd send us to Nuremberg for a change.'

All the boys in Hannes' form were in the Jungvolk, except Hügli, who was Swiss, and three others who were ineligible for health reasons. On Youth Days, when Jungvolk members were excused from attending school, Hügli and the 'palefaces', as they were called, were kept in class for special instruction in 'civics' by Professor Waldmeister.

'You'd be excused, wouldn't you, Kloth?'

Hannes was surprised but not displeased by the savagery of his own voice. He blinked up against the light, the way he had seen Rolf Sandmann blink.

'They might let me join the Jungvolk next year,' Kloth said. 'The doctor said I might get better by then.'

'I bet,' Hannes said. Kloth's ambitions did not interest him. He was hungry and hot and he had failed to detect Professor Waldmeister among the other teachers at the end of the playground.

Dr Gilbrecht was sending the pupils off with courteous good

wishes. He asked them to remember to disport themselves as
proud members of German youth, to remember the traditions
for which the school stood. His faint voice did not carry far.
Strands of hair, usually so neatly plastered across his head,
were blown about by a breeze and stood up in limp wisps.
Finally the headmaster raised his arm in a half-hearted salute
and stepped back. His place was taken by the progressive new
sports master, Herr Bussart, who wore a freshly pressed SA
uniform and spoke through a megaphone. In a high clerical voice
he declared the term ended. Then he commanded the school to
stand to attention.

'Our great Führer,' he shouted, 'Sieg — '

'Heil!' the school roared back.

'Sieg — '

'Heil!'

'Sieg — '

'Heil!'

Behind him the other masters rose. Hannes registered with
relief that Professor Waldmeister was among them. Herr
Bussart gave a signal. Masters and students joined to sing
the first two verses of the National Anthem. *Our country above
all, above all in the world* . . . Precisely four beats after the
sounding of the final note, they launched into the Horst Wessel
song. *Hold high the flag and close the ranks, the Storm Troopers
are marching!*

Hannes sang lustily. It was a good tune. Too bad one had
to hate it. After dismissal, Jürgen Kloth fell into step with
Hannes.

'I wanted to ask you something . . .' he began.

'I'm looking for somebody just now.'

Hannes did not slow his pace. Kloth got on his nerves.
Besides, he needed to talk to Professor Waldmeister. He
was standing by the school's iron gates chatting to a group of
older boys.

'I'm going to do a puppet play,' Kloth said. 'I've got my own
model theatre at last.'

'So what?'

'I thought we might learn off a marionette play by heart and put it on after school hours next term. I've got loads of puppets. Just need somebody to help me. It's fun once you get interested. I thought you might . . .'

'Can't do it,' Hannes told him briefly. 'Find yourself some-one else.'

He ran towards the gates, leaving Kloth standing. Kloth was a nuisance, always trying to worm himself into his good graces. He was also a threat.

Hannes came face to face with Professor Waldmeister.

'Sir, can I see you a minute, sir?'

'I'm leaving for a seaside holiday with the family,' Professor Waldmeister informed him with end-of-term jocularity. 'Should your questions concern your education, you're going to be unlucky!'

He cackled contentedly, showing two pelmets of pink gum and long, rather narrow teeth. Hannes noticed, not for the first time, that Professor Waldmeister, with his long top lip, prominent gums, and sparse, bristly hair, resembled a camel. Looking up at the teacher, he had to resist an almost irresistible impulse to giggle. As he began to speak, though, his heart pounded.

'It's only what you said in class, sir.'

'In class? I say a lot of things in class.' Over Hannes' head, the Professor exchanged pink smiles with passing students.

'It's about · . . about what you said . . .'

'Come along, I haven't got all day . . .'

Hannes swallowed. Had he lost his head completely, challenging Professor Waldmeister like this? His mother would never forgive him, if she knew. He had made a horrible mistake. There was no way out now.

'. . . about me being at the opera, sir,' he said lamely.

'Ah, yes, I remember. You weren't paying attention, I suggested you were tired because you were always going to the opera . . .'

'That's right, sir.'

'Well?'

'Well, sir, I don't go to the opera . . . I mean . . .'

'Rubbish! Of course you go to the opera!' The teacher's voice was tinged with irritation. 'Saw you there with my own eyes. Hopping down from the Upper Circle!'

So it *was* true. Hannes felt his stomach melting. Might as well be hung for a sheep as a lamb, he thought.

'Was I alone when you saw me, sir?'

'Alone? How should I know? I expect you were with your mother, or your aunt. It was *Carmen*, wasn't it? Beautiful work! Powerful! *Toreador – Toreado-o-or* . . .' Professor Waldmeister was conducting jauntily. 'A rather mediocre Don José, I thought. Let you into a secret, Hacker. I'm rather fond of opera myself. But one shouldn't overdo it at your age. The open air, Hacker! Marching through our beautiful countryside! That's the ticket!'

Professor Waldmeister turned away. Two masters stood behind him, claiming his attention.

'Yes, sir, thank you, sir.' Hannes wheeled round gratefully, bolted through the playground, flew up the steps of the school-house, hurried along the corridors into his class-room. Fooled the silly old sod, he sang to himself, doesn't know a damn thing! *Toreador, Toreado-o-or!*

He lifted the flap of his desk to collect his books, stuffed them into his leather satchel, thrust his arms through the loops, loudly shut the desk. Then he ran back into the corridor; soon he was lost in the stream of boys flowing out into the white sunshine. He felt so relieved, he was whistling the Horst Wessel song.

CHAPTER FOUR

Hannes' Friday visit to his grandmother was a ceremony with which nobody was allowed to interfere. His Jungvolk unit never met on Fridays, and when Rolf Sandmann asked him why he 'funked' the depot on a Friday, Hannes invented troublesome relations who had to be visited every week.

The ritual began at home. Hot from school, he changed into his grey flannel shorts, matching jacket and clean white shirt. Once in the street, he halted for a moment at the end of the arched passage, needing to make sure none of his friends were about. Then he sprinted over cobblestones and tram-rails towards the curve of Eppendorfer Baum. From there, he walked down an avenue of copper beech trees, carefully avoiding the black lines that separated paving stones, his secret method of making sure that nothing would happen to disturb the ceremony.

The Haynstrasse, where his grandmother lived, was a world removed from the depot – the tenements, courtyards, and smells of poverty of Falkenried. When they marched through the 'posh' districts of Eppendorf and Harvestehude on the way to camp, Rolf spoke of 'this nest of plutocrats'. Hannes agreed, though he knew it to be untrue. Along the west side of the Alster, the city's merchants had built their villas half a century ago as monuments to optimism. The houses, reflecting their owners' rich taste, their awe of culture, had erupted in a boastful hotchpotch of styles: Hellenic porticos, ivy-clad facades, arched windows, Spanish balconies. Roofs culminated in Gothic towers or turrets with copper steeples which in time turned into green witches' hats. 'English' lawns, with sundials, statuettes of

Pan and fountains with marble mermaids, sloped down to the Alster. Some of Rolf's mythical plutocrats still inhabited these palaces. Others had long ago abandoned them to speculators who converted them into offices and apartment houses.

Hannes believed his grandmother to be rooted in this world. He and his parents no longer were. They had been cast out from comfortable, middle-class life, ineluctably moving *down*. Hannes didn't know where their descent would end. Meanwhile his grandmother had survived in this world, which was not on the shores of the Alster but in an opulent corner building in the Haynstrasse – unfortunately situated a stone's throw from a certain red brick building – the Eppendorfer Realgymnasium. That proximity had become the bane of Hannes Hacker's life.

His grandmother occupied the third floor of the Haynstrasse building. Until two years ago, the white enamel plate nailed to the entrance had read 'ROSA ROSENTEICH – Masseuse'. Since then it had been tactfully changed to: 'MASSEUSE – third floor, right.'

Hannes walked past this sign, through the long, tiled entrance way. On both sides were gardens, wild and overgrown, where he and his friends had played cowboys and Indians long, long ago. A vanished age.

Outside the front door Hannes whistled the first few bars of *La Donn' è mobile*, his secret signal. Presently, a window opened, his grandmother was heard to whistle the end of the aria, keys came hurtling through the air. If he caught them, the ceremony was intact. All would be well. He hurried up carpeted stairs, inhaling muted odours of luxury: coffee, floor polish, fresh flowers, traces of scent.

Like his mother, Rosa had been trained as a nurse. Since the death of his grandfather she had supported herself by her own efforts. Hannes had never known his grandfather, a liberal-Jewish banana importer with a stately office, his *Kontor* in Hamburg by the harbour. He died in 1923, while inflation had raged; according to family legend he had suffered a lethal stroke while reading the financial section of his *Fremdenblatt*. The stocks and shares he left Rosa had become worthless paper, 'fit only to paper the walls' as his grandmother would have it.

In Rosa's sitting-room Hannes thought he detected the
spirit of his grandfather whose ordered, cosy world he held
in the highest regard. The room, hung with plush curtains,
was full of heavy mahogany furniture. Cut-glass vases were
set on lace doileys; there were porcelain poodles, potted
linden trees, a chaise-longue with a sealskin-rug, a booming
grandfather clock.

Hannes liked to imagine his grandfather, florid and bewhisk-
ered to judge from stiffly posed sepia photographs, lying
comfortably stretched out on the green chaise-longue after
a day at his *Kontor*, his lacquered shoes and spats protruding
from striped trousers, a pince-nez on his nose. Awaiting his
pleasure on the velvet pouffe beside him stood a small glass of
apricot brandy; a fat cigar glowed on the red crystal ashtray,
shaped like a swan.

Only recently had it occurred to Hannes that his grandfather
had never seen this flat. His grandmother had come to live
and work there after his death. Hannes had quickly dismissed
the thought from his mind. Rosa's sitting room *had* to be a
grandfather of a room. Here he felt safe, protected from a
hostile world.

After their ritual midday meal, if it was too cold to go out for
a walk, Hannes and his grandmother played cards or Monopoly
in the 'consulting room', where Rosa pummelled her clients. On
a marble-top dresser stood coloured jars, bottles and tubes of
creams and fluids that had always fascinated Hannes.

To make sure all these mysterious medications stood in their
appointed places was an important component of the weekly
ritual. In this small, enclosed world, far removed from the
menace of the depot, the conflicts of school-life, Hannes could
still find universal order.

Patches of sunlight quivered on the lake's glassy surface. The
afternoon was warm and cloudless, canoes and paddle-boats
glided silently through the water. The waltz from *The Merry
Widow* drifted like a mist from the Uhlenhoster Fährhaus, the
terrace café at the far end of the lake.

They were sitting on their habitual bench on the Streekbrücke, where white motor launches pulled up for passengers, then coughed away, disappearing beyond weeping willows.

Dappling the water with its broken reflection and half-hidden behind blooming hydrangea bushes, stood the house which Hannes had decided to inhabit when he was grown up. It was a great orange pudding of a house, with a row of white stone figurines running along its roof, like icing on top of a formal cake. Sometimes Hannes and his grandmother watched the people who lived in the orange villa. They sipped tea on their balcony and observed the boats passing below. These people had a strangely still, untroubled air about them, and were sometimes attended by a curtsying uniformed maid. One of the traditional games Hannes and his grandmother played on Fridays was to invent biographies for these balcony fortunates. Hannes constructed a prosperous shipbuilder's family. Rosa had invented a banana-importer whose wife was a violin virtuoso.

Hannes often speculated on how long it would take them all to die so that he could move in, make the dream house his own, and build a gymnasium in the hall.

His grandmother had closed her eyes. She inhaled the honey scent of the wild lilac which blossomed all around them. Hannes took out his mouth-organ and played a few tentative notes.

'I can never quite understand what you get out of these Friday afternoons,' she said, more to herself than to Hannes. 'You must want to be with your friends, doing things . . .'

'No,' he told her truthfully. 'I like being here with you.'

He glanced sideways at Rosa. Strange to think that she was nearly sixty – an old woman. He liked her sleek dark hair which she wore parted in the middle and brushed back into a bun; his father claimed she dyed it. She had the sharp, rather birdlike profile of his mother and Erika, but in her character Hannes could detect no family resemblance. There was something business-like and resilient about her. Despite an occasional overflowing effusiveness ('her Jewish side' Papa called it), she had a strong masculine streak which Hannes liked. It expressed itself in severe tweed suits and tiny dark-brown cigarillos. Hannes thought of her as the Queen of Spades.

'I suppose everything's all right at home, is it?' She opened her eyes. 'I never see any of you these days – except you, my darling.'

'More or less,' he said, rubbing his mouth-organ across a bare knee. 'Mother seems to have lost interest in everything. She's always got that headache of hers. Migraine. Doesn't even want to listen to the radio any more.'

'Don't you ever sit round a table and talk anymore?'

He shook his head.

'Mama's like Erika. They just want me to *pass*. To be one of *them*, you know. And then they resent me doing things I've got to do, like joining the gang down at the tram depot, or being in the Jungvolk and that. Everything I do is wrong.'

'Does Papa criticise you too?'

'Hardly knows I exist,' Hannes said bitterly. 'Erika says Mama hasn't had her hair done for over a year. He doesn't notice anything. All he cares about is being with his cronies down at Sandmann's, drinking beer and playing cards.'

'Your father's having a very hard time,' Rosa said. 'You must make allowances. He's a very sensitive man. So handsome when your mother met him, with that ginger moustache of his – all the girls' heads used to turn . . .'

'They don't turn now,' Hannes said.

'Have you tried to take an interest in his work? He's a very cultured man . . .'

'We've got nothing in common. He doesn't know an Opel from a Horch. He sneers because I take an interest in sport. And the books he wants me to read! Plays by Schiller and that – what d'you call it? – *David Copperfield*. Nobody's ever finished that, I bet. Dry stuff like that. And he says Edgar Wallace writes books for housemaids . . .'

'Which reminds me. I've got you a new one from the library.'

'Great! Gangster or jungle?'

'Gangster,' she said. 'Spoil you to death, don't I?'

She sighed. He looked at her sharply.

'What's the matter now? Anything wrong?'

'Nothing,' she said, patting his hand. 'Nothing, really . . . oh, and another thing, I've got us tickets for *Die Fledermaus*.'

A motor launch, painted a brilliant white and hung with bunting and a swastika flag, gurgled towards them. Hannes got up and waved his arms about. Another Friday tradition: he had to signal to each approaching boat that they were not passengers, that it could pass on without stopping. An infantile game, Hannes thought, but Rosa seemed to expect it. He went on with it to please her and keep the ritual intact. Evidently she wanted to think he was still a little boy.

'Bit of a problem,' Hannes said, after the boat had passed out of sight. 'That history master of ours, old Waldmeister. He knows something.'

'The *rishiss ponem*?'

Among her diminishing store of Jewish expressions, this one, meaning 'anti-semite face', was a favourite.

'The *rishiss ponem* saw us at the opera. That time you took me to see *Carmen*. We'd better not go again for a while.'

'Would Erika come?'

'We can always listen to opera on the radio.'

After a silence, she resumed:

'They're determined to take everything. Everything. Bit by bit. Before long they'll make us wear the Yellow Star and spit on us when we walk down the street. If you'd known this world when your mother was young, my Hannes . . . I'm so tired of waiting – waiting for everything to get worse and worse . . .'
She sighed.

'There's just one thing I still care about – I want to live long enough to see what will become of you.'

'I'll be all right,' he told her. 'They don't scare me. I can yell louder than any of them. Next week I might get my youth knife.'

'You really want this knife?'

She sounded incredulous.

'You bet. Just to prove I fooled them, know what I mean? To be eligible you've got to do the 60 metres in 12 seconds, a 2.75 metre long jump, a proper pack drill and at least one overnight camping trip. Done all that. Then you learn the Jungvolk rules off by heart and answer a couple of history questions and Bob's your Uncle.'

'You'll get it, my Hannes.' To reassure herself, she patted his arm. 'You'll get it.'

He looked up at her; her eyes were brimming. Unlike his mother, who was constantly on the verge of tears, Rosa never cried.

'Something *is* the matter, isn't it?'

The sun was still high in the sky; the people in the orange villa were still drinking tea, winding up a portable gramophone. Gustaf Gründgens and Hilde Hildebrandt were singing a jolly *Schlager* about High Society. As she began haltingly to tell him what was the matter, he remembered they hadn't played the dinosaur game that afternoon. It wasn't important – classifying people they saw into different categories of prehistoric monster – but an integral part of the ritual.

They had forgotten the dinosaurs; the ceremony was in pieces. Another boat was rumbling into sight. Hannes did not get up to wave it on. For all he cared it could stop there forever. To hell with it.

On the way back to the Haynstrasse, Hannes mechanically checked off all the cars they encountered. If he guessed correctly, the ceremony could still be saved. Horch . . . Ford . . . Mercedes-Benz . . . Citroën . . . Opel . . . Then he mistook a Bentley for a Rolls-Royce.

Passing a chemist who stood outside his shop in his white smock, he murmured 'Swimming Elasmosaurus'. His grandmother smiled wanly. The ritual was stone dead.

'Pretend it's nothing unusual,' she whispered as she unlocked her front-door. 'It could all be much worse.'

The first thing he noticed when he entered the sitting-room – even before he saw the man in uniform – was the smell of his cigar; not the sweet, slightly rancid odour of Rosa's cigarillos, but the biting smoke of a full-sized Havana.

The man sprawled out on the chaise-longue did not rise to greet him. In his late forties, heavy-set, with a flushed, rubbery face, he wore the brown uniform of the Storm Troopers. He had taken off his belt and leather strap, his tie hung unknotted from his collar.

'This is my grandson, Hannes Hacker,' Hannes heard his grandmother say. 'And this is Herr Bohrer.'

The SA man grinned sheepishly. He still made no move to rise. Hannes mumbled 'How do you do'. As he looked at the man's jackboots a precise image of lacquered black shoes and spats rolled across his mind.

Herr Bohrer waited until Rosa had left the room. Then he sat up, ran big, rough hands through his crop of sandy hair and walked across to the table.

'Don't look at me like that, boy,' he said. 'I only bark here. I never bite.'

He squashed his cigar stub into the red, swan-shaped ashtray. Hannes noticed that his fingernails were bitten down to jagged brown lines. Herr Bohrer had spilled specks of cigar ash all over the starched white tablecloth. Now he lowered his bullet head to try and blow them into the ashtray. He only succeeded in scattering still more ash across the table. Then, with the side of his hand, he tried to brush it into the swan. He left dark streaks running across the clean cloth. Noticing that Hannes had gravely observed his operations, Herr Bohrer grinned as if to apologise for his clumsiness.

'There's a tray and brush in the sideboard, Herr Bohrer.'

'Name's Fritz. Like the good old Fritz of history. Have you done him yet at school, Hans?'

'It's not Hans, it's Hannes. Short for Johannes. As in Johannes Brahms,' Hannes recited dryly. 'And I know all about Frederick the Great. Seen him on the pictures.'

'*Fredericus Rex, his Imperial Majesty . . .!*' Herr Bohrer thundered forth, underlining a march rhythm by hammering on the table. 'Know it?'

'We've marched to it often enough.'

'Marched? Where have you marched?'

'With the Jungvolk, of course.'

Herr Bohrer's mouth gaped open. He narrowed his eyes in simulation of cunning.

'You . . . marching with the Jungvolk?' He sounded incredulous. His attention was momentarily diverted. Rosa had entered with a tray of food, and now placed a dish with three fried eggs in front of Bohrer.

'Love fried eggs,' Bohrer exclaimed, rubbing his hands. He began to tackle his eggs, sinking the side of his fork into the yolks, then gulping them down like soup. 'I'll say this for you, Rosenteich, old girl, you know your way about a frying-pan.' His mouth still full of egg-yolk and bread, he attempted a grin. 'Never thought I'd take to this kosher grub. Just shows you . . .'

I could kill him, Hannes was thinking. It could be done. Quite easily. Just ask old Elasmosaurus for some arsenic to kill the rats in the cellar. The thug wouldn't even notice the bitter taste in his coffee. Wait till he's stone-dead, wrap him up in an old newspaper, chuck him in the dustbin at the corner. It could be done.

'Help yourself, Hannes,' his grandmother said, pointing to a plate with cakes.

'Not hungry, thanks.'

'Your grandson tells me he's in the Jungvolk,' Bohrer lifted his full cup to his lips. 'You people know a fiddle or two, don't you?'

'My grandfather fought with the Hussars,' Hannes said, and regretted it immediately.

'Sure,' Bohrer said mildly. 'I believe you. Another cup, Rosenteich, old girl, if you please.'

Hannes stared guiltily at his empty plate. All afternoon, while Rosa must have had this horror on her mind, he had prattled on about winning the knife.

Bohrer finished slurping his eggs, wiped his mouth on his brown sleeve, then eased himself down in his chair to pick his teeth with a split match. Hannes noticed the perspiration under his arm. No sooner had Rosa left the room with her tray than he farted. Hannes had nothing against farting. In camp one did it all the time. It was a manly thing to do. But in this room? *Nobody* had ever farted in this room.

'Your granny's OK,' he said, and stretched himself. 'First class.'

'You a client of hers?'

'Never lie on that slab of hers to let her tickle me, if that's what you mean.' He laughed. 'That's not to my taste, not in my line of business you might say.'

'What is in your line of business, then?'

Bohrer creased his rubbery face into another sheepish grin.

'Put it this way. I'm supervising your gran's business affairs. Protecting her interests and bodily welfare. Aryanisation, we call it.'

He sucked his teeth, then threw the broken match into the ashtray. When he got up to knot his tie, he looked enormously fat.

'I'm off,' he announced. 'Not to worry, my boy. Your little Jungvolk secret is safe as houses with Fritz Bohrer. Silent as the grave, that's me.'

When he had gone, Hannes walked to the window. In the wilderness of the garden below, the luscious summer green of the bushes was flecked with fading yellow light.

'It's finished,' he told himself. 'The End.' He felt a chill running through him, and shivered convulsively.

'You remember him, don't you?' Rosa asked him when she came back. 'Kröger's, the grocers. Their delivery man. I used to tip him every week.'

Hannes could detect no trace of bitterness in her voice. She appeared faintly amused.

'Is it official then, or just a sideline? Sort of racket?'

'He just turned up out of the blue, told me he hadn't come to deliver butter this time. He was in that uniform of his. Was I running a licensed business on these premises, he wanted to know.'

'What happened then?'

'I asked him in and gave him a cup of coffee. I was too frightened to do anything else. Then he asked me if I employed any Aryan women under forty-five. That was now against the law. I told him I didn't employ anybody. So anyway, finally he said the local lads, whoever they might be, knew all about me.

They took a serious view of a non-Aryan business being carried on "clandestinely" in Eppendorf. Gave the place a bad name, he said. Then he said he wasn't an anti-semite. That was the one part of the New Order he couldn't really go along with — '

'The nerve!'

'Arsehole' he had been on the point of saying. Hannes was fairly sure Rosa had never heard such a word in her life.

'Anyway, he said he'd have to "officialise the premises". The rest you know. This is now an Aryan establishment. I'm protected. I have a partner. Fifty-fifty.'

'Can't you do anything about it?'

'Go to the police? A Jewess complaining about the behaviour of an SA man? It'll give them the best laugh they've had for months. No, I'll have to manage as best I can . . .'

'It'll change everything, won't it? Our Fridays, everything . . .'

'Let's not talk about it. He's not here, is he? I'll feed that greedy schnorrer till his seams burst. We'll go next door now and have a nice little game of rummy. Pretend it hasn't happened. I've got you some of your favourite jellied lemon slices. Spoiling you to death.' She put her arm around his shoulder. 'But why not? We might all be dead tomorrow.'

She was fantastic. She really was.

CHAPTER FIVE

'There's old Hacker!'

Rolf Sandmann greeted Hannes by flicking a brown apple core into his face. He was standing in the doorway of his father's pub, the Jungenschaft's Saturday morning assembly point. His legs were placed wide apart, his hands rested lightly on the buckle of his belt. He looked alert, ready for action.

The sight of Rolf in uniform always made Hannes feel an impostor. He attempted a similar stance, felt like a shop dummy and groped for the security of a wall to lean against. His discomfort did not escape Rolf, who allowed himself the faintest of smiles as he peered down the street for late-comers.

Why did Rolf make him feel so inadequate? Hannes could detect no difference in their uniforms. They both wore the regulation black shorts and brown shirt, black tie and black peaked cap, leather strap drawn tight across shoulder and chest, the belt with its flash of lightning insignia. If there was a difference it was that Rolf's boots were dusty. His own were clean and polished.

Yet Rolf had this one advantage over him: *he had the knife*. It was attached to his belt in a leather sheath, the wooden handle with inlaid mother-of-pearl swastika gleaming above the silver glint of the hilt.

I'll get mine before long, Hannes assured himself. We'll be evens then.

'What's the matter with your shorts, Hacker?'

Rolf was scrutinising him with gritty authority.

'Shorts?' Hannes brushed them with the back of his hand. 'Nothing's the matter with them. Why?'

'They're miles too long.'

'At least his boots are regulation cleaned.' Another boy had spoken up. 'Yours are filthy.'

They all looked at the unknown speaker. He was neatly dressed, his uniform recently pressed. He had clean white knees. All of it revealed an upbringing that disapproved of playing in the street. A new member, Hannes surmised, one who clearly knew nothing of tram-yard despotism.

'Got them back from the repairers' this morning, if it concerns you,' Rolf explained. 'I'll get them polished up before we assemble. Nothing to worry your little head about.'

'Isn't it time we set off?' the newcomer wanted to know.

Rolf had now had time to compose himself.

'I decide when we march,' he said. He screwed up his eyes against the sun and began to whistle.

'Yes, sir, Herr Obergruppenführer,' the new boy mocked, unimpressed, leaving the other members of the Jungenschaft in suspense. How would Rolf handle this challenge?

'Where's your knife?' Rolf confronted the new boy.

'Expect to get it this week. I got transferred, so I'm . . .'

'So shut your bleedin' trap,' Rolf broke in with sudden vehemence. 'Know who I am? My old man's Blockwarden. Want me to report you? I'm in charge here. What do they call you, anyway?'

'Er – Kurt Friess.'

Hannes observed with dismay that the boy called Friess had already begun to acknowledge Rolf's authority.

'Where do you come from, Friess?'

'Well, we've just moved to Hoheluftchaussee 116 . . .'

'That explains it.' Rolf cocked his head to one side and winked at Hannes. 'Funny coincidence.'

'Certainly is,' Hannes agreed.

'Better watch it,' Rolf said. 'Know the tram depot corner of Falkenried? We don't want to see you there for a start. We've had you thoroughly investigated before you joined this Jungenschaft. Got some very interesting information on you, Freezy.'

'You don't even know me.' The new member looked confused. 'My name's not Freezy, either . . .'

'Don't let it go to your head, Freezy. Fall in. On the double. Into line.'

Rolf pulled the peak of his cap over one eye. The handful of boys that made up the Jungenschaft formed a straight line. The collapse of Kurt Friess was duly registered.

'Old Gärtner is missing,' someone said.

'Fähnleinführer Hinrichs will see to him,' Rolf said curtly. 'You know your orders, men. We'll march in formation to the harbour, landing stage number seven. There we'll link up with the other Jungenschaften from Eimsbüttel, Hoheluft-East and Eppendorf to re-form into a Jungzug. We will then proceed to the Hermann Göring camp, where we are to join our Fähnlein. Is that clear? 'Tention! Two deep! Right turn! Come on, Hacker, you're up in front with me. Freezy, you in the rear! Ready, one, two, three, MARCH, left, right, left, right, left . . .'

Marching at the head of the column with Rolf Sandmann at his side filled Hannes with uneasy pride. Eighteen thumping feet made an impressive sound. Presently Rolf suggested a marching song.

'What about "The Wanderer"?' Hannes asked.

'That's no marching song,' Rolf scoffed. 'That's for kids.'

'We haven't got a band. We could whistle for a change.'

'We'll do Horst Wessel,' Rolf decided. 'We all know the words. Make it nice and loud. Pass it on to the rear . . .'

Hannes signalled, arm outstretched. Voices were lifted, words came tumbling out, strong and clear. The nine boys of the Jungenschaft could have sung them in their sleep; they pitched their unbroken voices an octave lower, in emulation of the manly rasp of the Storm Troopers. Marching close to the gutter, between the pavement and the tram rails, they raised their voices whenever a tram passed to make themselves heard above the grind and clatter. Men and women stopped by the curb. Some raised their arms in salute as they watched the little group pass by, singing as they marched in the sunshine. Young children followed them on their route. Out of the corner of one eye, Hannes saw small beads of sweat forming on Rolf's top lip.

The Jungenschaft arrived at the harbour in mid-morning. They sat on their packs and started to unwrap sandwiches. Hannes peeled a banana; his eyes tried to pierce the smoke-laden yellow mist to observe the other side of the harbour area.

The outlines of the wharves and warehouses were blurred, but the tall cranes stood out clearly. Hannes thought of them as steel giraffes, dwarfing the men who laboured beneath them. In some places the sun cut through the haze, scattering flashes of light over steel and water. Small tugs chugged past the landing stages, dodging the green-and-white painted ferries. Rainbow-tinted grease flecked the water. A smell of fish, petrol and hops hung in the air.

Hannes' mind filled with images of seafaring adventure, of stowing away in a cargo ship, of concealment among sacks and crates, going to America as a cabin boy and coming home, a millionaire in a fur coat, chewing a fat cigar. He had read books about such things; there was one by Jack London that Rosa had given him last Christmas . . .

The port's vividness dimmed like cinema lights. Something hardened in his stomach, as he recalled the previous evening.

Why was his mother so helpless, so despondent?

'. . . all you can do is fiddle with that iron,' he had complained. 'Can't any of you *do* something? A Storm Trooper with a face like a pig sits at Rosa's table, feeding his face with fried eggs and what does this entire family do about it? Bugger all!'

His mother frowned, supporting her weight on her arms, but she said nothing. Strands of matted hair hung limply over her forehead.

'You look a sight,' Hannes told her, satisfying a sudden whim to hurt her. 'I'd be ashamed to be seen with you!'

She switched off her iron and left the kitchen. He sat down with his father's paper, glumly pencilling Olympic rings around the name of the New Zealander who had just won the 1500 metres.

Later Erika came in and clipped his ear. He crunched the paper into a ball and hurled it at the corner stove.

'I hope you're satisfied,' his sister told him. 'Your mother's lying on her bed, weeping her heart out. What did you say to her?'

'She's always bawling. I told her about Bohrer. She just went on ironing handkerchiefs. Nothing she could do about it. Not my fault if she looks like something the cat brought home.'

'Then sod off to play with your Rolf Sandmann and his little Jungvolk rats!'

'And you go play with your Georg! . . . Who made me join the Jungvolk in the first place? *She* did. Mama! She could have let me have a doctor's certificate like old Kloth's. She *wanted* me to join.'

'For whose sake I'd like to know?' Erika's lips twisted with scorn. 'I can just see your precious Rolfie's face if you didn't belong to his Jungenschaft. You're not fit to have such a mother. You disgust me, Hannes Hacker. Go on, get out into the street where you belong!'

Turned out like a dog, Hannes thought. Just because I was trying to help Rosa. I hate them all! He flung down his chair, hoping it would fall on Erika's feet, and slammed out of the house. But even before he reached the vaulted passage his anger had receded, leaving him choked with contrition.

He ambled over to the depot, but everybody had gone. No doubt to homes where they were appreciated. He spent the next quarter of an hour kicking a tennis ball against the stone wall, but it didn't satisfy him. It was far too late now to do something exciting. In the tenement blocks, silhouetted against a charcoal sky, squares of yellow light twinkled like Chinese lanterns. Down at Sandmann's, somebody was playing a harmonica. Hannes had stuffed the ball back into his pocket and gone home to bed without supper, pulling the sheet over his head . . .

'Look lively there, Hacker! Dreaming, are we? You're not at that fancy school of yours now. On the double!'

Hannes roused himself. He recognised the whine of Jungzugführer Anders' voice. They called him 'The Ram'. He had curly brown hair which fitted his head like a woolly wig, and the blunt, submissive profile of a sheep. Group-leader Anders was not cut out for Jungvolk work. Usually irritated and impatient, he wasn't even impressed by his own authority. Rolf Sandmann had long been convinced Anders was a Jew spying for the Bolsheviks.

'Fine bleedin' group leader,' he whispered to Hannes as they lined up at the quayside with the other Jungenschaften. 'That droopy nose. Bleedin' sheep's head. Ba-ah! Can't make out why Fähnleinführer Hinrichs tolerates him. Hasn't even noticed my boots this morning . . .'

While Anders conferred irritably with the ferry boat captain, Rolf decided the time had come to take care of those boots. Hannes' help was enlisted. Rolf claimed good reasons for not disturbing his own kit. While Hannes was hastily repacking for roll call, Rolf – boots freshly glistening like nobody else's – was brightly asking Group-leader Anders when kit inspection would be held today.

The forty members of the Jungzug, having shrieked out their names, were now released to swarm over the gangplank and up to the ferry's top deck. Older passengers hastily retreated to quarters below. High voices excitedly cut across each other.

'That big one with the red and white funnels, that's the *Cap Arcona*. One of ours.'

'The *Bremen*'s much bigger. She's ours as well.'

'That's a Swedish whaler over there.'

'Can't you recognise flags, idiot? It's Greek!'

'The Greeks got no whalers.'

'They have and all.'

The ferry drew away from the quay to make the river crossing. Hannes leant over the deck rail, watching the water curdle and foam under the stern wheel. The haze had begun to lift. Seagulls, their wings tipped with sunlight, swooped and circled and mewed. Spray washed over his face.

The Ram's voice droned orders through the ship's loud-speaker. The Jungzug was instructed to sing 'Arise, O German Eagle'.

Hannes bellowed with the rest. The sun was in his eyes, brine in his nostrils. The world had become beautiful.

The Jungzug marched, three-deep, through heathland. Led by the Ram, a flag-bearer, and a drummer, they strutted over wild, flowering hills, through sleepy villages, past old farmhouses.

Their thatched roofs sloped down so low, the boys pulled out straws out as they passed. The afternoon sun bore down on them, the straps of their packs cut through their shirts, bruising flesh.

'This counts as a 15-kilometre route-march, men,' Anders bleated. 'Don't think you're going on a school hike. Remember we're training you to become soldiers for the fatherland.'

Rolf and Hannes, marching side by side, spoke little. They were grimly preoccupied with demonstrating that the day's exertions could be taken in their stride.

'Where's old Freezy now?' Rolf asked.

'In the back somewhere.'

'Haven't finished with the little bastard. Remind me to take care of him, Hacker.'

'Bleedin' flies,' Hannes muttered, lifting his guard for a moment.

'Can't take it?' Rolf blinked knowingly at the sun. 'We haven't started yet.'

Anders was shouting an order. Some of the boys started to sing.

'Wasting our best song,' Rolf jeered. 'Shan't sing!'

Hannes' eyes strayed over the purple hills to the rows of slim, bending poplars on the horizon.

'I'm not singing, neither,' he reassured Rolf.

But the music seduced him, as it seduced them all. In the end he joined in lustily. He could feel the elastic of his stockings biting into his skin; he knew he could not stoop down to loosen its grip. Two pebbles cut into the soles of his feet. Tonight he would find blisters there. Beside him, Rolf was clearly suffering, too. That thought refreshed Hannes. He raised his voice:

> *Forward, Forward!*
> *Ring out the fanfares loud and clear!*
> *Forward, Forward!*
> *Our youth has no thought of fear!*
> *Fatherland, stand thou in bright array,*
> *Though we may perish on the way . . .*

Hannes used his forearm to brush sweat from his eyes. Soon they would come to the Youth Song's refrain. It always sent shivers through his body. Only two other pieces of music could do that to him: the Intermezzo from *Cavalleria Rusticana*, and the start of *Carmen*. The Youth Song was even better. Perhaps one could stop it affecting you if you could think about something else. Beside him Rolf was yelling:

> *Even though our goal is high,*
> *Youth will conquer it or die!*

That morning Mama had knotted his tie for him, kneeling in front of him to brush down his uniform shorts.

'God's sake,' he had reproached her. 'I can do that myself.'

'If the grass inside those tents is wet . . .'

What did women know? Mama would never understand why Nazi songs gave you the shivers or what boys like Rolf Sandmann were really like, or why one needed the knife. She lived in a world as remote as that overgrown garden in the Haynstrasse with its chipped sundial and scattered rhododendron blooms.

When Mama embraced him, he caught sight of her in the mirror – her arms wrapped around the boy in a brown Jungvolk uniform. He had quickly twisted away from her . . .

> *Our flag waves proudly in the van,*
> *We advance into the future man for man . . .*

There it was, the refrain. High in his nose Hannes felt the familiar tickle.

'What's the matter, Hacker, lost your voice?' Rolf's forehead glistened. Inspired by his own singing, his eyes shone.

> *We are marching for Hitler*
> *Through darkness and dread!*
> *Holding high our flag*
> *For Freedom and Bread!*

Trembling, Hannes joined in:

> *Our banner signals the new day,*
> *Our banner carries us to glory*
> *Our banner means more than our death!*

Feet tramped over the hard earth with renewed vigour. Group-leader Anders raised his arm, shouting another order.

'Good,' Rolf panted. 'Second verse.'

Hannes glanced at him but quickly averted his eyes. Rolf's mouth was open, his look clearly reflected that golden future – bloody, victorious, certain. How I hate your guts, Sandmann, Hannes thought. I hate you more than anybody or anything in the world.

> *Youth, youth, we are the future's soldiers!*
> *Youth, youth, heroes of tomorrow's deeds!*

Hannes now began to sing his own personal version of the chorus:

> *Jews, Jews, we are the future's soldiers!*
> *Jews, Jews, heroes of tomorrow's deeds!*

His eyes were moist with unwanted tears. What fools they all were! Couldn't even detect him singing a treacherous version of the lyric. They would never find out the truth about him. None of them. Ever. In his exhilaration, he forgot the load on his back.

> *Whoever still against us stands*
> *All shall fall beneath our hands!*

I'm going to get in with Erika and Georg and that lot, he decided while he sang. They're going to be proud of me. I know how to use a rifle. I'm going to pick out Hitler and Hess and Göring as they pass in their new Mercedes convertibles. I'm going to shoot to kill – right between the eyes. We'll storm the Chancellery in Berlin. We'll carry lighted torches. We'll get

Jesse Owens to lead us. The negro had won everything – long jump, hundred metres, two hundred metres. Nobody would ever catch up with Jesse Owens! Or with him for that matter!

And if they did? They'd march him to a brick wall. He'd hear them shout 'Fire!' That would be that. Glorious death!

> *Führer, we are pledged to thee,* they sang,
> *Comrades, prove your loyalty!*

Hannes had not realised how far they had marched. The country around them had changed. On both sides vast fields of rye stretched up towards the horizon. Swarms of midges danced crazily in the sun. He could smell the heat as it singed the corn.

'What time do we get to that bleedin' camp?' Rolf Sandmann grumbled beside him, sweat dribbling down his pink cheeks.

'What's up?' Hannes asked, eyes out front. 'Can't take it, Rolfie?'

CHAPTER SIX

The bugle sounded. Through a gap between the tent flaps, Hannes could see a narrow strip of blue sky. He threw off his blanket and got up.

'Rise and shine, Rolf. Six o'clock.'

In his sleep Rolf looked quite cherubic and defenceless, incapable of devising or inflicting hurt. He grunted and stretched, turned over and pulled the blanket over his head.

Hannes drew back the flap and looked out. It had rained during the night. A fluffy mist, like cotton wool, hovered just above the earth. On the horizon a few tattered clouds were slowly sucked into the blueness of the sky. The pointed white tents, about forty of them, were beginning to billow into life. Small figures darted about, somebody flapped a hand over his mouth, hollering like a Red Indian.

The other occupants of the tent, Freitag and Lessing, older boys who belonged to another Jungenschaft, were stirring now, swearing manfully as they rooted among their packs.

'Shake your bloody arse,' Lessing said, inhaling noisily through his nose. 'Come on, Blondie.'

Rolf blinked up at him.

'Who are you ordering about?'

'You, Blondie.'

Rolf was up in a flash, pulling on his trunks.

'You're not in charge of this tent, Lessing.'

Lessing was full of cold. His nostrils were reddened and sore, his speech blotted.

'I suppose you think you are,' he said.

'Fat chance,' Freitag said, establishing his role as Lessing's ally for Rolf's benefit. Like Lessing, Freitag was tall and fair. Soon they'd both move up to the senior organisation, the Hitler Youth. Hannes had previously noticed the elaborate, scientific way Freitag bit his finger-nails. He was at it again now, nibbling and chewing and biting, now the tips, now the corners, biting with his front teeth or using a gap between two molars as a lever. All the while his long white fingers moved with exaggerated daintiness, as if toying with a roast leg of chicken.

'We'll get the Ram to sort this out,' Rolf said confidently, 'I know my rights as Jungenschaft leader.'

'The Ram, is it?' Lessing sniffed grimly. 'Not by any chance referring to Group-leader Anders, are you? Think I'll call his attention to your description. Remind me, Freitag.'

'You wait,' Rolf said, long after the two older boys had left the tent, laughing. 'I'll get even with them.'

'Still got to get even with old Freezy,' Hannes pointed out.

'All in good time.' Busily tying his shoelaces, Rolf failed to detect the irony in Hannes' voice. 'I'll report Lessing to Fähnleinführer Hinrichs for calling him names. You heard him, Hacker. You're my witness.'

Their morning sprint took them through a small coniferous wood which sloped down to a narrow stream. Beneath their feet, the earth was slippery with pine needles. Sunlight dodged and feinted between tree trunks.

Hannes inhaled the clear morning air.

'Smells like Christmas,' he said, running.

'Never mind Christmas,' Rolf gasped beside him. 'Get to the head of that column.'

'What for? This isn't a competitive run.'

'Never get the knife with that shirky thinking.'

Rolf leapt ahead, Hannes followed meekly.

Later Rolf rested against a tree trunk, hands on hips, grinning and gasping, showing the exhausted humility of an Olympic runner.

'Beat you to it, Lessing,' he proclaimed.

'Hope you've left yourself with enough wind for PT,' Lessing snuffled.

The group-leader who put them through their morning exercises was an enthusiast. After the thirtieth knee-bend, Hannes felt faint. The group-leader promised they would enjoy breakfast all the more for their exertions.

Lined up at an old pump for water, Hannes filled his aluminium mug. On the way back to the tent, he drank half the contents, intended for washing. He found Rolf menacing Freitag with his filled cup.

'One drop touches me, Blondie, they'll have to retool you,' Freitag threatened. 'Make up your fucking mind to that.'

'Fine language,' Rolf said, emboldened by Lessing's absence. 'Haven't they told you about swearing in camp?'

'Sod off, Blondie.'

Freitag, satisfied that Rolf was no man of action, turned his back on him.

As he washed, Hannes wondered why Rolf had to spoil everything with pointless vendettas. Lessing and Freitag weren't so bad. They had a sense of humour, they swore like men. They had also crossed a certain line, that neither he nor Rolf had reached. They *knew* things, they were tuned in on the mysterious network of adult secrets . . .

Erika was in it, too, and like all adults she was determined to keep kids out. Catching her washing a small garment in the kitchen sink recently, he asked his sister what she was washing. She switched on that unmistakeable jamming signal, the adults' Keep Out sign. Told him it was nothing little boys should want to know about. He never did find out what Erika had washed that day. Freitag and Lessing could probably tell him, if he asked. He promised himself to investigate that secret world denied him. First, though, he'd have to win the knife. After that he would be able to stand up to them all.

Lessing stepped into the tent and snapped his fingers.

'On the double, men. Inspection in two minutes.'

'Don't have to snuffle camp routine to me,' Rolf snapped. 'I carry the knife, you know.'

'He carries the knife, you know.' Lessing grinned across

at Freitag. 'Fancy us forgetting that. Make a note of that, shall we?'

'Bake a dote of dat, shall we?' Rolf retorted bravely. 'Bake a dote of dat, Hacker.'

'Come on Rolfie,' Hannes said anxiously. 'Let's get the blankets folded.'

'That's right, Rolfie,' Freitag jeered in a falsetto. 'Be a good little boy, fold blanket.'

They broke into raucous laughter. Hannes longed to see Rolf's humbling prolonged, his trouncing witnessed by the absent Schemel and Schmitt. After that, nobody at the depot would ever again accept Rolf Sandmann's pretensions. Odd thing, that. One always had to pretend to be on one side, while in one's heart, one was on the side opposite.

'Watch it!' Lessing warned. 'Hinrichs is taking inspection. Sandmann, straighten your collar. Hacker, what are you dreaming about?'

They stood rigidly to attention as one of the group-leaders drew back the flaps. Fähnleinführer Hinrichs entered the tent.

'At ease, gentlemen.'

Staring at Hinrichs, Rolf's eyes flickered with reverence. The Fähnleinführer, flanked by two group-leaders, had tied a non-regulation yellow silk scarf around his neck. Clear, blue eyes gazed at each boy in turn. Hinrichs had fresh, dimpled skin and wavy, platinum hair. He walked with the languorous grace of a cat. When he practised his apologetic smile, which Rolf often tried to copy, he showed three gold fillings. He was a very experienced member of the Jungvolk and quite old really – at least twenty-one, Hannes guessed.

Hinrichs bowed with humility.

'Good-looking tent, don't you think?' he asked the group-leaders. 'Let's see your fingernails – er, Hacker, is it?'

Hannes held out trembling hands, Fähnleinführer Hinrichs did not even bother to glance at them.

'The beginning of all culture,' he said, addressing the tent in general, 'is clean ears, clean feet and clean fingernails.'

He turned to go.

'Sir,' Rolf called out. Hannes was impressed by his daring. 'Sir, I'd like you to put on record who's in charge in this tent.'

'In charge? I had the impression this was a happy tent.'

'Yes, sir.'

Hinrichs turned to exchange a few mumbled words with the Ram, whose blunt profile thrust forward eagerly.

'Lessing is in charge,' the Fähnleinführer decided. 'Seniority. Does that break your heart, Sandmann?'

Rolf blushed. 'No, sir, not at all. A technical point, sir.'

'Excellent. Glad to have been of service.'

Fähnleinführer Hinrichs' blue eyes rested on Rolf for a moment, then he clicked his heels and lifted one eyebrow. 'Gentlemen, Heil Hitler!'

The flap was drawn aside. Hinrichs and the group-leaders stepped out to move on to the next tent.

So that was how Rolf liked to see himself, Hannes thought. *Gentlemen, Heil Hitler!*

'Let that be a lesson to you, Sandmann.' Lessing sniffed with satisfaction. 'You, too, Hacker. You'll learn, the both of you.'

'Not taking orders from you, friend.'

Rolf was too preoccupied imitating Hinrichs' voice to watch Freitag. He was a fraction of a second late dodging the blow. Hannes watched, open-mouthed, as Freitag's clenched right fist embedded itself in Rolf's stomach. It was like a slow-motion film: Rolf crumpled up, gasping as he held his front with both hands. His head lolled between twisted knees.

'Just watch it,' Freitag said, 'that's all, boy. That's all.'

'That hurt,' Hannes said, bending down to help his friend. Still – it wouldn't have done Schmitt and Schemel any harm to witness the scene . . .

The hundred and sixty members of the Fähnlein stood bareheaded in the sun ardently looking up as the flag rose on its pole. Then they solemnly spoke the familiar words of Dedication.

'I swear,' Hannes mumbled with the others, 'to serve our leader Adolf Hitler faithfully and selflessly. I swear to do my best for the unity and comradeship of the fatherland's youth.

I swear obedience to the Leader of German Youth and to the leaders of our organisation. I swear by our holy flag that I shall always try to be worthy of it. So help me God.'

Drums rolled, they launched into the Horst Wessel song. On an empty stomach, it could be an emotional experience. Hannes thought of *Hitlerjunge Quex*, of the blood trickling to the ground. Perhaps there really was something to all that stuff, just a tiny bit, that could be wholly understood only if one was really one of them, not just pretending.

The song came to an end, the Fähnlein was dismissed. The leaders stepped into their tents, the boys scattered across the meadow, yelling and hooting, celebrating their hunger.

They've got to give me the knife this time, Hannes thought as he trotted towards the steaming cauldrons of milk and coffee. I'll get it tomorrow. I'll wear it on the way home. He saw himself gliding through the night air towards the harbour lights, his hand firmly gripping the handle.

He burst into a run.

'On June 28th, 1919, a handful of German traitors put their signatures to a shameful scrap of paper, on which our enemies dictated the brutal terms they called the Treaty of Versailles.'

Fähnleinführer Hinrichs balanced his body elegantly on the edge of a trestle table. Sunburned finger-tips absently tugged at the ends of his silk scarf, his modulated voice never rose above a purr. The boys listened eagerly. This was no dry school history lesson. This was the real thing, a briefing for the future's soldiers.

'That day, gentlemen,' Hinrichs went on, 'will go down in history as the moment of the fatherland's greatest disgrace – the day of national humiliation *we* have been chosen to avenge.'

His eyes moved sternly along the rows of uniformed boys who sat cross-legged in the grass; the sun beat on their bare heads. Rolf's eyes had that glassy look that made Hannes feel uneasy – as if somehow his own safety was in jeopardy.

'The Treaty of Versailles was unjust because it did not reflect the outcome of the Great War. Who really won that war? Whose armies stood in the field when others had retreated or lay dead on the battlefield? Whose navy held sway over the North Sea and the Atlantic? Whose air force boasted heroes like Manfred von Richthofen?'

His voice sunk to a whisper, a prayer. The boys craned their necks to catch words spoken with tenderness.

'The fatherland defeated its enemies in battle. Yet those hard fought victories were signed away seventeen years ago by traitors, who wished to sell our nation into slavery.'

Fähnleinführer Hinrichs stared down at his jackboots; wisps of his silvery hair trembled in the breeze.

'Had they driven a dagger between the shoulder-blades of every fighting soldier in the field, they could not have dealt our fatherland a more treacherous blow. For fourteen years we had to stand by passively while our enemies bled us white. The British stole our colonies. The French required us to pay milliards of francs. And why? Because we had dared to defend ourselves against a world armed to the teeth.'

For the first time since he began, Fähnleinführer Hinrichs' gold fillings became visible.

'Reparations! We, who defended ourselves on three fronts simultaneously, *we* were blamed for the war! But let us be quite clear on one point. Whose money-bags made a war against Germany possible in the first place? And, for that matter, who would not allow their own lily-white hands to be soiled with the blood and muck of battle?'

Fähnleinführer Hinrichs' forefinger indicated a simplified Semitic profile. He waited for the laughter to subside before he went on more stridently:

'Correct, gentlemen! So never let us waver in our task! We must do more than wait for the day of justice, when we can once more engage the enemy on the field of battle. Wherever we go, we must carry our awareness of our destiny in our hearts. We must feel it in the very marrow of our bones, show it in every action, every plan, every word! Today, you may think you are on holiday. Well, gentlemen, no decent German can rest in peace until justice dawns. Every breath we draw must be staked on one thing, and one thing only – ultimate victory! The

Führer wills it. We obey. Thank you, gentlemen, for listening so attentively.'

Fähnleinführer Hinrichs' features relaxed into an apologetic smile. 'And now may we see a little action? Cavalry Exercises! Dismiss!'

The group-leaders began to move among the boys, splitting them up into teams.

'Hacker,' Rolf shouted excitedly. 'You're my horse!'

All around them, boys were climbing on one another's shoulders. Rolf held Hannes down while he mounted him. Each piggy-back team had to dislodge riders from the opposing team, disqualifying them from further taking part in the battle. At the final whistle, the team with the greatest number of surviving riders was declared victorious.

'Let's get Lessing and Freitag!' Rolf yelled into Hannes' ear, grinding invisible spurs into his side. 'Those sodding Frogs! Let's tread 'em underfoot, smash 'em into the ground! Defeat the enemy! Down with the Yids! Revenge for Marseilles!'

Bent double under Rolf's weight, Hannes stumbled blindly into the direction his rider was prodding him.

From the edge of the battlefield the Ram advised correct procedure:

'Only riders must fall! Fallen horses do not count! Fallen horses do not count!'

'Here they come!' Rolf cried, tightening his grip around Hannes' neck.

Panting, Hannes galloped into the whirling mêlée of legs and arms. Above him, Rolf shrieked triumphantly as he clawed at opponents, scratching cheeks, kicking stomachs, punching ribs. Hannes sweated. In glorious pain, he closed his eyes. With a little imagination, one could believe one was leading a charge, rumbling forward in a formation of tanks, or driving a bayonet into an enemy belly. The pressure of Rolf's weight on his back increased but still he advanced, thrust forward by Rolf's battle cries.

'French swine! Revenge for Marseilles! Down with the Yids!'

Rolf had got himself surrounded. Blows rained down on

Hannes. He could hear the Ram's voice piercing the tumult. 'Riderless horses have to leave the battlefield without delay!'

'Not fair,' Rolf protested. 'All against one, bloody lot of Yids!'

Rolf's arm was throttling him. A boot grazed his knee and drew blood. A punch landed on his head. Sweat dribbled into his open mouth. Two pairs of legs, dimly recognised as belonging to Freitag and Lessing, converged on him. Rolf renewed his protests. Suddenly he lost his grip, and Hannes his balance; they sprawled on the ground. A whistle sounded.

'Sandmann, Hacker! Out!'

They picked themselves up, limping to the edge of the meadow, feeling sore and proud.

'We did all right,' Hannes said. 'Still got a few men battling on!'

'There they go,' Rolf cried, 'look . . . over there!'

He pointed in the direction of the shrinking battlefield. Freitag and Lessing and their respective riders were rolling about in the grass. Lessing was breathing into his hands. His sensitive nose was bleeding.

'Ah-hah . . . Ah-hah . . . Ahahahaaa . . .' Rolf screeched in a weird parody of malicious laughter. 'Ahahaaa . . . serves you right, got yourself a bloody nose, that'll teach you!'

The warriors rested; they exposed their wounds to the breeze and the sun.

'Now you know what it's like,' Rolf said. 'War.'

'You don't get yourself killed this way.'

'Don't kid yourself.' To Rolf the battle had been totally real. 'Know of one camp, some boy drowned. Water battle. Got to take risks. Like in a real war.'

'Think there's going to be war?'

'Hope so. Heard old Hinrichs, didn't you? Asking for it, aren't they?'

'Who is?'

Rolf had taken off his boots. He was massaging his shins. 'Reds fired on our warships off the coast of Spain. Don't you read the paper? Your father worked on one once, didn't he?'

'Don't mind fighting,' Hannes said quickly. 'I just don't want poison gas sprayed all over me.'

'They'll never dare use it. My dad says so. They use poison gas, we'll bomb them to smithereens.'

'High explosives?'

'Dive bombers.'

'The French got bombers.'

'We'll always beat them, don't you worry. My dad says they're dirty, always thinking about girls and that.'

'What about the English?'

'They'll come in with us, my dad says. They're against the Jews and the Communists as much as we are. I can't bloody wait to join up.'

Enthusiastically, he sprayed the meadow with an imaginary machine-gun.

'Thought you was going to join the Air Force?'

'Might. As a bombardier. Or the SS.'

'*They* don't do any fighting,' Hannes ventured.

'Against the wall . . . Ta-ta-ta-ta-ta.'

Rolf fired another prolonged salvo, hands quivering. 'Got 'em.' He stood up. 'Dinner time.'

'Schemel wouldn't be much good at this, would he?' Hannes heard himself asking obsequiously as he tried to keep in step with Rolf. It wasn't often that Rolf was so friendly. One had to make the most of it. While the mood lingered.

'Nor that bloody Asthma. Can't stand that bloke, can you?'

'Nar,' Hannes said. 'Makes me sick.'

Night fell, the Fähnlein was gathered around a huge crackling fire. Sparks hurled through the gloom like fireflies. Legs folded underneath him, Hannes squatted beside Rolf, listening to Fähnleinführer Hinrichs reading from a textbook.

'It happened in the year 1919. The German fatherland lay bleeding, betrayed by enemies, fiendish elements striving to destroy what last vestiges of German strength they could find. Then from the steadfast battalions of battle-worn German fighters, there arose a simple soldier and man of the people,

Adolf Hitler. With total devotion he strove against the rapacity of enemies within and without, against the devilish Treaty of Versailles. As he cast magic inspiration over our people, the field-grey columns turned into brown battalions, and their struggle brought forth its magnificent fruit – the glorious Third Reich.'

As he watched firelight flickering over the page of Hinrichs' book, Hannes' attention absconded. His joints ached, his legs were covered with scratches; he felt drowsy yet refreshed. He had knocked up a good score at target practice, the Ram told him he was getting to be useful with a rifle. Later they had swum in the shallows beyond a wood. Lessing had given Rolf a treble-ducking he wasn't likely to forget. Then he had caught those two kids behind the gorse bushes. If he hadn't seen it with his own eyes he wouldn't have believed it. The memory of that scene was indelibly engraved on his mind. Nobody ever told you anything, nobody explained. Not the things that mattered, anyway.

'Thank you, gentlemen.'

Fähnleinführer Hinrichs had closed his book and handed it to one of the group-leaders.

'I want to leave you with this thought. Here at Hermann Göring Camp, we are just one Fähnlein. But across the length and breadth of our fatherland, in Saxony, in Brandenburg, along the Elbe and the Rhine, other Fähnlein are gathered before their camp fires, dedicating themselves to the future. In an epoch such as ours, you will agree, it is truly exciting and beautiful to be alive and young.'

The boys rose from the grass. Muscles hurt, their joints creaked as they strolled over to the flagpole and once more assembled in formation.

'I could certainly use some sleep,' Hannes yawned.

'Sssh – they're hauling down the flag,' Rolf told him.

They stood with heads bowed, hands folded behind them. Somewhere beyond the silhouetted tents, a boy blew his bugle. Hannes could smell the grass, their battlefield, and hear the whirring of the crickets. Fähnleinführer Hinrichs' hand touched the flagpole.

'We will carry on the struggle begun by our fathers,' he intoned. 'We will steel our bodies and dedicate our hearts for the sake of future generations. Repeat after me . . .'

He used the most velvety of voices, halting after each phrase to allow the boys to repeat it.

'In the name of the two million dead of the war . . . in the name of all those who fell so that National Socialism might live . . . in the name of Horst Wessel and the other heroes of our movement . . . we swear that we know no other duty than to serve our fatherland, no greater happiness than to lay down our lives for our Führer, so that Germany may live . . .'

The last phrase was repeated. Hinrichs inhaled deeply, then raised his voice to an unexpected, exultant shout. Hannes felt goose-pimples breaking out on his arms and legs. It sounded like a dog howling at the moon.

'Germany must live,' the voice soared, 'even if we have to die!'

'Germany must live,' one hundred and sixty voices roared back, in unison, 'even if we have to die!'

'Our flag is tomorrow!'

'Our flag is tomorrow!'

'Our flag means more to us than death!'

'Our flag means more to us than death!'

The solitary fanfare sounded again. With all eyes upon it, the flag's limp silhouette slowly descended.

The tent smelled of canvas, oranges and sweat. Rolf was hiding behind his pack, whistling. Lessing and Freitag read by the light of their pocket torches. A mild night wind hummed through the heather. Hannes got undressed, stretched himself under his blanket, closed sore eyes. Freitag and Lessing could be heard tittering over their newspaper, which crackled as pages were turned. He heard a match being struck, scented fumes drifted across the tent. The bastards were smoking!

'What's so funny?' Hannes asked, raising himself up to peer through the darkness.

'Smoking is forbidden,' he added when no answer came.

'Show him the cartoon,' Lessing snuffled. A newspaper page crushed into a ball landed on Hannes' blanket. Rolf turned towards him and directed his torch onto the paper. He, too, held a hot fag-end in his fist. No wonder he had been so quiet.

'It's only *Der Stürmer*,' Hannes said. 'Can see that stuck up at the corner of Löwenstrasse and Abendrothsweg every day. How about a fag for me, then?'

'Let him get his own,' Freitag said.

'I got half of one somewhere,' Lessing grunted. 'Here, let him be sick on that.'

Hannes caught the white cylinder with his hand and placed it carefully between his lips. Rolf lit a match for him, he inhaled. The tobacco tasted bitter, but not unpleasant. He waited for something to happen. Nothing did. He didn't even feel sick.

'Look at that!' Rolf exclaimed awe-struck. Light from his torch flickered across the page of *Der Stürmer*, came to rest on a pen-and-ink cartoon. It showed a short-legged Jew with protruding nose and stomach, lounging in an armchair. One hand held a book marked 'Talmud', the other caressed the naked breast of a blonde girl with plaits. The girl's face mirrored acute suffering, the Jew grinned. Saliva dripped from his thick, sausage-like lips.

Rolf read out the caption: 'Never underestimate the rapacity, the uncontrolled sexuality of the Jew. The teachings of the Talmud compel him to pollute German women and girls.'

'Your type, Blondie?' Lessing sniggered in the dark.

'Nah, seen it before. My dad gets the paper at home. It's not a real girl, my dad says. More a symbol, like.'

'Like a bear,' Hannes breathed, still studying the cartoon.

'What?'

'Everybody looks like some sort of animal. Haven't you noticed? There's Anders who's like a sheep, and . . .'

He stopped abruptly, buried his cigarette stub in the ground beside him. He had caught himself only just in time. Animal likenesses only concerned his other world: Waldmeister, the camel; Bohrer, the pig; Elasmosaurus, the chemist . . . Touching his forehead, he felt a film of perspiration. He stared at Rolf's face: a ghostly shimmer behind the glare of his torch. He hadn't even been listening. A narrow escape. Quickly he pointed to another caption on the page. It was under a drawing of the owner of the *Stürmer*, Julius Streicher, showing the fat man receiving a bunch of flowers from a group of ardent children.

Hannes read out:

> *He prints the Stürmer, good and true*
> *The Jews would like to beat him black and blue*
> *They hate his guts and cry 'For shame'*
> *To Streicher it is all the same*
> *He fights the Yids with every drop of blood*
> *The whole world reckons he does good.*

Above the drawing was printed in large letters: 'THE JEW IS OUR MISFORTUNE'.

'The eight hundred tomorrow, Rolf,' Hannes whispered. 'Think anybody got a chance besides Woodruff?'

But *Der Stürmer* was continuing to engage Rolf's attention. Or was he only *pretending* to read, while ruminating about Hannes' unwise remark about people resembling animals?

'I bet I could tell you a thing or two about the goings on in this camp,' Hannes whispered, 'things you don't know about.'

He realised he was borrowing Rolf's own technique of claiming secret sources of information. Rolf allowed himself a faint sneer.

'You don't know anything I don't.'

'Bet I do.'

'Bet you don't.'

'Quiet!' Freitag shouted in the darkness. 'What's all the bleedin' whispering about? Reveille's at six. Go to sleep.'

'Quiet yourself,' Rolf yelled back. Then his voice dropped to a hush. 'Whatever you think you know, you'd better tell me, Hacker. I'm in charge of this Jungenschaft, remember!'

'It's got nothing to do with that.'

Lowering his voice still further, Hannes reported what he had seen behind the gorse-bushes that afternoon.

'See who they were?' Rolf wanted to know.

'I didn't stay to watch that long.'

'They have to be reported. Don't want skunks like that in our Fähnlein.'

So Rolf knew all about it!

'Bet you've never seen anybody do that,' Hannes challenged him.

'Schmitt does it.'

'He never!'

'Admits it as well. I wouldn't have him in my Jungenschaft. His family are degenerates, my dad says. I could tell you stories . . . My dad gets to know about things like that . . . You're a bit backward, aren't you, Hacker? Bet you never ever seen your sister without clothes on.'

Hannes was puzzled. 'What's that got to do with it?'

'With what?'

'With what we were talking about.'

'I don't know what *you* were talking about. I was talking about girls and that.'

'Talk about girls tomorrow,' Freitag grumbled wearily. 'Shut your gobs or I'll have you before Hinrichs, the both of you.'

'Bet you never kissed Lore Meinke,' Rolf hissed.

'You haven't either.'

'Have. Lots of times.'

'On the mouth?'

'Nearly. She liked it as well. I'm her No. 1, she says.'

'Did she say what I was?'

'Yes. No. 2.'

'Old Schemel likes Lore best as well.'

'Fat chance. He can have Inge Ahrens when you've finished with her.'

'Now look, you two!' It was Lessing's blocked voice this time. 'If you don't stop this whispering, I'll have to report you to Hinrichs first thing in the morning. I mean it. Pipe down and get to sleep.'

'Better go to sleep,' Rolf said.

'All right. Night, then, Rolfie.'

'Night.'

Rolf wasn't so bad really, once he forgot his private wars. All that stuff about 'getting even' with people. He'd forgotten all about Freezy; now he was cadging cigarettes from Lessing and Freitag, deadly enemies of a few hours before.

Hannes stretched his legs, wrapped himself in his blanket. Tomorrow they'll have to give me the knife, he thought. I've sung and fought and shouted, I've been just as good as anybody in camp. Can't do more than I've done today.

The wind was rolling against the canvas. He felt good and sleepy. Fancy Rolf trying to link up that dirty stuff with Erika. What a nerve! Erika. . .

He hadn't thought about her once, not all the time he'd been in camp. Nor about Georg or their secret plans. He hadn't even nosed out useful information to give them. All he'd done was enjoy himself. He was the worst of traitors. He deserved to be lined up against a brick wall and shot at dawn. No, not yet. Hadn't he promised Rosa that he'd be all right? It was all she lived for, she'd told him: to see him grow into a man. That damn Bohrer. Mucking about in her consulting-room, among all those coloured jars and bottles? Picking them up with his clumsy paws, smashing them . . . Fried eggs! Horrible!

He turned over.

Go to sleep, he told himself. Tomorrow they'd have to march fifteen kilometres . . . Scratches and blisters . . . So much nicer to sit with Rosa in the sun on the jetty . . .

He thought of his new knife in its sheath, hilt glinting, and the green and white ferry rocking in a dark harbour . . .

CHAPTER SEVEN

Walking down the Hoheluftchaussee, Hannes tried to keep one step ahead of Anna Panse. If the worst came to the worst and they were detected together, he could pretend the girl was a stranger.

'Mustn't be late for the picture,' he explained gruffly. Anna wore a beige overcoat and gloves. A bright red leather handbag with a brass lock dangled on straps from her arm. To go to a cinema with a popular girl like Lore Meinke would have added to his standing at the depot, but the Lore Meinkes of this world were never thrust on one by one's mother.

'Can't possibly keep up with you at this pace,' Anna Panse grumbled.

She certainly tried hard enough. Her round, overfed face registered sulks. A broad, beribboned pigtail hung down her back, plump legs bulged in white stockings – how could Mama fail to appreciate that to be seen walking down the Hoheluftchaussee with Anna Panse was suicide. The red handbag alone was enough to turn him into a laughing stock forever. The one tolerable thing about Anna Panse was her name. The centre-forward of Eimsbüttel, a genius, was called Panse. No relation, alas.

Why should he be victimised, his position endangered, just because Frau Panse and his mother wanted 'the children' out of the way while they discussed business?

Years ago, Anna's mother had worked as a maid at Rosa's. Hannes was sworn never to mention this to Anna. Frau Panse was married to a wealthy party member now. They lived in a villa on the banks of the Alster. Once a month she wanted to show that nothing had changed in her regard for the Hackers. She was driven in a Mercedes to Falkenried with orders for carpet fringes for Mama, usually leaving as quickly as courtesy allowed. Hannes hated those fringes, a form of concealed charity. They often kept his mother in the kitchen until long after midnight, her face burning.

Frau Panse's attempts to 'help' weren't compensated by the enforced presence of Anna. She spent her time at the Hackers boasting about the things she possessed: *her* bicycle, *her* typewriter, *her* gold watch, an enormous doll's house she called 'my mansion', an endless succession of new purses, gloves, hats, belts. None of these treasures could cure her boredom which expressed itself in tantrums. Still, Anna Panse had a sweet tooth. She was usually good for a marzipan bar.

'I can't for the life of me understand why your house always smells so awful.' She waddled beside him. 'Makes me quite sick. Horrid.'

'I suppose *your* house never smells.'

'Certainly not. We use disinfectant.'

If only one could put on a bandage at times like this, like that Invisible Man he had just been reading about. Rosa had taken the book out of the library for him. If they had given him the knife things might be different. He'd stand up to anybody then. Next time, the Ram had promised, next time lucky, Hacker! As if luck came into it. No, they had something on him, they *suspected* . . .

He thought he heard loud, derisive laughter behind him. Was that Schmitt's voice? Forcing himself not to look, he plunged on. Anna was swinging her red handbag. With every step she took it knocked against his side.

'My father took us to the theatre last week,' she said. 'Best seats in the house. Your father no longer gets press tickets, does he?'

Hannes did not wish to reply. They had passed beyond that danger zone where somebody from the depot might recognise them. Soon they would be swallowed up by the disinfected darkness of the Capitol Cinema. That would make Anna Panse feel at home and he would be safe at last.

'You never bother to make conversation,' Anna muttered

plaintively. 'I shan't go out with you next time my mother
wants me to. I only come for the car-ride in the Mercedes,
if you must know. You should see the car my father uses for
business. A Maybach. It has a speaking tube. You can talk to
the driver without him looking round at you. And there's a little
table in the back for playing cards.'

She prattled on, one step behind him. Hannes thought of the
times he had been invited to the Panse villa to 'play' with Anna.
She only knew primitive card games and lost interest the moment
she started to lose, humming and trilling and playing more and
more slowly. Finally she would throw all her cards in the air and
collapse, lying on the carpet with her mouth open, pretending to
be dead. You couldn't really talk to Anna Panse, let alone flirt
with her, as you could talk and flirt with Lore Meinke, who was
not only *attractive* but *knew a thing or two* . . .

'We've arrived – hadn't you noticed?'

Anna stood in front of the cinema's display case.

'Look,' she said. 'All Next Week: Hans Albers. Everybody
says my father looks like Hans Albers.'

'Your father looks like Emil Jannings,' Hannes grumbled. He
dug into his pocket for the money Mama had given him 'to take
Anna out'.

'I'll pay, if you don't mind,' Anna said and quickly walked
through the sweetly perfumed foyer. 'My father says you're
not to spend money on me; you can't afford it.'

'Give us a lemon jelly,' he pleaded when they were seated.

'Give *me* a lemon jelly,' she corrected him. 'It hardly shows
that you go to your swanky old Realgymnasium, I must say. Just
one then. Oh! It's starting.'

Hannes looked despondently at the screen. Some of the
picture's sub-titles were so smudged as to be indecipherable.
The story, when you got the hang of it, was about Shirley
Temple and two men, one in a grey uniform, who was her
father, and another in a black one who was not. There was a
war, but a very slow, old-fashioned American one, with nobody
getting killed. In the end, Shirley Temple stopped what little
fighting there was, and everybody cried. Even *Triumph of the
Will* had been more exciting.

He walked out into white daylight with a blinding headache.

'Isn't she adorable?' Anna squealed. 'Oooh – you've got a sugar moustache.'

'From *one* lemon jelly?' Then: 'I'll walk you back to the Alster.'

'No, you don't. I'm to call for Mummy at your place.' She consulted her wrist-watch importantly. 'We'll take a Number Two tram. Don't worry, I'll pay.'

The word 'tram' pierced his muddled thoughts like an arrow. If she insisted on taking the tram, they would have to pass the depot. Unthinkable! Anna Panse, fat Anna Panse in her beige coat, her podgy hands encased in beige gloves, her red handbag dangling from her arm, marching across the length of the yard, while he was in obsequious attendance a step or two behind! At this time of the afternoon the depot would be crawling with people he knew. The Hoheluft gang might be there. Even if Rolf wasn't, Schemel was sure to report to him what he had seen.

'We'll walk,' he said. 'Help you to get rid of all that fat.'

'I'm not fat!' Anna cried. 'I'll tell my mum of you. I'll never ever come out with you again!'

'We'll walk,' he repeated sternly.

'In that case I'm first having an ice cream at Hedwig's Ice Café.'

'All right then.'

Buying a cone and licking it in the street wasn't good enough for Anna Panse. She had to go to a proper ice-cream parlour, sit down at a table, take off her gloves. After scanning the menu, she ordered vanilla for him, a strawberry and lemon ice for herself. She wolfed it down, grabbing the only chocolate biscuit in the silver bowl on the table. Then she opened her handbag, took out some money, and asked the waitress to keep the change.

'It's jolly expensive going out with you, Hannes,' she remarked when they were out in the street again. 'My father has just bought an ice-cream machine. It's heaven. By the way, he thinks you're jolly lucky to have me spend my time with you. Lots of people wouldn't, he says. Needn't tell you why, need I?'

She stopped abruptly, afraid she had gone too far. Hannes quickened his step. That's how it was now. You had to stand for stuff like that. Only three years ago – less than five weeks before all the trouble started – there had been that last memorable Christmas Eve. There was roast goose and red cabbage and a bottle of red wine on the table. Rosa had come and a few of father's relatives. They all kept well away now. The family lived in a nice, airy flat then, with a view of a football field. There had been a tall Christmas tree, laden with coloured baubles and curled wax candles and chocolate rings on a string. His father – flushed and laughing after his office party – had worn an elegant pin-striped suit and his bow-tie; Mama had her hair permed and wore new ear-rings. There had been many presents, including a book from Frau Panse for him: *Sport Through the Ages*, and the tree had turned on a silver turntable and played '*Silent Night, Holy Night*'.

He had managed to circumvent the tram-yard and was navigating Anna through the arched passage. About to congratulate himself on his cleverness, he suddenly heard Rolf's unmistakable whistle. The passage walls amplified the sound. Hannes sprinted ahead of Anna, as he had promised himself if the worst came to the worst. But he had left Rolf's bicycle out of his calculations.

> . . . *dark or fair—*
> *I like them best when bare* . . .

Rolf sang as he swished past them. At the end of the passage he swerved and squeezed his handlebar brakes. Then he laughed, the shrill, maniacal 'hah-aha-haa' Hannes had heard after the piggy-back battle, when Freitag and Lessing had rolled about in the grass. The sight of the fat girl with her red handbag trundling after Hannes was even better. Rich stuff indeed. Rolf was not fooled by Hannes's sprint or by the desperately innocent smile he attempted. Rolf quickly pedalled through the passage again, hands folded behind him, whistling shrilly as he turned the corner.

The worst had happened. Hannes looked at Anna Panse with helpless rage as she strode past him.

'What on earth was the matter with that lout?' she asked

as they climbed the staircase. 'Why did he laugh at you like that?'

'Laughed?' Hannes asked, taking three steps at a time. 'Didn't hear anyone laugh. What are you talking about?'

The tableau that awaited them in the kitchen left no doubt: a new crisis had materialised while they were at the cinema. Anna seemed to be oblivious to the tenseness in the atmosphere, inanely chattering away about Shirley Temple. Frau Panse, fur coat trailing on the kitchen floor, embraced her. Over Anna's shoulder, she stared at Hannes gloomily, the way people looked at you when they are about to reveal a disaster.

Papa stood with his back turned to Frau Panse, facing the mirror, pedantically clipping his moustache. His mother was bent over the table, fingernail idly tracing patterns on the wax cloth.

'Annalein,' Frau Panse said, at last, 'time we went home.'

She hugged Hannes briefly, then they were gone, Anna's high-pitched chatter receding down the staircase.

'Did you like the film?' Mama asked him in a self-consciously bland voice. It confirmed Hannes' suspicion: something was very wrong indeed.

'Kid's stuff,' he said. 'Shirley Temple. You know.'

He didn't feel like asking what had happened. Rolf Sandmann cycling through the passage the very moment he and Anna Panse were walking home! No doubt Rolf was already regaling the gang with all the grisly details. Fat girl. Red handbag. White stockings. Schemel would be jeering maliciously for weeks . . .

'I'm going to be arrested,' Papa suddenly said, snipping away at the ends of his moustache. 'That's what the Panse creature came over to tell us.'

'To warn us,' his mother added.

'What's he done, then?'

Hannes studied his father's bemused smile in the mirror. It was all happening on a stage, a long way off.

Mama said, 'What have any of us done?'

'Frau Panse is an old gossip, Mama.'

'Her husband gets certain information at the Rathaus. Your father's file got passed around.'

The scissors were going click-click in front of the mirror. Hannes' eyes refused to focus. His father was giving some sort of performance, pretending to be brave.

'Frau Panse thinks,' Mama said, 'that someone must have denounced us. Radio Moscow. One of the neighbours.'

Her hands were clenched; Hannes noticed the dark arches of her fingernails. She was fighting tears. If only she wouldn't always bawl.

'False alarm,' Hannes said. 'Papa hasn't done anything.'

'He's married to me.'

Mama now burst into tears. Her head came to rest on her forearm. Papa stood behind her, looking embarrassed, listlessly stroking her hair. Why doesn't she have a shampoo now and again, Hannes thought. Why can't she look the way she used to?

'I shall tell them nothing. There is nothing they can do to me.' His father took a deep breath. '*Semper fidelis*, that's my motto.'

He walked to the window-box, broke off the stem and bloom of a geranium and inserted the red flower into his button-hole. Then he looked up at the kitchen clock.

'I think I'll just . . .'

He was off to Sandmann's again!

'You'll want something to eat first,' Mama said, getting to her feet heavily, noisily blowing her nose on her apron. Why did she have to do these disgusting things? What would Rosa have said?

'Have a lie down, why don't you?' Papa said, kissing her lightly on her temple. 'Take an aspirin. The boy can get his own supper for once.'

Hannes read a look of pained resignation on his mother's face. Couldn't she at least argue with him?

'All right, you go, dear.'

She was speaking to Papa as if he were a little boy. Have your fun, she seemed to be saying, I know there's nothing to keep you here. Papa nimbly slipped out of the room. Presently they heard the front door close.

'I think I will have a lie down,' Mama said. 'Maybe you'll ask Erika when she comes home to get your . . .'

Her voice trailed. How sorry she felt for herself!

Hannes exploded: 'Maybe she'll get my supper, maybe she won't. Who cares? Erika's got Georg, Father's got Sandmann's, you've got your sodding headaches. I can look after myself, thanks.'

'Why do you talk to me like that?'

He sensed how reproachfully Mama would be gazing at him now, waiting for some explanation for that outburst. How easy it would be to fall into her arms, allow her to pet you and tell you how much she loved you, that nothing else mattered. So easy, yet he couldn't do it.

'It's true,' he said, avoiding her eyes, 'you don't give a damn what happens to me. None of you. I'm the nuisance around here, I just make everything more difficult . . .'

He paused, hoping she would contradict him. She said nothing. Hot rage consumed all reason.

'You hate me! Why don't you admit it? You wish I were dead. You wish I'd never been born. You and Papa. That's why you make me go to camp, why you send me off with a cow like Anna Panse.'

His mother's silence was slow torture, burning into him like a hot needle. Had she been close enough, he might have reached out to hit her.

'You've all changed. Look at you! You and your bloody tablets. You *want* things to get worse! I can't stand the sight of you!'

'That's what they've done to you,' Mama managed to say.

She was quite alone with her grief. Yes, she wanted it to be this way! Perhaps she was even enjoying it . . .

'Didn't really mean that,' he said. 'Sorry.'

But Mama had quietly left the kitchen. He heard the lino creaking next door; the bed groaned as she lay down on it.

His eyes had fastened onto a headline in the newspaper his father had left behind. Germany had won the epée contest in the Pentathlon. Now we needed only one more gold medal to join the Americans at the top of the table. First Rolf and Anna's red handbag. Then Papa threatened, the row with Mama. Now this.

He rose from the table, ran water into the kettle. While it boiled up, he cut himself a slice of brown bread, smeared margarine on it. Was it wrong to feel hungry at a time like this? The bread was crisp and fresh. He munched happily.

As he poured the boiling water over the leaves of peppermint tea, he had an idea. Maybe he could save Papa. Mama didn't know where to start. He took the tray into her bedroom. When she had one of her headaches she needed peppermint tea. She could take her tablets with it. She liked coffee even more, but Hannes found coffee too complicated to make.

'I'm going to Sandmann's as well,' he announced, all anger drained away. 'Got an idea. I'm going to warn Papa.'

His mother looked up distraught. She warmed her hands on the teapot.

'I don't understand . . .'

'Papa's in danger, I think I know why. It's Sandmann himself who's got him into this. He's the Blockwarden. It's his job to spy on people and get them arrested.'

'Don't, Hannes.' His mother was frowning. 'This isn't one of your rubbishy Edgar Wallace stories . . .'

'I'm going down all the same.'

'Please don't. If Papa wants to be by himself for a while . . .'

'Drink your tea. Got your tablets? Shan't be long.'

He slammed the door behind him. Mama had already forgiven him. Stay active, he told himself. It was exciting, turning ideas into action. Why did everybody treat him like an idiot? Sending him out with that half-wit of a girl, when a real crisis was brewing! And a fat lot she knew about Edgar Wallace.

Sandmann's was crowded. It always smelled of beer and gravy and smoke here. Enamel advertisements for mustard and tobacco were nailed to the walls. A man with a wooden leg sat on a chair near the door, playing the accordion, a large Alsatian stretched out in front of him. Men sat around scrubbed tables and played Skat, their glasses resting on soiled cardboard beer-mats.

Behind the bar Sandmann manipulated his beer-pumps, moustache bristling, his bald head gleaming under a row of naked lights. Now and then he wiped his hands on his leather apron. He greeted arrivals by touching his temple with his forefinger. Beside him a grey-haired crone chopped herrings, bringing down her knife on the wooden platter with staccato precision. The tip of her tongue projected from her lips. Her faced was flushed with concentration. In his mind Hannes saw the old woman hacking away with relish not at herrings but at human bodies. What a thought! But in a place like this anything was possible.

'Looking for Rolfie, lad?' Sandmann asked, scraping the head off a tankard of beer. Under his dark walrus moustache, his lips parted in a grin. His sleeves were rolled up to reveal tattoo marks on his arm. Rolf liked to boast that his dad had once been a seaman. Now he's an informer, Hannes thought. All the Sandmanns had this rotten streak. Why couldn't Papa see the truth staring him in the face?

'My father here, Herr Sandmann?'

'Over there, Hannes.'

He had always imagined his father at the centre of a carousing group of cronies when he went down to Sandmann's. In fact, Papa sat alone at a small table near the pub's back door, staring into a very small glass of grog, biting the end of his empty cigarette holder. The red flower in his buttonhole looked already wilted. He seemed to be muttering to himself. A wave of shame swept over Hannes. It was obvious what Papa was doing. He was rehearsing what he was going to say when they came for him.

'Hello, Dad!'

His father looked up, frowned, did not seem to recognise his son. Then he became flustered and angry.

'What the devil are you doing here? Can't a man go anywhere without . . .'

'I've got to talk to you a minute.'

'Don't whisper! Are you mad? What's the matter with you?'

'I only came to warn you . . .'

'Don't whisper here, I tell you.'

'It's Sandmann . . . He's Blockwarden, isn't he? I'm sure he denounced you. That's what I came down to tell you.'

'Rubbish! Come a bit closer. As for Sandmann, he has no idea

. . . I mean about your mother . . . about us. Would he let me sit here, drinking on credit, if he had?'

Hannes stared at his father. Realising his mistake, he put his hand to his mouth. What a hare-brained idea he'd had! Of course Sandmann didn't know anything. If he did, then Rolf knew! . . . His eyes smarted, the smoke was almost impenetrable. The man playing the harmonica had started to bawl an old sailor's song.

'Go on up,' his father said, 'go on, go back to your mother.' He was waving Hannes away as one waves away a yapping stray dog. 'Never do anything like this again. Take your mother a cup of her peppermint tea.'

'Can't I get you another drink?'

'No, go away. I need to concentrate.'

'Sorry, Dad.'

Hannes turned to go, glancing at Sandmann who smiled benignly, eating a hot Frankfurter, grinding the end into a heap of mustard on a cardboard plate. The old woman was still decimating her herrings. No wonder Rolf was a leader! He had won his knife, he had no family problems, he didn't have to feel shame or fear. There was no Jewish grandmother to keep quiet about, no mother with headaches, who sent him out with dreadful girls like Anna Panse. His father was prosperous and happy to talk to him. At the door, Hannes looked back at his own father. His little glass was empty now, he had started to mumble again, lips moving rapidly under the finely clipped moustache.

'Had something to eat?' Erika asked him. 'Mama told me you made her some peppermint tea. That was nice of you . . .'

'I had a sandwich. Did she tell you . . .?'

'Don't bother your head about it, not yet. It may be just another round-up scare. They do it to frighten us. After all, what's Papa done?'

'That's what I said, and everybody screamed at me.'

Hannes stood by the open window, enviously gazing at the neat squares of yellow light opposite. Why couldn't he be part of one of those placid, uncomplicated families? An old man was squatting behind the window-ledge in his shirt sleeves, reading his paper and smoking his pipe. In another square, a large family sat round the kitchen table, eating supper. The father was in SA uniform, the children's loud voices floated through the open window and dispersed in the still summer air. In the passage leading to the next courtyard a couple stood embraced, undeterred by a pack of boys rattling past them on scooters. In the distance, Hannes could hear the clanking of trams as they shunted into the depot. If he listened hard enough, he told himself, he might detect the voices of Rolf and Schmitt and Schemel, cackling over the incident of the red handbag.

That's how life treated you. Make one mistake, step out of line just once, walk through a passage with a fat girl, and nothing you had ever done was remembered. He looked up at the sooty evening sky. He should be down there now, in the tram yard, arguing his case, explaining Anna Panse away, laughing at the red handbag *with* them, before the whole thing festered in Rolf's mind and became serious.

Erika came over and rested her elbows on the sill.

'I'm going to have a bath,' she said. 'Off you go next door.'

'Just tell me this. Why did Mama ever marry him in the first place?'

'You don't ask questions like that.'

'Why not?'

'You're not old enough to understand.'

'That's what you think,' he scoffed. 'He's sorry he ever married her, isn't he?'

'Give it a rest.'

'. . . and she's sorry, too. For him.'

'You should see some married couples,' Erika said. 'The Elsters next door row all evening and throw things at each other. How would you like parents like that?'

'If it weren't for Mama he'd still be a Bohemian, and wear bow-ties and work for a newspaper.'

Erika didn't answer. Didn't she want to discuss serious things with him? In a while, she'd show him her Teddy Bear frown. Now she wanted her bath. She had no idea how much he knew about life. What he had seen at camp: girls didn't know such things even existed. And there were words she wouldn't

know. He had a good mind to try them out on her. Instead
he said:

'Bertha Heller's husband divorced her, didn't he?'

'He'll never divorce Mama. He'll never do that.'

'Lots of men in Papa's position are doing it just to keep
their jobs.'

Hannes thought of his father sitting alone at his table,
muttering to himself. Was he thinking of leaving them? No
wonder he could no longer bear to call them by their Christian
names. He and Erika probably stood between him and what he
wanted from life.

'Erika,' he said suddenly, 'I've got to meet this Georg
of yours.'

'What for?'

'You never bring him here. Where do you go?'

'He's got a room.' She blushed. 'Don't tell Mama.'

''Course not.'

Dorn came into his mind. Another problem. A danger. A link.
*The Man Who Knew Too Much . . . The Four Just Men . . . The
Gaunt Stranger . . .*

'I want to ask him – things,' he added.

He felt her arm touch his shoulder. They sat together on the
window sill, looking out into the fading light, listening to the
evening sounds. In the yard below, girls were skipping rope. A
radio jangled *Love Makes the World Go Round*. A pair of horses
was pulling a beer-wagon over cobblestones. The pressure of
Erika's arm felt strangely comforting. She's my only ally, he
thought.

'Georg,' he said. 'How about tomorrow?'

'Let me have my bath.'

He slipped down from the window sill, picked up his father's
newspaper, went into his bedroom. There, he opened the
paper, neatly folded it back at the sports section. He let the
Olympic results and tables absorb and envelop him. It was very
comforting.

CHAPTER EIGHT

With marching strides Georg piloted Hannes and Erika through the narrow lanes of the fair. In one hand he held his pipe, the other, large and rough, clasped Erika's waist, fondling her when he thought Hannes wasn't looking.

Georg was not as Hannes had imagined him to be. When Erika had talked about him, she seemed to refer to someone dark and sinister-looking, with heavy-lidded eyes and bushy eyebrows. Hannes expected him to walk with a stoop, a man who was a cross between a mysterious Edgar Wallace hero and a film spy.

He turned out to be no different from the workmen who sat around at Sandmann's playing Skat. He wore corduroy trousers, an open-necked shirt and a scratched leather jacket. He spoke with a fruity Hamburg accent. He wasn't even young. About thirty, Hannes guessed, a bit old to be a hero, certainly too old to go around with his sister. Nobody could call him handsome. He was short and stumpy, and almost bald. He had a shiny red face and crisply curly hair. When he laughed, he showed a set of teeth white and regular enough to be false.

Georg had not taken them to the Dom, the sprawling amusement park on the Heiligengeistfeld, but to a shabby suburban fun-fair, set on some waste ground near the paint factory where he worked. Tinny music drew them through a sweet doughnut-scented mist from roundabout to roundabout. Hannes ploughed through the air on a giant swing; he enjoyed driving the dodgems, imagining he was Rosemeyer butting into anyone too slow in getting off the mark.

In Georg's company, Erika's Teddy-Bear sternness dissolved

into yielding and fervour. Her eyes flickered as she clutched his hand. She wore lipstick, but most of it had come off on the giant lolly Georg had bought her.

'What's next on the menu?' he asked after they had washed down sizzling Frankfurters and warm rolls with fizzy lemonade.

'Haven't been on the ghost train.'

'Lad's right,' Georg said. 'Must do ghost train.'

'You do ghost train,' Erika said, mimicking Georg's accent. 'I hate being frightened. I'll wait outside. Go on, you two.'

'And lose my chance to slip me hand where it shouldn't be in the dark when lad isn't looking? Not likely.'

He laughed, pretending to defend himself against Erika, who was pummelling him with small, ineffectual fists. Finally, she buried her flushed face into Georg's leather jacket.

'Shouldn't talk like that in front of the boy.'

'He's in the Jungvolk, isn't he? Bet he could tell *us* a thing or two.'

'You bet,' Hannes confirmed proudly.

They came to a halt outside a gaudy façade. Large letters dripping red paint proclaimed the ghost train's attractions.

'Dance of the Skeletons,' Hannes read out. 'Murder! Torture! Bloodbaths! Thirty Pfennigs' worth of darkness for you and your girl! True Horror! Forget your daily cares here!'

'I'm going to like this,' Hannes said.

'We'll have a plateful,' Georg agreed. 'You'll be sorry, Erika. Come on, lad.'

Georg led Hannes to a row of small wooden cars, each just wide enough for two, which were about to be propelled into the Unknown. Hannes got into one of the cars while Georg held out some money. An attendant took it, then pushed them through twin doors. They rattled through darkness, gathering speed. Sirens wailed, blending with the screams of murder victims, the cackle of lunatics. Cobwebs tickled their faces, whips licked their cheeks. Illuminated skeletons, shooting up from nowhere, stretched out fleshless bones. They drove straight into the arms of a blood-spattered vampire, turned at right angles, almost crashed into a one-eyed giant, who held a club raised over his head, bringing it down within inches of their faces. Tableaux of torture and decapitation flashed by, sirens screamed. Suddenly they slammed through the doors again – back to sanity.

'Smashing,' Hannes said.

'Lovely.' Georg pounded Hannes' shoulder. 'Erika missed something good. Where is she?'

'Over there . . . with her back to us.'

Hannes spotted her in a small group outside a booth further down the lane. With her head under its white beret cocked to one side, she listened to the blandishments of a cadaverous barker in a battered top hat. From time to time the man coughed pitifully into his fist, then praised his 'American All-Star Wondershow – straight from Broadway, New York'. His eyes roved listlessly along the upturned faces of his audience.

'Listen,' Hannes said, holding Georg back by his leather sleeve. 'Before we get back to Erika, I've got to warn you about something.'

'Warn me?'

Georg was about to laugh again, but Hannes tightened his grip. 'Ever heard of a fellow called Dorn? Lives in Hoheluft.'

'What of it?'

He only wanted to find Erika again. They were being jostled in the middle of the lane. Behind them the ghost train wailed, doors slammed.

'He's got it in for you, Georg. You're being watched.'

'So what? Just another wanker in uniform. His father and I belonged to the same union once. Now he's on the dole, with a sideline spying for Blockwarden. I'm told youngster takes after him, acts as go-between for SA lads and schoolgirls.'

'He'd stop at nothing,' Hannes confirmed.

'Just a little bully,' Georg laughed. 'Come on. Let's catch up with your sister before she finds herself someone better-looking than me.'

Can't do more, Hannes thought. I warned him.

Georg drove them back to his little place on his motor-cycle. Hannes sat in the blimp-shaped side-car, newly painted blue and yellow, while Erika crouched behind Georg, arms tightly wrapped around his waist, eyes closed against the wind.

The flat, where Georg lodged with a couple of old-age pensioners, was in a grey tenement building off the Hoheluftchaussee. The walls were ash-coloured, cracks like spiders' legs ran down from the ceiling. Georg knew how to make such a place habitable. He'd covered a low divan with a purple spread that might have been a sail once. There were stained coloured cushions, the walls were plastered with photographs from an old calendar, mountain views of Switzerland. On a chair in the far corner stood a wind-up gramophone with a wooden lid and a stack of records next to it. Some of them, lacking the usual paper envelopes, had bits chipped off the edges. A soap-box, garishly painted green and orange, served as a book-case. The narrow window looked out on a cobbled backyard. Cats prowled, dogs lay stretched out in shafts of fading sunlight.

It didn't add up to Hannes' idea of a clandestine headquarters. His eyes swept vainly round the little room for a clue to Georg's dangerous activities.

While Georg was in the kitchen making coffee, Erika and Hannes sat round a mahogany table in the middle of the room, bare except for a jam-jar filled with water and a few wild flowers – buttercups, daisies, dandelions from the green patches in the courtyard.

'This is where you go in the evening?' Hannes asked his sister.

She nodded. 'You promised not to tell.'

'Not to worry,' he told her. He felt so richly laden with secrets, one more confidence made no difference. 'You're safe.'

Georg had come back into the room with a steaming coffee-pot and the evening paper.

'Norwegians beat us at soccer.'

Hannes was up in a flash, seizing the paper, greedily gobbling up the report.

'Two goals to nothing!' he jeered.

'Happy when your country takes a beating?' Georg asked, pouring coffee.

'Aren't you?'

Georg shook his head. 'I'd like to be as proud of my country's achievements as the next man. That's not chauvinism, that's patriotism. Never was anything wrong with that. Don't let 'em twist your mind, lad. We're the patriots. Not them.'

'Don't want us, I mean them, to win the Games, do you?'

'Couldn't care less, lad.' Georg's free hand was squeezing Erika's knee under the table. Then he lifted his cup to his lips. 'They'll end up top of the table anyhow.'

'Nobody *wins* the Olympics, do they?' Erika asked.

'They do this time,' Georg laughed, 'or Reichssportführer Tschammer von Osten gets his cards.'

'You mean they can fiddle it?' Hannes asked.

Now they were getting down to it. Here was real inside information being passed on. Papa never talked to him like this. Perhaps he never knew anything important. Georg seemed to know a lot . . . Even Erika, who wasn't interested in sport, looked concerned. What a pity he could never tell Rolf about any of this.

'They don't have to cheat,' Georg said, puffing at his pipe. 'What happens, they find they've come second or third, so they'll pull some fancy new competition out of the bag – dung-carving, sack-racing, what have you. Three guesses who'll be competing with the great German dung-carvers and sack-racers. A couple of Japs to make it look good. Comes time for points to be totted up, including gold for dung-carving, sack-racing etcetera, guess who's climbed to top of table . . .'

'Americans won't stand for that, will they?'

'They stood for us marching into Rhineland, they stood for Abyssinia, they're standing for our mates being shipped to KZs by the cartload. Expect they'll stand for a bit of dung-carving and sack-racing as well.'

'So they're all scared of us?' Hannes asked. Happy to have some information of his own to impart he added: 'The Communists fired on our warships off the coast of Spain last week.'

Georg shrugged and puffed. 'War is war.'

'Is there going to be a war?'

'Somebody's got to fight the wicked Bolshevik. Germans to the front! Strong man at the helm, that's what they all want!'

Was Georg being sarcastic? You never could tell. So far he hadn't really said anything really dangerous. Never ever mentioned Him. Georg was clearly practised in keeping his lips buttoned.

'That's enough politics.' Georg winked at Hannes as he squeezed Erika. 'Plenty of time when you're both as old and bald as me. Let's have some music.'

Funny sort of revolutionary leader, Hannes pondered. He liked Georg, he just hadn't turned out to be what he'd expected. He and Erika weren't really serious; no whispered exchanges about running messages or printing leaflets. Or was Georg merely testing him?

'What sort of music do you like?'

'What have you got?'

'This and that.'

'Be careful, Georg,' Erika warned.

It might have been Mama talking to his father. Was there something subversive about Georg's records? He was winding up the gramophone, which wheezed and rumbled. The first record sounded old and scratchy. The singer was hoarse, Hannes found it hard to follow the words.

Georg smiled as he turned the record over.

'How did you like that?'

'Not so loud this time,' Erika began before Hannes could reply.

Georg wound up the machine again. Then he leant against the wall, pensively rubbing his chin.

Georg was trying to tell him something through his records, but exactly what? Hannes had never heard music like it. It wasn't classical music, nor popular songs. Some of the numbers were in a fast march tempo, others dragged like American blues – it sounded like jazz, folksong, military band music all mixed up. The words, when Hannes could make them out through the syncopated din, were like street shouts, tenement slang bawled through smoke and soot. The singers sounded bitter and desperate.

'Banned stuff, is it?' Hannes asked.

'You bet.'

'Thought as much.'

Georg wiped a record with his leather sleeve.

'Degenerate they call this stuff. It's real opera – performed all over the world.'

Hannes wasn't sure what 'degenerate' meant, but he knew they hadn't been listening to opera. Georg didn't know everything. The song Hannes liked best was the one about this man who was emigrating to Brazil to throw coffee into the ocean, and was then deported to Canada, where he burned wheat – all to keep world prices up! They were Communist songs, that much Hannes understood. Perhaps that's what the underground organisation sang in its secret hide-outs.

'Propaganda?' he asked.

'Poetry,' Georg replied ardently. 'Fellow called Bert Brecht wrote some of it.'

'He still alive?'

Georg shrugged. 'Gone to Canada to burn wheat, I dare say.' His face suddenly exploded into laughter, cheeks bulging, glowing like red Jonathan apples. He closed the lid of the gramophone.

'Mustn't tell anybody about hearing those records here,' Erika warned him.

'As if I would.'

After all the noise, the room suddenly seemed very quiet. Georg sat down close to Erika. Her hands were folded over the white beret, as it lay next to her coffee cup. A sinking sun brushed the frames of the window with gold, their faces were glowing – the colour of a blood orange.

'I wish there was something I could do . . .' Hannes said.

'Nothing you can do lad. Nothing even an old man like me can do. There's such a lot of us and yet . . .' Georg sucked at his cold pipe. 'Nothing we can do makes a scrap of difference.'

'I'm not much better than they are,' Hannes said. It took him a second or two to realise he had spoken his thoughts aloud. Georg and Erika were sitting close together now; two heads, framed by the window, tipped with dying light. Everything seemed to be receding again, as it had done the day before. There was nothing to grip, nothing to hold on to.

'I'm not much better,' he said again. 'I do all the things they do . . .'

'Mustn't worry about that, Hannes lad.' Georg's voice came from far away. 'Just carry on best you can. Shout as loud as they do. Play their daft games, sing their rubbishy songs. Just don't let them mess your mind up, see? That's the only thing we can do. Any of us.' He tapped his temple with two fingers. 'Keep a clear head. And remember where you belong.'

Hannes nodded. He had hoped for a more inspiring message. Light in the room was fading quickly now. Georg scratched about in the bowl of his pipe with a penknife. Nobody spoke. Erika looked tired, her slack lower lip projected slightly. All that remained of her red lipstick was a flaking smudge of colour.

It seemed to Hannes they were no longer alone. A fourth person had stolen into the room. Erika and Georg seemed hypnotised by the inaudible voice of the newcomer.

They were waiting for him to go, drawing away from him. Awed by the invisible interloper, they were no longer concerned with Hannes' presence.

He looked at the divan, at the purple covering, at Erika and Georg who had turned to wax. It was so dark in the room now. In the shadows, his sister's mouth had opened, but she didn't speak. Something was prodding Hannes' mind, demanding to be remembered, but he shook it off.

'I'm going now,' he said, hoping they would beg him to stay to discuss the secret plan in which his own part was vital. 'Mama will worry.'

'Shan't be long,' Erika said.

Georg got up. His right hand shot out, Hannes felt his hand gripped and quickly let go again.

'Thanks for everything. Spending all that money at the fairground. Night then, Erika.'

'Remember what I told you, Hannes.' Georg tapped his temple again. 'See you soon, lad.'

'So long then.'

Hannes fled down the gloomy staircase, jumping three or four steps at a time. That's that then, he repeated to himself. That's that. That's that. *Remember where you belong.* At the time he had known exactly what Georg meant. Now he was not so sure. Belong where? With Erika and Georg, who wanted to be left alone to lie on the purple coverlet in their darkening room? With his mother and father to whom he was just a problem? With Rolf and the Ram and Fähnleinführer Hinrichs who handed out the knife? That, at least, gave you a certain safeness. School? The depot? Enemies lurked everywhere. Only the lilac on the Streekbrücke seemed capable of calming his anxieties. And that was now spoiled by Bohrer . . .

'Hacker! Yes, you! Hacker!'

Hannes froze, forgetting where he was or where he was going. He had left the sombre tenement block behind, and taken the tube to Hoheluftbrücke. Now as he walked down Hoheluftchaussee, he heard hob-nailed boots close at his heels. An arm grabbed him and swung him round.

'What's the hurry, boy?' Dorn asked. He wore a pair of over-long frayed trousers, probably his father's, a faded green shirt and gym shoes. He grinned, slightly out of breath, showing his repulsive teeth. Girls must be blind to go out with him, Hannes thought.

'I'm going home. What's it to you?'

'This ain't your lousy depot, Hacker. When I ask a civil question I want a civil answer. Want me to call my mates?'

'I'm late,' Hannes said.

'Been with that fellow Koch, have you?'

'Been watching Altona 93.'

'Altona 93 ain't playing today, silly sod. You been with that Red.'

Dorn reached out, Hannes instinctively lowered his head. Dorn's fist shot up to skid painfully over his face. Hannes wondered if his nose had started to bleed, but took care not to put his hand to his face.

'Don't know any Reds,' he said.

Dorn grinned, rubbing his fist.

'You been to Georg Koch's. Saw you coming out of his doorway, didn't I? Your sister there with him?'

'Don't know,' Hannes said. 'Wasn't there.'

'Wasn't there? I bet. How did they do it?' Dorn formed a ring with his left thumb and forefinger and stirred in it with the middle finger of his right. 'Or doggy fashion?'

'Don't know what you're on about, Dorn.'

He turned to go, but collided with Dorn's outstretched arm.

'You're all right, Hacker.' Dorn ran a hand softly over Hannes' hair. 'I could use you. Want to do me a favour? Ask Erika to meet me down by the building-shed, corner of Bismarckstrasse, right? She'll know. Tomorrow at nine. Let you have a nice packet of fat, round, fully-packed Junos if she turns up. If she don't, I wouldn't like to be in your shoes, mate.'

He lowered his arm, Hannes pushed past him. Dorn's dry cackle rang in his ears as he crossed the road. He kicked a pebble, watching it land on a tram rail. Shan't push it off this time, he thought, so the next tram would get derailed and capsize, with everybody getting turfed out into the street. I don't care.

He ran on down the Lehmweg, stuffing his hands deeper into his pockets. Suddenly he became aware of a drone overhead. He stopped, looked up into the sky, now the colour of watered blue school ink.

A huge monster purred overhead, a mysterious, unknown species of dinosaur. It was the *Hindenburg*. The tiny cabin, a growth on the Zeppelin's vast bulk, was lit up. It looked to be on fire. Then it disappeared, with surprising speed, over the roofs of the Hoheluftchaussee. Hannes started to run. It was dark, he shivered. Something dreadful was about to happen. He was in the ghost train, smashing though twin doors, colliding with devils, monsters, skeletons, vampires . . .

CHAPTER NINE

Darkness had closed in on the depot. The lamps over the garage gates cast a gauzy light over the group; Hannes could see the lights reflected as yellow pinpoints in Lore Meinke's eyes. She was gripping the handlebars of Rolf's bicycle, squirming and giggling with barely containable excitement.

Rolf had his court assembled about him – Schmitt, Schemel, a couple of girls, two younger lads whom Rolf was training as henchmen. Even Jürgen Kloth, who had not yet departed for the seaside was there, determined to stay close to his leader and miss nothing. As they waited for Rolf's next move, Hannes felt the atmosphere charged with electricity, as if someone had wired their group to the trams that clanked past. At any moment there could be an explosion, a blue flash, a catastrophe . . .

Lore's mother did not often allow her daughter to stay out late. Hannes adored Lore. She was slender, narrow shouldered, with a lightly freckled face; a fringe cut across her forehead. She had grey eyes spotted with yellow, and a knowing air. Thinking of Lore Meinke produced in Hannes a voluptuous daydream: he was alone with her in a railway carriage, travelling to some hot remote beach, where they would shelter together under a large pink sunshade.

Unfortunately, Lore was in love with Rolf Sandmann. With anguish, Hannes watched her endorsing his pathetic jokes with giggles, tolerating his crudest intrigues. Whenever Rolf kicked his tennis ball along the length of the yard so that the crippled Schemel could fetch it back like a dog, Hannes noticed a special way she had of twisting her body. What delighted her most were Rolf's constant hints that he possessed secret information about each of them. If revealed, this could land them all in serious trouble. Listening to Rolf's catalogue of threats, Lore sounded her chopped-off giggle, twisting her knees and shoulders with shy abandon.

Hannes had long ago resigned himself to the fact that Lore was regarded as Rolf's property. It was only natural, after all: the leader got the best girl. Lore was a prize that went with Rolf's, position. How could one compete if one didn't even have the knife?

While Rolf was balancing on his bicycle, confident that all initiatives emanated from him, Hannes felt a deepening anxiety. Rosa was coming round to pay one of her rare visits to Falkenried. Any minute now she might loom up in the yard and find herself confronted with Rolf Sandmann. His carefully separated twin worlds would be smashed. Hannes took a deep breath, tried to reassure himself. Rosa would have more sense than to greet him openly. He was losing his grip, surrendering too easily to fear: first that false alarm about his father; then the scare about the red handbag, an incident which Rolf seemed to have generously overlooked. To avoid panic in future, he would have to apply a stricter discipline to his thinking. The Jungvolk was supposed to turn you into men of steel – *soldiers of the future* . . .

The bubble of tension finally burst when Rolf fell off his bicycle. He hit the ground with an agonising yell, grazing his knee. He screwed up his eyes in pain, began limping about the yard, begging for sympathy. Placing his arms around the shoulders of Lore and her friend Inge Ahrens, Rolf was borne into a nearby doorway.

While Lore turned herself into a nurse, tying a handkerchief around Rolf's injured knee, Jürgen Kloth drew Hannes aside. He had now assembled all the necessary equipment to give a performance in his puppet theatre.

'What's that got to do with me?' Hannes asked. 'Told you I wasn't interested in that stuff.'

Rolf was groaning in the doorway.

'Try spitting on it,' Schmitt advised.

The dimly lit doorway, Hannes realised, was situated in direct line between the arched passageway and his own front door.

Rosa would *have* to come this way. Was Kloth trying to set a trap for him? His damn puppets could go to hell.

'Must have broken something,' Rolf whined. 'Must have.'

Lore put fingertips with wondrously clean fingernails between her handkerchief and Rolf's scraped knee.

'Hadn't I better call your father?' she asked.

'I can take pain,' Rolf assured her, drawing in his breath as he prised himself up again. He dug his teeth into his bottom lip, as he limped heavily towards the dimly lit staircase.

'Now we're here, Rolfie,' Kloth suggested in a conspiratory whisper, 'how about a game – you know, like the other week – forfeits and things?'

The girls giggled; 'forfeits' meant scampering up to the third floor, to be kissed by favoured boys, and to pretend to be kissed by others, who were too proud to complain afterwards of the deception.

'What about it, Rolfie?' Schmitt asked obsequiously. Though Hannes knew that no girl would ever honour Schmitt's claims, he had clearly not given up hope.

'Not in the mood for any of that,' Lore Meinke declared, wrinkling up her freckled nose disdainfully. She turned to burrow her head into Inge's shoulder; their bodies undulated together in a performance of some private joke the boys could not understand.

Hannes recalled what Rolf had confided to him under canvas: Lore had kissed several boys *on the mouth*. She had confessed, moreover, that she liked it. Hannes had not been able to confirm this, but suspected it to be true.

Recognising Hannes as his closest rival, Rolf had tried for some time to divert his attention to the blue-eyed, snub-nosed Inge Ahrens. Inge had stiff yellow pigtails, Rolf had nicknamed her Angora. Hannes knew Angora liked him; she probably considered herself entitled to him – by virtue of their respective standing in the group. But he wasn't remotely interested in Inge Ahrens. Nor was he impressed when Rolf pointed out to him the chalked-up 'IA loves HH' legend on a passage wall. Hannes wanted Lore Meinke. He would wait for Lore forever, rather than be lumbered with Angora.

'You *would* suggest games like that, Asthma,' Rolf said, forgetting that it was he who habitually organised kissing games – at least when Lore Meinke had a rare evening of liberty. 'I suppose,' he added, 'that's what they're all like in your posh part of the world.'

'You go on and on about that,' Jürgen Kloth reproached his leader. 'Your folks run a pub, mine have a cake shop. What's the difference, except that your dad makes more money?'

'My dad makes an honest living.' Rolf could not allow such insubordination to pass unpunished. 'That's why he's Blockwarden. Don't want any of your girls' games here, Asthma! Got it?'

'Eats cake all day, then wants to snog all night,' Schmitt contributed supportively.

Schemel kicked his unencumbered leg gleefully. When excited he had a habit of foaming at the mouth.

'What do you want to play, cripple?' Rolf asked him.

'Me?' Schemel recognised the signal: he had to suggest the game that Rolf wanted played. 'I want to play Emperor,' Schemel cried dutifully.

'So what are you grinning about, Hacker?' Rolf frowned. 'Got something cooked up with your posh school pal?'

Hannes sensed danger. 'I'm playing Emperor,' he said quickly.

'Right then, it's decided,' Rolf declared with finality, 'Emperor it is.'

'Emperor' was Rolf's invention, his own version of a popularity poll. It began with each player going 'out' in turn, the rest had to scribble an anonymous rating of between one and ten on a scrap of paper. Each player then had his total scrawled on the wall in chalk. The boy with the highest number of points was declared Emperor. This entitled him to choose his Empress. The boy with the lowest total was named 'Slave' and commanded by the Emperor to do his bidding – like emptying dustbins, cadging cigarettes, or standing on his head for as long as the Emperor deemed fit.

Hannes admired Rolf's cunning in devising a game which

needed no skill, and did not require him to share spoils. No one but Rolf had ever been Emperor.

Following tradition, Rolf elected himself as the first to go out, while the others crouched in the doorway with bits of paper and Jürgen Kloth's silver pencil. Jürgen Kloth was despised for this possession. He also usually ended up the wretched Slave. Yet once again he produced the tell-tale pencil, the emblem of wealth, with its store of refills and concealed india-rubber. He wrote out his rating in neat handwriting. Next, it was Lore Meinke's turn.

'Not allowed,' she admonished Hannes, who tried to peep over her shoulder. He inhaled the scent of her hair, that played no small part in the reverie of the train, the white beach, and the sunshade.

'She's putting a nine again,' Inge called out treacherously. 'She always does for Rolf Sandmann.'

'Don't neither,' Lore blushed, nibbling the pencil with grave concentration.

'Hurry up with that pencil,' Schmitt squealed. 'We all got to have our turn.'

'I'm putting a seven for a change,' Lore declared, passing on the pencil.

'Rolfie won't like that,' Schemel warned.

Hannes felt intoxicated with hope. 'Bloody silly game if everybody always puts the same number. I'm putting a two.'

'You wouldn't dare,' Kloth exclaimed. 'Rolfie would know it was you.'

'He will if you tell him,' Angora pointed out.

'Have to,' Schemel retorted. 'Rolfie's always been Emperor.'

You'll never be Emperor in a million years, Hannes thought.

'Stick your bloody game,' Schmitt suddenly cried, flicking the pencil into Schemel's lap. 'Catch!'

'Hey!' Kloth protested. 'That's mine.'

'You and your sodding pencil, Asthma!'

The game was disintegrating before it had properly begun. With Rolf's premature reappearance came final collapse. He was frowning, his hand dug deep into his pocket.

'You all blind?' he demanded. 'They're coming this way – the Hoheluft mob!'

'Hacker put a two, Rolfie!' Schemel yelled.

'We hadn't even finished,' Kloth protested.

'Sod that,' Rolf muttered, gravely pre-occupied. 'They're coming through the passage. You and your girls' games! I need my knee looked at. Might be gangrene.'

He was off.

'Bloody well stay and face the music for once,' Hannes felt a sudden exhilaration of revolt boiling up within him.

'What's up with you, Hacker?' Rolf asked him sharply. A moustache of perspiration glistened over his top lip.

'He put a two,' Schemel cried again. 'I saw it.'

Hannes' mind was only partly absorbed by this verbal exchange. He knew: the sensible thing was to run for it *now*, before Rosa appeared, even if it meant enduring inevitable jeers. In his place, Rolf would have done it without a moment's qualm. In any case, Dorn and his men weren't after Rolf. He'd want to know why Erika hadn't turned up at the building shed. Had he made a mistake not giving her that message? You couldn't expose your own sister to a monster like Dorn, could you? That was white slavery! It was bad enough to know how things stood between Erika and Georg. Dorn as well? No, he had done the right thing.

'Keep your nose out of other people's business, Hacker,' Rolf was saying. 'We all know the score where you're concerned.'

'Who does?'

'Werner here, Jürgen, Schmitt, the lot of us. Why not ask them?' Rolf was girding himself for the kind of stand-up row he needed to assert his leadership. 'Where's your fat girl friend tonight? We all seen you!'

Now that Rolf had spoken the dreaded words – a formal indictment – it did not seem quite as terrible as Hannes had feared.

'You didn't see anything,' he said. He got no further because Dorn and his usual lieutenants stood in the doorway, barring all escape attempts.

'What's this?' Dorn grinned, showing green-flecked teeth. 'Depot dwarfs playing Doctors and Nurses?'

He was in Hitler Youth regalia, his swastika armband spotless, cap drawn menacingly over one eye, thumbs behind his leather belt. Torn between winning his quarrel with Hannes and standing up to Dorn, Rolf summoned up an uneasy grin, which quickly faded into a grimace of fear.

'Ain't supposed to wear uniform this time of night,' Schmitt piped up. 'Against orders.'

'You stink! Ever tried soap?'

Lore Meinke giggled and clasped Inge Ahrens' waist.

'Who are these girlies?' Dorn asked sternly, Schmitt having stayed silent. They were all leaning against the pitted wall now, as if waiting for the firing-squad. Rolf furtively eyed the doorway, speculating on a possible withdrawal because of his injury.

'They just live around here,' Jürgen Kloth explained. 'And I'm not scared of your uniform, Dorn. Schmitt's right. You're not supposed to wear it after eight o'clock unless you're on duty.'

'Ain't even in the Jungvolk,' Schemel exclaimed. By now ingratiation with authority was automatic for him.

'Name?' Dorn asked Kloth.

'Jürgen Kloth.'

'Jürgen Kloth,' Dorn echoed, crinkling his lips in parody of Kloth's superior accent. He fingered Kloth's chin, then ran a fist over the boy's face. Kloth put thumb and finger to his nose.

Hannes' remaining hope was that, before Rosa's imminent arrival, somebody would come down the staircase to complain about the noise and disperse the group. But the grown-ups seemed as frightened of Dorn as this pathetic lot down here.

'Any further questions?' Dorn asked.

'I'm off home,' Rolf announced. 'Broke my kneecap just before you came.'

'You still run these pygmies?' Dorn asked him incredulously.

Rolf nodded. He momentarily forgot his knee, his hands went to his waist in a gesture of restored authority.

'That's right,' Schemel said. 'Rolfie's Emperor.'

'He's what?' Dorn cocked his head sideways and cupped his ear. His two lieutenants, lounging against the wall, guffawed.

'It's a game,' Hannes volunteered.

'Didn't ask you, Hacker. Still got a bone to pick with you. Haven't forgotten you, friend.'

'A game, just a game,' Schemel echoed.

'What sort of a game?' Dorn asked him. 'You tell us, Leo.'

A look of terror filled Schemel's eyes. The name 'Leo' somehow seethed with unknown menace. He scratched his chin, begging moral support from Rolf, who now sat at the foot of the stairs, face in his hands, eyes averted.

'Not much good at explaining games,' Schemel muttered, fearfully ogling his interrogator. 'Forfeits and that.'

Dorn's pals roared with laughter. Lore clutched Angora's arms and started hopping from one foot to another.

'What's the matter with you anyway, Leo?' Dorn asked, 'You got rickets or something?'

'Infantile Paralysis,' Schemel proudly proclaimed and stood to attention.

'So what are you so pleased about? You look like a Yid to me.'

Now Dorn had them all on his side. Rolf was hooting with laughter. Schmitt and Kloth sniggered, the girls had to lean on one another for support. Hannes opened his mouth and tried to laugh with them, but no sound came. What if Rosa chose this moment to come through the passageway? Her arrival was far overdue. It had become imperative to shift them all, including Dorn and his gang, from that doorway. There was not a moment to lose.

'Come on, Leo,' Dorn said, 'tell us about this dirty game of yours.'

Schemel tried, but his babble didn't make sense. Dorn wasn't listening anyway. He was looking Lore Meinke up and down.

'It's all Jürgen Kloth's idea,' Schemel concluded.

'No, it isn't,' Hannes said. 'But I got an idea. Why don't we . . .'

'We always use his pencil,' Schemel insisted.

Dorn hadn't heard Hannes.

'What do these girls have to do?'

'One of them becomes Empress.'

Dorn sucked his teeth, then exchanged glances with his

henchmen. Now he approached Rolf, who still sat at the foot of the staircase, trying to look unconcerned.

'You dwarfs are in real trouble,' Dorn announced. 'Playing subversive games. That's forbidden by Government decree.'

'Only a silly old game,' Schmitt said.

'Have to report the lot of you. You two girls are quite depraved, aren't you? Let the boys take you upstairs, do you?'

'Certainly not. Do we, Inge?'

'Who's your Fähnleinführer, Sandmann?'

'Hinrichs. No good you blaming me for this, Dorn. I never wanted to play that stupid game. Ask them. I did it as a favour.'

Hannes had been anxiously peering out of the doorway. Now he turned towards Rolf. 'Favour to whom? You never complain when you're Emperor, I've noticed.'

'Right, Hacker.' Rolf melodramatically narrowed his eyes. 'I'll get you for this. We all know about you.'

Rolf was bluffing, of course. He was always bluffing. He knew nothing.

'Hacker's just jealous,' Schemel consoled Rolf. 'He's after Lore Meinke.'

'You wait,' Rolf reiterated, glaring at Hannes and sagely nodding his head.

'Pipe down,' Dorn bawled. 'It's like a bloody Jews' school around here. Want me to send a report to Hinrichs, Sandmann, yes or no?'

'No,' Rolf said meekly.

'Right then, as a member of your senior organisation, I'll deal with this matter myself.' He sniffed with satisfaction. 'Have to have a trial.'

'Another game?' Schmitt wanted to know. 'Like "Traitors"?'

'This ain't no game. From now on you won't be playing unauthorised games without proper supervision from me. Disgrace to the neighbourhood, you lot.'

'I'm going,' Lore Meinke said tentatively. 'Coming, Inge?'

'The girls stay put.'

Hannes heard steps approaching. Fresh panic gripped him. But it was only an old man shuffling by. Something had to be done, before they were confronted by Rosa. He took a deep breath.

'No privacy here,' he said, squarely facing Dorn. 'People coming and going all the time. Got to hold this trial somewhere else.'

'Suits me,' Dorn agreed sardonically. 'Got a hotel-room tucked away somewhere, Hacker?'

Hannes sensed relief. Here was a chance to kill several birds with one stone. Helping to get this trial organised would help Rosa to avoid danger. It also meant appeasing Rolf, who still sat brooding at the foot of the staircase. Finally, it might be a way of getting himself into Dorn's good books.

'Over by the depot,' he said, with newly found authority. 'There's a bit of a garden behind the garage. Nobody ever goes there.'

'All right, let's move,' Dorn commanded. 'Follow in a single file. Girls as well.'

They marched off dutifully. A chestnut tree grew in the middle of what was hardly more than a patch of weeds. Housewives dumped their rubbish here when the dustbins were full. The smell was ripe and fruity.

'Needn't think you're so smart, Hacker,' Rolf muttered to Hannes in passing. 'I knew about this place as well. We all did.'

'You're my chief witness,' Dorn said, prising Lore Meinke away from Angora, then pushing her roughly against the tree. 'Get a rope,' he ordered.

High windows sent a shimmer of light into the garden. Lore Meinke, her initial courage rapidly dissolving, whimpered softly, wiping her eyes with the back of her hand. Watching her, Hannes became aware of a feeling of triumph. He had succeeded in luring them all away from the doorway. He had more resource than any of them. No-one would now be able to witness Rosa's arrival. True, Lore was being temporarily sacrificed, like a squaw in a Western, but it was Rolf's place to protect her, not his.

Inge Ahrens stamped her foot.

'You rotten lot,' she complained. 'Lore's Mum's expecting her home.'

'How old are you, Lore?' Dorn asked.

'Thirteen and a bit.'

'Brothers or sisters?'

'No.'

'What does your father do?'

'He's dead.'

'Member of the BDM?'

'Yes.'

'Been to camp with them?'

'Couple of times.'

'Mixed camp?'

'No, just girls.'

'Are you Aryan?'

A sudden wild hope rose in Hannes.

'One hundred per cent,' Lore replied

Which wasn't necessarily true. If she had a Jewish grandmother, she would never admit it, certainly not to Dorn. Meanwhile, Rolf was studiously observing Dorn's technique. One thing was clear: they would never play Emperor again. After this it would be 'Trial'. And, unless Dorn now took over the gang completely, who could dispute Rolf's right to be inquisitor?

'Why did you play this forbidden game, Lore?' Dorn continued.

'Never knew it was forbidden.'

'You let these boys kiss you?'

'Not telling.'

'Your BDM group leader will be sent your file. Who instigated this disgusting game?'

'Don't know. Honestly.'

'Who wanted to play Emperor?'

'Don't remember. Please let me go home now, please, Dorn. I'll get into such trouble if I'm home late.'

'Should have thought of that before you joined these disgraceful activities.'

Schmitt tittered. He was enjoying himself. So, Hannes suspected, were they all. Rolf hadn't even tried to rescue Lore. Anyway, Dorn wasn't doing her any real harm. It was just another game.

Lore covered her face with her hands. Her narrow shoulders quivered.

'I'm waiting,' Dorn said patiently. 'Whose idea was it?'

'Don't remember.'

'Yes you do, rabbit.' Dorn took three steps towards the tree, then quite unexpectedly slapped the girl hard across the face. Lore flinched, then broke into choked sobs.

'What you want to do that for, Dorn?' Hannes asked.

Dorn ignored him. He was still facing the girl.

'I warned you this was no game,' he told her. He ran his hand through Lore's hair. 'We've got to clean up Eppendorf, girl. Got our orders. Karl-Heinz!' He turned to his first lieutenant. 'Call her mother down.'

'No, don't do that! Please! I'll tell you what you want to know! It was him!' She pointed at the astonished Werner Schemel. 'It's always him.'

Schemel grinned shiftily. He seemed unaware that in the fine spectacle he had been watching, he was suddenly cast as the villain.

'Go home,' Dorn told Lore. 'You're all right.' He reached out for her, but she eluded him deftly and fled from the garden, still sobbing.

'Wait for me, Lore!' Inge Ahrens ran after her friend. 'Don't be rotten.'

'Your turn, Leo,' Dorn announced dryly. 'Against that tree, boy.'

'Me?' Schemel still seemed oblivious that he had been indicted. Limping forward, he stumbled over some weeds. 'Why me? I never did nothing.'

'You heard the girl,' Dorn told him. 'Go on, against the tree.'

'I'm a cripple,' Schemel protested. Panic dawned at last. 'Don't believe her, do you? I got a doctor's certificate. I'm sick. Rolfie knows . . .'

Dorn turned to the others. 'You heard the witness, men. You know the charge. You know the facts. Don't want to prolong this trial unnecessarily. Guilty or not guilty? One at a time.'

'Guilty,' Rolf declared. 'You heard Lore. You suggested that game.'

'Rolfie, you rotten swine,' Schemel bleated. 'You dirty rotten swine . . .'

'What about you others?' Dorn grinned encouragement.

'Guilty,' they cried in unison.

'Hacker?'

'Guilty.'

'Guilty,' Kloth whispered, lowering his head.

'You rotten sods . . .' Schemel whined.

Dorn adjusted his cap.

'You're a disgrace to the neighbourhood, Leo. I'll give you a light sentence allowing for the fact that you're crippled. Don't want to see you join in any activity here for the next fortnight. That understood? One false move, I'll change the sentence to house-arrest. Now apologise to the rest for instigating a filthy game.'

Schemel wiped his mouth, clearly relieved by the lightness of the sentence.

'Sorry I instigated a filthy game,' he began cheerfully, then stopped abruptly.

'HANNES!'

Turning his head, Hannes instantly recognised the slight figure who came running into the garden.

'Erika . . .' he stuttered. 'What . . . Why . . .'

Dorn bowed from the waist and gallantly touched his cap the way he'd seen Willi Forst salute women at the pictures. 'Good evening, Fräulein Erika . . .'

Erika pretended not to notice. 'I've been looking everywhere for you, Hannes! How much longer do you intend to keep Rosa waiting?'

'Oh, dear,' Schmitt sang in a falsetto. 'Mustn't keep Rosa waiting, must we?'

'Who's Rosa?' Rolf grinned. 'Your fat friend with the red handbag, is it?'

'Come along now,' Erika said.

'I'll come when I'm ready.'

'You'll come now. Supper's on the table.'

How could she do this to him? How could she treat him like an idiot in front of all his friends? Important things were happening. Schemel was being punished. There was a new challenge to Rolf's leadership. How could Erika burst in on this world of action and decision with nagging chatter about supper? He would never forgive her for this. Never. Dorn could have her. Any time.

'We all going home?' he asked Dorn, trying to save face.

'No,' Dorn said, 'we ain't all going home. Not just yet, Erika.'

The others tittered.

'Not just yet, Erika,' they chorused. It sounded just like the title of a popular song.

'I'll be back in a minute,' Hannes hesitated, then turned to follow his sister who was striding towards the yard.

'Not just yet, Erika,' they shouted.

'Buy you an ice-cream next time, Erika,' Dorn bawled after her. 'Vanilla!'

Hannes meekly followed his sister. She had ruined everything. They had done with Lore, with Schemel. In his absence they would now dispose of him. Dorn still had it in for him. He had failed to set up that date. And Rolf would want to get even. They were probably planning to follow him home, eavesdropping outside the front door while they had supper, plotting to attack Rosa when she came out . . .

'Horrible little yobs,' Erika muttered in the passage. 'It's not often Rosa comes to see us. And you can't even be bothered to be there when she does.'

In the little garden they had started to sing. Hannes could hear them quite clearly – that popular song about the love-life of sailors from the Hans Albers' film *Bombs on Monte Carlo*. Their voices swept up into the night sky; he could separate the different strands of sound: Dorn, Rolf, Schmitt, Karl-Heinz . . . even Schemel was joining in now.

'What's the matter?' At the far end of the passage Erika turned. 'Why are you standing there like that?'

'I'm not coming up.'

'Don't be silly, Hannes. Told you, supper's on the table.'

'Don't want any supper.'

They faced each other in the dimly lit passage.

'Bloody Hell, Hannes. Rosa's waiting.'

'Let her wait. Not coming. Don't want to see her!'

He turned, drawn back to the source of the singing.

'Hannes,' she yelled after him. 'Hannes!'

Let her scream, he thought, running still faster. Every step was bringing him closer to those insistent voices. None of this was Erika's damned business, he thought, it's not she who's in trouble, it's me. It's me.

CHAPTER TEN

Next morning Hannes found two strange men sitting at the kitchen table. One was middle-aged and squat, with a snout of a nose and a button mouth fitted with a cold cigar-stub. He wore a trilby hat and kept his hands buried in his raincoat pockets. The other, younger man, with a blue-chinned waiter's face, wore a shiny blue serge suit. He kept slapping the table with soiled leather gloves. Both men looked bleary-eyed, numbed with a night's sleeplessness and smoking.

'My son.'

His father introduced him in a tremulous voice. Standing by the open window, he was fiddling with his collar stud. His mother stood at the stove, keeping her eyes averted. Hannes guessed she had been crying again.

The two men glanced up at Hannes but showed no interest. The waiter grunted a greeting; his colleague leant back in his chair and put a match to his cold cigar.

'Let's have some more coffee, mother,' he grumbled, holding out his cup with unsteady hand. 'Need something to keep me awake.'

'I'm ready for you, gentlemen.'

His father tried bravado, presenting himself in his best black suit which he was required to wear behind the glove counter at Tietz on the Jungfernstieg.

'You're our last call before we hand over to the day shift. Time for another cup.'

'I'd just as soon get this over with,' his father said. 'You have told me nothing. No charge has been read out to me. I don't even know . . . I mean, I have a job . . . I mean, will they . . .'

He broke off in mid sentence and sat down. The older man burped, then mumbled an apology. Hannes found he could watch the scene with detachment. His father was afraid, but it was all happening a long, long way off. A useful trick, once you mastered it: you could switch people into the distance by turning round a pair of imaginary opera glasses.

It was all so ordinary, so undramatic. One man was drinking coffee, the other played with his gloves. On the window-boxes some sparrows were hopping about against a deep blue backdrop, pecking at crumbs. A fine morning; the air that blew into the kitchen tasted fresh and salty.

'Look here.' Hannes' father had pulled a tattered piece of paper out of his wallet. 'This is for your superiors.' He flung it down on the table. 'It will show them who they're dealing with. This is obviously a mistake. My grandfather fought at Sedan . . . My . . .'

He mopped his forehead, then caught his wife's silencing look. The older man studied the family tree. His cigar had gone cold again. It suddenly occurred to Hannes that the two men looked a bit like Laurel and Hardy. He had to look away to stop himself from laughing.

'Most impressive,' the older man said. 'Family tree, Waldemar. Fought at Sedan.' He pushed the paper across to his younger colleague, who sneered mildly and handed it back.

'Could you at least let me see a warrant, gentlemen?' His father began again. 'After all, anybody can burst in here before breakfast and claim they're from the Gestapo. Surely, I can demand . . .'

'We don't bother about scraps of paper,' the older man said cosily. 'Might have been good enough in the days of Weimar. We're free of all that red tape now, Herr Hacker. We all know what we're doing. So don't you get yourself into an uproar. You done nothing wrong, then you got nothing to worry about, right?'

'My daughter's employers are an old-established firm of solicitors. I shall ask my wife to get in touch with them.'

The other man extracted a card from a shabby leather wallet.

'Erika Hacker, born April the twenty-ninth, nineteen nineteen,' he read out. 'Schuster and Mitternacht Partners.' He returned the card into the wallet which he stuffed back into his breast pocket. 'They won't break a leg for you, Herr Hacker. Not up on a criminal charge, are you?'

'You're asking *me?*' his father expostulated. 'How can I be on *any* charge? I've never been politically involved. Never voted Communist. I'm a *feuilleton* writer, not a political journalist. I'm pure German. My family can be traced back three hundred years.' He fingered the ends of his moustache, then touched the knot of his tie. 'I served in the army, fought as a mere boy at Tannenberg. Still . . .' He chuckled nervously. 'I suppose all that counts for nothing any more.'

'Shouldn't be so free and easy with your confessions, Herr Hacker,' the older man said gently, as he put another futile match to his charred cigar. He rose; crouching, he drained his cup. 'Probably just want to find out what you're doing these days. Card indexes. That sort of thing.'

'Shall I pack something, some sandwiches . . .?'

'No, mother, that won't be necessary. Come along, Herr Hacker. Best put your overcoat on. Don't want people in the street to laugh at us, do we?'

Ludwig Hacker looked down at his neat black suit as the younger man helped him into his raincoat.

He looks seedy, Hannes thought. And he's doing everything wrong. Everything. Nobody respects him. They're laughing at him. When they come for me, I'll do it all differently. With dignity. And not so much chat.

'Haven't you even got a car?' His father sounded exasperated.

'What for? It's only round the corner. Cars are already on the day shift, anyway.'

'Next time we'll bring our Bentley,' the younger man said.

Papa stood in the doorframe. His raincoat had shrunk, the sleeves rucked up almost to his elbows.

'No need for lengthy goodbyes,' he said at last. 'Back for supper.'

After their steps had echoed away, Hannes sat down next to his mother and put his arm around her.

'They won't keep him long, Mama. You heard them. If it was really serious, they'd have sent along someone more important.'

His mother poured herself another cup of coffee.

'I'm going to wash up and lie down,' she told him, absently stroking his hand. 'You think you could go round to Erika's office?'

'I'll see to it. Go and rest.'

She pressed his hand again and dragged herself next door, her pill bottle rattling in her apron pocket. Hannes started washing up the breakfast things. Later he brought her a glass of peppermint tea.

'I just thought,' he told her, sitting down on the bed, slipping upturned palms under his thighs. 'Papa's one hundred per cent Aryan. What can they do to him? With one of us it'd be different.' He got up to stir her tea. 'I'm glad it isn't you, Mama.'

'I thought it had all blown over.' Tears strangled her words. 'False alarm.'

'Never mind,' Hannes said.

'If they do something to Erika, I'll do away with myself.'

Why Erika, he thought. If it was me, she'd grin and bear it, I suppose.

'Must be that Georg of hers they're after. They've taken Papa to pump him for information. Why can't Erika be more careful?'

'They won't find out anything about Georg,' Hannes reassured his mother. 'It's Rosa I'm worried about.'

'You didn't seem all that worried when she came over last night. Why did you . . .'

'Couldn't help it. She say anything about Bohrer?'

'Don't think she wanted to talk about it.'

She had split two flat white tablets with her thumbnail, then swallowed them with draughts of tea. The curtains weren't drawn, the sky was startling in its blueness. Hannes picked up the empty glass and stared through it. In the morning light, her skin looked puffy and greasy. There were stains on her apron.

Why don't I love her anymore, he asked himself. She's let herself go. Not my fault.

He tried hard to concentrate on an image of lilac bushes and the jetty, substituting Mama for Rosa. For a moment, he saw Mama as her old, immaculate self, a string of pearls around her neck, paying real attention to what he was saying. Then Rosa came to join them. Now they were all blissfully together, watching the boats gliding by . . .

Why can't it be like that again, he wondered. Can't she see I want her to be as she used to be? What did I do to stop her from being what she was?

'I've got an idea,' he said excitedly. 'Why don't we have a little outing, spend the day in the open air? Just the two of us. It's such a lovely day. We could take a boat out on the Alster. Haven't done that for ages. Or a trip down the Elbe . . . we could take sandwiches, it won't be expensive.'

'Today?' She looked baffled, even alarmed. 'You want to go out – today of all days?'

'We don't go anywhere on other days either, do we?'

'How can you expect me to . . .?'

'Just thought it might do you some good,' he said tersely.

No good. She didn't understand. He got off the bed. Rosa would have understood. She would have taken him down to the Alster or on the river. Together they would have watched the boats rocking on the water and enjoyed the spectacle, feeling sad together. Mama never saw the point of things like that. That was her trouble. She was afraid of shared emotion. She wanted to feel sad alone.

'I don't understand you any more,' she said.

He sensed a constriction high up in his nose. He managed to fight back tears. There was a ring at the door.

'I'll go,' he told her. 'Take your pills. If you really think that's the best we can do for Papa.'

He slammed the bedroom door. Wish I were dead, he thought.

It was Rolf Sandmann who stood on the threshold, spruce in his Jungvolk uniform.

'You're late, Hacker. Sling your uniform on.'

'What for?'

Rolf was hiding an object behind his back.

'Don't tell me you've forgotten! Jungzug has been called out. Strength through Joy! Collection day!'

He produced the concealed tin and rattled it in Hannes' face.

'Go on, get changed.'

Reluctantly, Hannes invited his friend inside. Wouldn't do for Rolf to look too closely at Mama. She might inadvertently give the show away about Papa's arrest.

'You alone?' Rolf asked.

'My mother's lying down.'

'In the morning?'

'Feeling a bit sick.'

Hannes took him into the sitting room; their beds were still airing. Rolf sniffed.

'You sleep here? . . . Your sister as well?'

'Sometimes,' Hannes said vaguely. 'Wait here. Shan't be long.'

He tried to explain the new situation to his mother. Rolf had started to examine the books Erika kept by her bedside.

'Strength through Joy. Have I got to go?'

His mother had raised herself up.

'Don't want him to start asking questions, do you?'

'I want to look after you, Mama. And go to Erika's office!'

'I'll phone Erika from a booth. Don't worry. Put your uniform on.'

'Don't want to.'

'Mustn't keep him waiting.'

I don't handle these things much better than Papa, he thought angrily. Walking back to the other room he discovered the source of his anger: he was *eager* to go out. Into the sun with Rolf, wearing uniform, rattling collection boxes . . .

He found Rolf studying a postcard.

'What you got there?'

Rolf stabbed the inside of his cheek with his tongue. 'Wouldn't you like to know?'

'You been rummaging among my sister's things?'

'Keep your eyes skinned,' Rolf quoted Fähnleinführer Hinrichs. 'Forgotten already?'

Hannes belted his shorts as he strode across the room.

'Give it to me, whatever it is.'

Rolf narrowed his eyes. 'This is all very interesting. Old Hinrichs was right. Never know, do you?'

'What are you talking about?'

'So who writes to your sister from Palestine?'

'Give me that,' Hannes cried hoarsely.

Rolf was waving the postcard above Hannes' head. How could Erika have been so careless? He suddenly remembered: the card was from Uncle Peter and Aunt Ida, blast them. Erika must have forgotten to tear it up, was probably using it as a bookmark. It was the worst thing that had ever happened.

Rolf grinned.

'Didn't know you had Jew friends.'

'Got no Jew friends.'

'Stamp says Palestine, Hacker. Come to think of it, I could use it for my collection.'

What had those stupid old people written on that card? If he could only remember . . . Whatever it was, by now Rolf was sure to have read it.

'Give me that card, Rolfie. I'll steam the stamp off for you.'

'I give it back, you'll keep it.' Rolf winked. 'I know you.'

'I wouldn't.'

'Jungvolk Honour?'

Rolf was using the card to fan himself.

'Keep the bloody thing,' Hannes stuffed his hands in his pockets. 'I'm not swearing oaths because of a stupid old postcard. Keep the sodding thing.'

'Don't worry, I will.'

Hannes had turned his back on Rolf. Now he swerved abruptly to fling himself at him. Before he could recover, Hannes had snatched the postcard from him. He ran to the window, tore the card into small pieces.

'You bastard,' Rolf cried, 'what you want to go and do that for? I only wanted the stupid stamp.'

'Teach you to take your nose out of my sister's things,' Hannes told him. 'It wasn't Palestine anyway. It was Egypt. Can't even read.'

'It was Palestine all right,' Rolf sucked his gums pensively. He hadn't recovered from Hannes' unexpected show of violence. 'Won't forget that in a hurry, Hacker. We'll remember that.'

'Do what you bloody well like.' Hannes knotted his tie. The evidence was destroyed. Things weren't any worse than before. 'You're not coming here to do your spying . . .'

'What's the matter, Hannes?'

His mother stood in the doorway, blinking. Then she brushed some hair from her forehead. 'You boys fighting?'

'It's only that birthday card Erika had from Egypt,' Hannes said.

'Egypt?' Mama repeated dimly.

'It was from Palestine, wasn't it? I saw it.'

She swallowed, then smiled at Rolf.

'No, dear, Hannes is right. From Egypt. Erika's birthday. From Egypt.'

'It wasn't a birthday card and it wasn't from Egypt,' Rolf said stubbornly. 'I only wanted the stamp. Hannes tore the card up. Don't know why.'

'Why didn't you tell me you were a stamp-collector, Rolf?' Hannes watched his mother open a drawer to look for the folder which contained their papers. She's gone mad, Hannes thought. She wants to land us all in a KZ.

'Here you are, Rolf,' Mama was saying. She selected a letter from the folder. 'Here's one from Portugal. We have friends there.'

Rolf watched her tearing the corner off an envelope and handing it to him.

'Thank you, Frau Hacker.'

Hannes surveyed his uniform in the mirror.

'Be back lunch-time,' he told his mother. Then he turned to Rolf. He needed to be sure the incident was closed. 'Won't we, Rolfie?'

'Let's get a move on, then. Got the whole of Eppendorfer Weg to cover.'

'But it's Friday.'

Mama's words hit Hannes like a cold shower.

'So it is.' He *had* forgotten. He grinned conspiratorily at Rolf. 'Those old relatives again. From Winterhude.'

'Thought you said they lived in Uhlenhorst?' Rolf asked. Luckily, he was in a hurry. He clicked his heels. 'Thanks again for that Portuguese stamp, Frau Hacker.'

'Quite all right. Hope you both collect a lot of money.'

At the door, Hannes turned to signal thanks to his mother, but she was already trudging back to her bedroom. Ahead of him, Rolf Sandemann was clattering down the stairs with metal-tipped boots, whistling tunelessly.

Herr Bohrer lay on Rosa's chaise-longue in shirt-sleeves and breeches, hands folded behind his head. When Hannes entered, he exploded with coarse laughter.

'Now I've seen everything.' He released one hand from behind his head to point a stubby finger at Hannes. 'You Rosenteichs know a trick or two, don't you?'

'My name's Hacker,' Hannes said dryly, as he sat down at the table. 'Told you last time I was in the Jungvolk.'

Bohrer shook his head and began to laugh again. This time he only managed a cackle.

'How're they treating you then, your Jungvolk pals? Do they know their luck?' He sat up and scratched in his cropped hair.

'Collecting for Strength through Joy this morning.'

'That's the style.' Bohrer heaved himself across to the table and rubbed his hands. Rosa had brought in the food; he piled his plate high. Hannes watched him shovelling food into his mouth, eating everything with casual relish. He consumed enormous quantities of white bread with his meal; his flabby red face glistened.

'Why don't you bring that pretty sister of yours round to see your granny?' Bohrer asked presently, scooping up the last of the gravy with bread.

'Because you're here,' Hannes told him.

'I've shot people for less than that,' Bohrer said, pointing his dripping knife at Hannes. 'Watch your step, Jewboy.'

'You've never shot anybody in your life, Bohrer,' Rosa told him. 'You couldn't kill a fly.'

Hannes looked up from his plate. Her bantering tone disturbed him. How could she talk to him like that, as if he had become some sort of lodger, or as if they were married?

'Should have known me in the old days,' Bohrer said, helping himself to more food. 'I'm one of the old guard. What we got in this country today, *we* fought for it. People like to forget that. We never got nothing served on a plate. Might have got a knife stuck in our backs for our pains. Pitched battles we fought against the Commies. Broke up their meetings, kicked the bastards' arses, tore down their flags.' He wagged his head nostalgically. 'Those were the days all right. Didn't even mind delivering your eggs and cheese then, Rosenteich, old girl. Knew our day would come. At night we had our real fun. Meeting the lads, deciding on the next job, code words, plans, instructions from on high. Now who gets all the cushy jobs? Intellectuals! Blokes who never lifted a finger. The old fighters are forgotten, have to fend for themselves. So I say, grab what you can. The days of comradeship are over, finished. Just look around you . . . The blokes from the SS are the masters now. Bunch of queers. That's all they are. Everybody knows that.'

'Wouldn't shout that from the rooftops,' Rosa said, evidently used to similar outbursts.

'I'll say anything I please. Don't give a shit if that old sod of a Blockwarden hears me, neither. He's another one of them. Let him try to denounce me, if he dares . . .'

'You'll shoot him as well, will you?'

Talking to him as to a spoiled child! Rosa was no longer scared of him. It was all wrong. As soon as he could, Hannes went to the consulting-room. Here, at least, nothing had changed. The bottles and tubes and jars stood in their appointed places. He slithered along the polished parquet floor, inhaled the clean, cold, medical smell. Then he walked over to the window to look down into the garden, at the rotting wooden bench among the weeds. The afternoon sun streamed through the foliage, onto the sundial. Overhead white clouds bulged, then collided; flies buzzed against glass; a maid washed up by an open window, singing a *Schlager*. Hannes leant out and shut his eyes, guiltily enjoying the sweet poison of melancholy.

He hadn't heard Rosa come into the room. She stood behind him, ran her hand through his hair.

'It's Papa you're worried about, isn't it? Mama rang me this morning.'

He continued to stare out of the window. Too difficult to explain.

'He'll be back in a day or two,' she said. 'They're always rounding up people. It doesn't necessarily mean an arrest.'

Then she gently broke the news to him: there would be no walk to the jetty this afternoon.

He looked at her uncomprehendingly. 'But it's Friday . . .'

The jars and tubes and bottles were all in place on the marble slab. On the way, he had carefully avoided every crack between paving stones. When he had whistled their aria, she had responded.

'I've got to see a few customers.'

'But you never work on Friday afternoons . . .'

'Have to. This is a gentile undertaking now.' She jerked her thumb in the direction of the other room. 'He insists. Nothing I can do about it. A Christian firm works on Friday afternoons. I'm not permitted to take clients on week-ends any more.'

'You get your oldest customers on Sundays . . .'

'He wants to play boss. Comes from having been an errand-boy too long.'

'You're very understanding all of a sudden,' he said bitterly.

She sighed. 'I have to make the best of it.'

When the door-bell rang, Rosa left him to admit a client.

Later it clouded over, a light Hamburg drizzle glazed the pavements. While Rosa worked, Hannes played Old Maid with Bohrer. It was the only card game he knew, that and Poker. Bohrer made a tiresome partner, humming and drumming on the table, crunching boiled sweets and making the cards sticky. He took as long to make up his mind as Anna Panse.

'Don't you find it gets a bit boring here?' Hannes asked him.

'It does a bit.' Bohrer clumsily shuffled the pack. 'She does her best.'

'You're in on a racket, aren't you?' Hannes asked. He also felt unafraid of Bohrer, a man who couldn't even play Rummy.

'Chap's got to live, Jewboy. No law against it.'

'You'd get into trouble if I reported you to headquarters,' Hannes told him. 'Your turn, go on.'

Bohrer picked a card from the pack, flipping up a second card in error. 'Who's to report me?' he asked. 'I offer your grandmother protection. She's not complaining. She's still working.'

'Talking of rackets,' Hannes said. 'I know you get girls to pick up old Jews in the street. When the men go with them, the girls turn them in.'

'What do you expect? Racial pollution is a serious offence. You ain't got it right, anyway. The girls, what they do, they go up to these old sods, they make out they're Jewish themselves. That's how the Yids fall for it in the first place.'

'Your turn.'

'Some girls, they don't bother to hand the bastards over. Squeeze them dry on their own account. One girl, she put it across the same Yid twice. *Twice!* Like it says in *Der Stürmer.* They can never get enough.'

'Wouldn't say that in front of my grandmother.'

'Well, you're not really one of them, are you? The chosen people, I mean.'

'You're a fine lot,' Hannes found his courage mounting. 'This morning they arrested my father. He's one hundred per cent Aryan as well. That was a heart, not a diamond.'

'Ram-di-dam, Ram-di-dam,' Bohrer trumpeted, staring at his hand. 'If he's done nothing wrong, they'll send him back. Stands to reason.'

'Hearts,' Hannes reminded him.

'Sorry mate,' Herr Bohrer said. 'My turn, is it?'

*   *   *

It wasn't until later, when the drizzle had stopped, that Hannes got another opportunity to talk to Rosa. Bohrer had gone for a beer. Rosa was hanging up her smock in the consulting room.

'I forgot to apologise for last night,' he said contritely. 'I just couldn't leave my friends at the depot. There was a bit of trouble.'

'I understand, Hannes.' She sank down on a straight-backed chair and lit a cigarillo. 'Mustn't worry so much. Got cross because we couldn't go down to the jetty today. If we *had* gone, we'd have been caught in the rain.'

He sat down opposite her.

'How do you stand that pig all day?'

'Could have been worse.' She leant back, inhaled smoke. 'He's not brutal. I haven't had to look after anybody for a long time.'

'Well, you don't have to look after me any more.'

She looked up startled. He searched for something to say. He did not want to waste more of their precious time together with explanations and talk about Bohrer. Even when he wasn't there, Bohrer came between them. When they sat by the jetty on a fine afternoon, conversation just rippled along on almost nothing – fragments of old games, private jokes, words he had mispronounced as a little boy, scraps of opera plots, dinosaurs.

He looked out on the dripping leaves in the garden. Incredible how one could outgrow all that in one afternoon.

'He can't just leave us, can he?'

'Papa? Don't even think about it. He loves your mother.'

'I suppose so,' Hannes said.

'I remember Ludwig Hacker when he first came to see us. They met during the war, when your mother was a Red Cross nurse. He had been wounded. He was young and dashing, an officer. I would have preferred her to marry a Jewish boy, but, well . . . they were strange times. Later, he came to visit us on Sundays. He'd sit in our garden with us, reading out his poems. He could be very witty . . .'

'Poor old Papa,' Hannes said.

'He'll be back in a day or two. Bound to be. Try talking to him. Tell him you love him.'

For a while they were silent.

'It's going to get worse, isn't it? Everything, I mean. The worst hasn't happened yet, has it? Not by a long chalk.'

She rose.

'I'll have to get Bohrer's supper started. Try not to worry so much.'

'Better get home,' Hannes said. 'Rain's stopped anyway.'

He turned up the collar of his uniform. There was still a fine drizzle. Rosa no longer answered his questions. It was just a waste of time going to the Haynstrasse now. Rosa had changed, just as Mama and his father had changed. They were drifting further and further away, treating him like a child. Rosa didn't really want to be bothered with him anymore, that's what had happened.

He decided to make a detour. He walked through Schröders Park, where Rosa had taken him long, long ago, when he still wanted to play in the little sandpit. Nobody played there today, it was too wet. In a dark hut, under a dripping thatched roof, a young Kindergarten teacher was reading to her charges.

Outside the Kellinghusenstrasse swimming baths he stopped. Might as well go in there and drown myself, he thought. That would solve a lot of problems. Rolf would finally realise he'd lost his best friend. Mama would have something real to cry about, which would bring her closer to Papa.

'If only we had known,' they would keep saying as they sat in the kitchen.

There was one obstacle. Once one was dead, how could one ever know what the others said or did? Being dead wasn't necessarily better than being alive. What happened? You got buried, they shovelled earth on your coffin, women wore black veils. But what happened to *you*? That stuff about going to heaven and becoming an angel was fairytale rubbish for infants. Like Father Christmas. Erika had explained it to him once. There wasn't a God in Heaven. Nothing, she had told him, *nothing* – that's what happened to you. You became what you had been before you were born. A Nothing. He could imagine it: a large cube filled with grey vapour; you crept inside it and stayed there forever.

Nothing. A useful thing to remember.

CHAPTER ELEVEN

Lore Meinke clawed his arm, as they roared through twin doors and past illuminated skeletons. They were in the dark. In an empty tram racing over the Alster. Under a red beech tree Lore slid along the polished seat, further and further away from him. The fairground barker with the battered top hat turned and grinned at them. He was driving the tram. 'That's Death', Lore sang in her corner. A tune from *Carmen*. The driver turned his back on them. Now he mowed down the weeds in Rosa's garden. Lore stumbled out of the tram, wading through the lake, the barker at her heels. Then he was racing up the staircase of Rosa's house. It was getting darker all the time. He screamed, knowing he was dreaming, wanting to wake up to save himself. In the sitting room, Waldmeister was feeding a sparrow on the window-box. No, it wasn't a dream. He went into the consulting-room, the jars and bottles lay smashed on the floor, the fluids mingling and congealing on the parquet floor. A pterodactyl hovered behind the window-sill; Waldmeister recited: 'We must never go back again, come back, back again . . .'

Hannes opened his eyes, staring into his mother's face.

'Papa's back!'

Dazed, he ran into the kitchen. Erika had already gone to her office. His father, bathrobe pulled over his good suit, towel slung around his shoulders, shaved in front of the mirror.

'Surprised, my boy?' he asked the mirror.

'Glad you're back, Papa.'

Hannes hesitated. Should he come nearer? It could still be part of his nightmare.

'Was it awful?'

'Awful?' his father echoed.

'Did they keep you in prison all night?'

'Yes, I spent the night in a cell.' His father spoke with measured solemnity. 'It wasn't pleasant. I don't want to talk about it . . . However, they won't bother us again, I think I made sure of that.'

'Did they tell you why they let you go?'

'They didn't even tell me why they arrested me.' His eyes strayed past Hannes, as if his next statement was not intended for his ears. 'Their efficiency is a complete myth. I was passed from pillar to post. Kindergarten Kafka.' He wiped soap off his face with a towel. 'Perhaps if one could get a commission from an American paper . . .'

Hannes' eyes fastened on the folded newspaper, propped up against the coffee pot. He leant across the table, desperate to know the previous day's results. The paper was not open at the sports page, alas.

'They got nothing out of me,' Papa was saying. Hannes looked up in time to see his mother hugging Papa, nibbling at his fist. 'I know their little minds. I'm not to be intimidated by such primitive methods. The waste though, the futility . . .'

They heard a key turning, then hushed voices gliding along the corridor. Erika stood in the door – with Georg.

'We thought you'd gone to the office, Erika.'

'Papa, this is a friend of mine . . .'

'Koch's the name, Georg Koch. Pleased to meet you, Herr Hacker.'

Georg strode forward to shake Ludwig Hacker's hand. Then he grinned at Hannes.

'All right, lad?'

Georg started to explain why he had come. Hannes snatched up his father's paper. The other voices washed against his ears as he devoured the latest reports. Germany had won another gold medal, for the 2,000-metre tandem bicycle race! Dung-carving, if you please! Germany and America now shared first place in the table, with $71^{1}/_{2}$ points each. Then came Finland, Sweden, France, Italy – in that order. Trying to concentrate, Hannes cupped his hands over his ears, extracting from the tables their intoxicating power. His mind conjured up the Badenweiler March to counterpoint the results, a package of mounting excitement. Voices kept bursting through.

'Useless to press me further, Herr Koch,' Papa was saying. 'Your name was never mentioned.'

Georg scratched his head.

'They wouldn't just ask you outright, Herr Hacker. They're too smart for that. They'd just drop a hint, they might ask you "Does your daughter see anybody behind your back?" – that sort of thing.'

Ludwig Hacker managed a trapped smile.

'I'm perfectly capable of remembering what I was asked, Herr Koch . . .'

'Don't ask him any more questions now. He's tired.'

'It's a question of life or death for Georg.' Erika put on her Teddy-bear frown. 'Won't you try and remember, Papa?'

'Stop badgering me, girl! It's fantastic! I arrive home after an ordeal, only to be confronted by a complete stranger . . .' He waved his arm about. 'For all I know, you may have been sent to report on me, Herr Koch! An *agent provocateur*! I was ordered not to discuss my interrogation!'

Georg nodded solemnly.

'I understand what you've been through. Thanks all the same. So long, lad. Good day, Frau Hacker. Sorry about this . . .'

'So long, Georg,' Hannes called out, eyes fixed on the sports page. Should he have told Georg about Dorn? He'd left it too late.

'Can't say I care for that gentleman,' Papa said while Erika took Georg to the front door. 'Did you know about him?'

'They've been seeing each other for months, Ludwig. Surely you've heard us talk about him.'

'Nothing of the kind. I've been kept in the dark as usual.'

Did he want to assert himself after his 'ordeal'? Or was it just a sleepless night that had made him so irritable?

'If you took more of an interest . . .'

'It's up to you to see that your daughter doesn't get into bad company. I should have thought my own burden was heavy enough as it is.'

'Georg's not a bad chap, Ludwig.'

'I know his type. He's twice her age. I won't have him here again. That's final.'

'*Pas devant le garçon*, Ludwig . . .'

'Oh, for God's sake, Mama!' Hannes caught his father's exact tone of itchy exasperation. 'I know that much French. Think I don't know about Georg and Erika?'

Erika came back. 'You're not much help, Papa, are you?'

'That's what I've come home to!' Papa's face quivered with self-pity. Two round pink patches coloured his cheeks. 'Nobody asks me how I feel. Instead, I find myself interrogated by an illiterate oaf . . .'

'Ludwig, please stop . . . I can't stand it . . . my head . . .'

I'm dreaming this, Hannes told himself. I was dreaming when Professor Waldmeister was feeding the sparrows. This is no different.

'Oh, I'll stop,' his father shouted. 'I'll stop. And that's not the only thing I'll stop. Speak to that man again, my girl, and I'll report him to the authorities. I mean it. Do you think I'm going to stand by while you endanger the whole family for the sake of some squalid affair? He's a Communist, isn't he? Yes, I thought so. Can't pull the wool over my eyes! Not much help indeed . . .!' He ripped his dressing-gown off and bustled round the table. 'Can't wait for me to be carted off to a KZ, can you?'

Hannes watched his mother pursue Papa out of the kitchen. He and Erika exchanged grimaces. The recriminations continued next door. Papa's voice rose in righteous indignation, undeterred by Mama's appeasing tones. Presently they heard their father storm out, slamming all available doors behind him. Had he worked himself into such a rage just to have an excuse for going down to Sandmann's so soon after being sent home?

Erika hurried to her mother's room, so Hannes was able to concentrate on the sports page again. But the tables had become cold and sterile. He knew now that he was not asleep.

'A good doctor, that's what she needs,' Erika said as she came back into the kitchen. 'Doesn't want to run to the expense, she says. Papa hasn't even noticed that she's ill.'

She poured water into a kettle, placed it on the stove. Then she sat down and gazed at Hannes dejectedly.

'You don't know how lucky you are.'

'Lucky? Why?'

'You're too young to understand what's going on here.'

Always the same reason for not trusting him! That's why Erika had never told him what Georg did in the Underground. Nobody trusted him.

'I've got a good idea about what happened,' he said. 'It's Dorn. He got Papa arrested so that they could squeeze him dry to get dope on Georg.'

She looked like a cross Teddy-bear again.

'This isn't a rubbishy film! What's Dorn got to do with Georg?'

'A lot! Remember when you took me to the funfair? Afterwards, Dorn was waiting for me. He knew you and Georg were out together. Asked me to tell you he wanted to see you. That building shed, Bismarckstrasse. I never gave you the message. Now he's out to get Georg.'

'How old is this Dorn?' Erika asked. 'Kid of fourteen? Who'd listen to him?'

'He's at least fifteen,' Hannes told her. 'Big noise in the Hitler Youth. He's taking over the local gangs single-handed!'

'Just a lout, that's all he is.'

Erika looked half puzzled. Was she flattered that Dorn should be interested in her? Thoughtfully, she was twisting her long hair around her fingers. You never could tell for sure what girls were thinking . . .

'Better not tell Papa.' She got up to pour boiling water into the percolator. 'He'll only think we're ganging up on him. Not that I believe you.'

'It's true . . . Listen, Erika, I had a horrible nightmare just now . . .'

'What?'

'I was in the ghost-train —!'

'Oh, for God's sake.'

'Perhaps there is a hell after all, Erika.'

'Told you. That's just superstition. God doesn't exist. The Devil doesn't exist. It's just stuff invented by the churches to keep people quiet. Anyway, the church is hand in glove with the murderers running this country.'

Hannes was wrestling with less temporal problems.

'It's possible, though, that you come back after you're dead in a different form, isn't it? As an animal or something.'

'Reincarnation is just another superstition.' Erika rinsed out a cup and dried it with a tea-cloth. 'Dead is dead. The end. Finito. I've told you that before.'

'You mean you stay in your coffin for ever and ever and ever and ever and ever?'

Erika was vigorously polishing the cup. Her face was set in a deep frown. She was in no mood to dispense bromides.

'If you must know, your flesh is eaten by worms, then the worms are eaten by bigger worms, while your bones turn to dust.'

Hannes stared at her, seeking confirmation that she was joking.

'That's horrible,' he said at last. 'You can't mean it.'

'Believe there's a heaven and a hell if you must. I can't stop you.'

'I bet you're just repeating what Georg told you. This worm theory is what the Commies believe, isn't it?'

'You won't think it's so horrible when you get older.'

'Bet *you* think it's horrible.'

'Stop saying "Bet".'

I'm twelve now, he thought, nearly thirteen. If I live to a normal old age, say seventy-two, then I've already had a sixth of my life, a fairly large slice out of a layer cake. Every morning one woke up with a few more crumbs of cake eaten away, and nobody even bothered to think about it!

'You and Georg don't know everything,' he said defiantly. 'It's anybody's guess what goes on in the Universe.'

'I'd better have a word with your friend Dorn.'

He stared at her incredulously. She was pouring out coffee,

her head lowered as she watched the dark brown liquid pour from the spout.

'You really want to go out with Dorn?'

'Of course I don't. What do you take me for? Just don't tell Georg. He wouldn't understand . . .'

'He's supposed to be awful with girls. I could tell you a few things I'd rather not think about.'

'I only want to make sure there's nothing in what you say.'

'I know where to find him,' Hannes said.

They decided he should drop a hint to Dorn that Erika would be hanging out laundry in their wash-kitchen next morning.

'And don't make it sound like a date either,' she told him.

Hannes never got as far as the Bismarckstrasse. Tempted to look in on the depot to see if anything untoward was happening, he found everyone grouped around a uniformed Dorn. They all looked up to him as if he were a monument. They were plotting! Strange that nobody had called Hannes down. Alarming, in fact. As he came closer, he noticed Werner Schemel gesticulating and laughing. Evidently Dorn's sentence on him had been suspended. He tapped Rolf's shoulder.

'What's up?' Hannes hoped he sounded grimly casual.

Rolf put a finger to his lips while he continued to gaze up at Dorn. Wasn't he talking? Did he mean to drag out that Palestine stamp crisis? Had Rolf perhaps denounced him to Dorn? That would explain why they had not called him down.

'What's going on?' he asked Jürgen Kloth, who loitered on the outskirts of the group.

'Big stuff,' Jürgen whispered. 'You in on this as well?'

'Who said I wasn't?'

Hannes noticed several new faces in the group: scruffy urchins from the Hoheluftchaussee. Had Rolf allowed the depot gang to become absorbed by Dorn's outfit?

'Decided to join us, Hacker?' Dorn drew back his lips, revealing his revolting teeth. He chortled mirthlessly. 'Or do you see yourself as a neutral observer?'

Hannes stiffened. 'Nobody told me anything was on. I'm not neutral.'

'Don't want *him*, do we?'

Werner Schemel was clearly restored to favour.

'Want your brains bashed in?'

'Better not try anything. We know all about you, don't we Rolfie?'

Rolf whistled; his cheeks quivered. Schemel had clearly prematurely revealed something he had been told in confidence. Was it really about the stamp? Had they been speculating on the significance of the postcard?

'You're all right, Hacker,' Dorn said. Hannes warmed to the leader's conciliatory tone. 'You can come in on this. If you want to, that is.'

'You bet I do.'

So Dorn knew nothing. Rolf had kept quiet. When it came to the test, he was still his best friend.

'Come to think of it, we can lose you, Leo,' Dorn said. 'What good would you be?'

'He could keep a look-out for coppers,' Schmitt suggested.

'Don't need that.' Unmindful of his uniform, Dorn extracted a cigarette from his brown shirt pocket. One of his lieutenants struck a match. What a nerve! Hannes watched him blow smoke in Werner Schemel's face. 'I know the copper on this beat from the boycott days. He won't interfere, not if he knows what's good for him. I'll send him to Sandmann for a free beer, OK?'

'What about souvenirs?' Schmitt asked.

'You just do as you're told, Skunky! What do they teach you in your Fähnlein? This is political action. There will be no confiscations, that understood? Only known Yid shopkeeper in the vicinity. We're going to ask him if he'd mind taking his business elsewhere, OK? Don't need kosher butchers in Eppendorf no more, do we? I've got authority for this operation from the SA, so I want it done right. If you depot dwarfs can't conform to discipline, drop out now.'

Hannes knew there was no way out. The situation had changed. Gone were the days when Rolf was in charge and decided for their small group whether to play football or Emperor or just stand around and gossip. They had become part of a greater whole.

'We got rid of the Reds and the Social Democrats. Now it's the turn of the Yids.'

'The Yids! The Yids!'

Werner Schemel, overcome by the significance of the situation, broke into a clumsy, impromptu dance.

'That settles it,' Dorn exclaimed, flicking his cigarette at Schemel. 'You're out. You're infantile. Go on, cripple, sod off.'

'What . . . why . . .' Schemel stammered.

'Anybody else here not in the Jungvolk?'

Jürgen Kloth raised his hand hesitantly and looked around for a comrade in misfortune.

'Hard luck, Asthma,' Rolf grinned.

'You're out as well, Kloth,' Dorn commanded. 'Go on, both of you, sod off. Can't take responsibility for bleedin' invalids.'

'Why can't I be in on this?' Kloth appealed. 'Tell him Rolfie.'

'Tell him what?' Rolf said. 'Piss off, freak. We got work to do.'

Kloth and Schemel took a few backward steps, hoping to follow events from the touchlines. Dorn ordered them off. Hannes watched them retreat along the tramlines like whipped dogs.

'Let's get on with it.' Dorn spoke softly. They had to close ranks to hear him. 'First, we need red paint. Need a volunteer. Hacker, how about you?'

'Got no money on me,' Hannes said.

'You know Meissner's, the ironmongers, don't you?' Hannes caught the coin that Dorn tossed across to him. 'Tin of vermilion paint. Make sure the tin opens easily. Don't want to be lumbered with tools. What are you waiting for? Want you running all the way, matey.'

Hannes hesitated. 'Coming, Rolfie?'

'Never you mind Rolfie. You got your orders.'

'You heard,' Rolf said.

He could still have saved himself – if it hadn't been for the coin in his hand. If he didn't come back with paint, they'd brand him a thief as well as a coward. If Dorn reported him to Hinrichs there might be Jungvolk repercussions. In which case he'd never get the knife.

The assistant at Meissner's didn't even look at him as he

handed the tin across the counter. Hannes held it by its wire
handle as he broke into a steady trot. *Want you running all the
way*. Better think of nothing. Easy if you half-closed your eyes.
Nothing. There it was, the grey cube, the vapour.

When he got back the others had dispersed. There was
only Rolf.

'Gimme the paint,' he greeted Hannes breathlessly. 'My
orders are to give it to Dorn. You're to get up on that wall
behind the garage. Whistle three times if you see anything
suspicious.'

Hannes followed Rolf through the patch of waste ground, then
clawed his way up to the top of the brick wall. There he squatted
down, arms folded. He had an excellent view of their target.

'Everything going according to plan,' Rolf reported. Hannes
thought it appropriate to express disappointment. They had to
do the donkey work – the others were having all the fun.

'Keep your eyes skinned,' Rolf advised.

Siegfried Levi's Kosher Butcher had been subjected to minor
ambushes before – Rolf had once planted a soft banana skin on
the threshold – but this was the first properly orchestrated
operation against the establishment. Dorn could certainly get
things done. Levi, a bespectacled hedgehog of a man in a dark
suit and hat, stood by the shop window, waiting for customers.
Hannes wondered if there could be many besides Rosa.

'Now for some action,' Rolf hissed. 'Lucky sods.'

Dorn and four of his Hoheluft gang had come into view, walking past the shopfront. Whistling self-consciously, they dodged
into the adjoining doorway and waited. After a few moments, the
second detachment, headed by Karl-Heinz, turned the corner
and marched straight into the shop. While Siegfried Levi was
dealing with them, Dorn's group emerged from their doorway
to take up position outside the shop window. Dorn rasped out
an order. One of his minions calmly opened the tin of red paint
and flung half of its contents against the shopfront.

'You watching?' Rolf asked Hannes excitedly.

The second group had now come out of the shop, pulling
Siegfried Levi with them by the scruff of his neck. They dragged
him to his window to acquaint him with their comrades' work.

Then they lifted the shopkeeper's hand and placed it hard against the streaming liquid. Dorn barked out a further order. Tightly held, the Jew began to smear the letter 'J' on the glass. There was not enough paint on his hands to complete the word. Karl-Heinz alertly splashed the remainder of the paint against the window. Some of it spattered against Levi; his trembling red hand smudged out the required letters.

A few bystanders had stopped to watch. When Levi had written out JUDE, he was frog-marched back into the shop. Schmitt took aim before throwing a pebble against the window. It cracked the glass but did not break it.

'All right, men,' Dorn yelled. 'Back to base!'

The two groups assembled, examining their clothes for traces of red paint. Then they cantered away round the corner.

The bystanders stepped forward hesitantly to inspect the damage; they were presently joined by the shopkeeper himself, his rather long arms held away from his body. He was shaking his head in disbelief; the onlookers took care not to stand too close to him.

A gust of wind blew dust into Hannes' eyes. Bloody fool, he thought, turning away. Couldn't Levi at least have changed his name? Or rubbed out those three Hebrew letters painted on the glass? Why present himself as a sitting target?

'That's that,' Rolf said as he climbed down from the wall. 'Should have smashed the window, though.'

At the depot, Kloth and Schemel rejoined the group.

Those who had taken an active part in the operation breathlessly recapitulated events to the others.

'Good work,' Rolf said, slapping Dorn on the shoulder.

'Not a bad little operation.' Dorn clasped his waist, accepting plaudits. 'Others would have waited till nightfall. We did it in broad daylight.'

'Better not show his face again in the Löwenstrasse,' Rolf said. 'That was just a foretaste.'

'So what did you do, Rolfie?' Schemel asked sarcastically. 'Sat on the wall and did nothing, you and Hacker. We saw you!'

The sight of Schemel's crooked smile disappearing behind Dorn's protecting back sent the blood shooting to Hannes' face.

'Say that again!'

'Wasn't talking to you, Hacker!'

'You insulted my mate!'

'Your mate? Since when?'

Hannes no longer saw Schemel's travesty of a smile. The faces around him dissolved into a blur. He lunged out blindly, his fist hitting Schemel's soft face.

'I'll do you,' he heard himself shout. 'Sodding little bastard!'

Before Schemel could drag himself away, howling with shock rather than pain, Hannes landed another jab. Then he thrust his knee up into Schemel's groin. Looking down at the squirming body of the cripple, he grunted with satisfaction. The others stared, stunned by Hannes' unexpected paroxysm.

'What was all that in aid of?' Jürgen Kloth asked, helping Schemel to his feet. 'He didn't mean anything.'

'Cool off, Hacker.' Dorn followed up. 'Go on, put your head under the tap!'

Hannes felt isolated. Couldn't they appreciate why he had to teach Werner Schemel a lesson? Now Dorn had turned on him, Dorn of all people! Slowly he sauntered through the yard. Just for that, he wasn't going to tell him anything. He'd never know how close he'd come to that date with Erika . . .

Resentment boiling up in him again, Hannes thrust his hands into his pockets and ambled through the draughty passageway. Don't give a damn anymore, he thought. About anything. They could jump in the lake for all he cared. The lot of them.

CHAPTER TWELVE

Camouflaged with twigs of heather tied to their caps, they stealthily advanced up the hillside. Then they crouched in the undergrowth, ears close to the ground, waiting for the signal to attack.

'Wait for my whistle, North Troop,' the Ram had commanded. 'South and North must co-ordinate their bombardments precisely. When you hear me call out "Zero", withdraw the pin, count ten, aim. Judge your distance. The enemy is entrenched on the summit. Your job is to destroy him. Capture the flag! The grenade must explode in the air!'

They held their breaths, waiting for the signal. The Ram, who wore a larger sprig of heather than the others, crawled forward, then raised his arm: 'Four, three, two, one, ZERO!'

With steady fingers, Hannes withdrew the pin from his dummy grenade, pitched it high in the direction of the gorse bushes high on the hill. Then he snuggled close to the ground, listening to the wooden missiles as they hummed over his head. The Ram blew his whistle again.

'Attack!' he yelled. 'Attack!'

Intent on capturing the summit, North Troop stormed up the incline, matching the shouts that drifted over from the other side.

'Don't drag behind!' the Ram bleated. 'You two idiots, keep your heads down! Becker! Stay where you are! You're dead!'

Hannes followed Rolf to the head of the advancing column. As he ran, he experienced the feeling that it had all happened to him before. Running through tall grass, out of breath, pursued by a horde of hollering plumed enemies, brandishing tomahawks. Summer holidays on another planet . . .

'The dead must stay on the ground!' the Ram screamed.

The defenders had formed a wall of uniforms around the flagpole, aiming wooden rifles at the camouflaged attackers, who streamed up the hillside.

Rolf and Hannes were amongst the first to reach the summit. They threw themselves bodily against the enemy, battling with half-closed eyes for possession of the rifles, working their opponents over with fists. Hannes dived into the mêlée with gusto, saw the coveted flagpole break in two. A defender snatched away the half with the flag attached; joining up with his comrades, he retreated down the far side of the hill, bellowing victory.

The Jungzug leaders blew their whistles. The attacking side had been narrowly defeated. Victors and losers picked themselves up, straggled back into camp, arguing the decision.

'We won really,' Rolf declared. 'We butchered them with those grenades. Bull's eye every time.'

Back in the tent they nursed their wounds. Freitag discovered a bleeding ankle, Lessing displayed his shirt, ripped by a knife.

'Could have split me like a peashell,' he boasted.

Hannes washed, then polished his boots until the black leather sent back a blurred reflection of his face. He folded his blankets, polished his buckle, washed his comb out under the pump, combed his hair. Finally he checked that his pack was in order, everything in its appointed place. If you kept objects meticulously separated, they wouldn't let you down. That way lay security.

Later they queued with aluminium mugs for their midday meal. Hannes crinkled his nose.

'Hot-pot again,' he groaned. 'Don't half stink.'

'Soldier's grub,' Rolf told him. 'Can't afford to be fussy about food in the army. Might as well get used to it.'

Horseflies danced over the glittering vats of vegetable soup with whole potatoes and bits of fat bacon swimming to the brim. Hannes could not suppress a retch.

'Let's see you get through that,' Rolf smirked.

Hannes went through the motions of eating. When he thought nobody was looking he spilled half the contents of his bowl under the table. You were not allowed to leave food uneaten.

'Can't get it down,' he said.

'Me neither,' Rolf admitted.

'I'll eat yours up, Rolfie,' Freezy, the newcomer, offered.

'No, I'm eating Rolfie's,' Schmitt insisted. 'I'll eat the lot up.'

'I offered first,' Friess insisted.

'You can have mine, Freezy.'

'Eat it yourself, Hacker.'

Evidently Friess had no wish to curry favour with him.

'Makes you want to throw up,' Rolf said, watching Friess eating.

'I'll eat the lot,' Schmitt repeated, pointing his spoon at Friess: 'First time in camp and crawling up Rolfie's arse already.'

'Shut your face.' Rolf took out a Sarotti chocolate bar, unwrapped it and started to chew meditatively. 'Friess is OK.' He looked up at the sun, half-closing his eyes.

'There's going to be changes,' he said. 'At the depot, I mean. Cutting out all that kid's stuff. Girls and that. Lore Meinke. You can forget her for a start, Hacker.'

'Dorn goes out with girls,' Hannes pointed out.

'Don't like Dorn, do you?'

'He's all right.'

'He's tough.'

'I said he was all right.'

'Come to that, there's a few things we don't like about *you*, Hacker.'

'Such as what?'

'Such as keeping things secret. You seem to be in a sort of daze half the time. Sort of sly, cunning.'

'So are you!'

'Only telling you what Dorn says. He thinks he knows what's the matter with you.'

'There's nothing the matter with me,' Hannes said quickly.

Rolf was in his element, nibbling away, spoiling everything, even out here, in camp, where he didn't have a proper audience.

I'd have a good time if it wasn't for Rolf, Hannes ruminated.
Ought to get myself a transfer to another Fähnlein. At the far
end of the trestle table, a group had started to sing, beating out
the march rhythm with their spoons.

> *The world's rotting bones were trembling,*
> *In fear of the great red war.*
> *We've broken the terror for them,*
> *For us, it was victory once more!*

Hannes gazed at the singing faces. He knew none of them.
The swelling sickness that had destroyed life at the depot was
rampant here as well. It wasn't just Hinrichs' Fähnlein which
had assembled at the Hermann Göring camp, it was a whole
Jungstamm, six hundred strong. Whichever way you looked,
you saw hostile strangers.

It was like being in a small boat out in the middle of the Alster.
The water was spreading, overflowing its banks, rolling back
the land, growing into an ocean. But you stayed where you
were, out alone on that threatening sea, with no land in sight
anywhere.

Everyone had taken up the tune. Hannes, glad to be distracted, joined in with zest:

> *And on and on we shall march now*
> *Let everything fall apart:*
> *Today we rule our country*
> *Tomorrow the world!*

'We have been honoured by the presence of Unterbannführer
Kanzl. His renown as an old fighter of the movement will be
familiar to you.'

Head stuck through the tent flaps, scratching his woolly hair,
the Ram looked more than ever like a sheep.

'Putting on a show for him. Need volunteers. Sandmann!
Hacker! Do anything? Impressions? Play an instrument?'

There was no reply.

'Don't want our Jungzug to lag behind. How about you, Sandmann? You sing, don't you? You scream loud enough.'

'Sorry sir, my voice is breaking.'

'Hadn't noticed. You, Hacker? Can't you do anything?'

'Sorry, sir.'

'Nothing at all?'

'He plays the mouth-organ, sir,' Rolf said.

Trust Rolf to betray him!

'Use your nut, Hacker. Up for the knife, aren't you?'

'Yes, sir.'

'Well, can you play the bloody thing or can't you?'

'I can't sir. Honest.'

'What did you want to tell him that for?' Hannes asked Rolf after the Ram had stomped out of the tent to find performers elsewhere.

'There you go, being devious again. You play, don't you? One of your worst faults, Hacker.'

'None of your business.'

'I'm still in charge of this Jungenschaft, in case you'd forgotten.'

'Didn't volunteer yourself, though, Sandmann, did you?' Lessing's cold appeared to be permanent. 'Pretty lame lot, aren't you?'

'We don't do culture,' Rolf told him icily. 'We concentrate on keeping fit.'

'Never heard of the leadership principle?' Freitag asked, little finger rooting between his teeth. 'Anything we're ordered to do, we do it. Got that?'

The show for Unterbannführer Kanzl was held in the open air. The boys sat cross-legged in the heather, the rows stretching back from a wooden platform which served as a stage. Sitting a few rows behind the guest of honour and Fähnleinführer Hinrichs, Hannes observed their profiles whenever they turned their heads to mumble something to each other.

Unterbannführer Kanzl was big and burly with black hair parted in the middle and plastered down with brilliantine.

Strong eyebrows met over an eagle nose. He wore four silver stars on his epaulettes. He seemed on very friendly terms with the velvety Hinrichs. When the performance was bad, the Unterbannführer pursed his lips indulgently; when he was amused he slapped his thighs.

He appeared to be particularly entertained by the shadow-play. It was mimed behind a white sheet, illuminated by headlights from the Unterbannführer's car. The play was called *Isidor*. Its two characters represented Average Citizen Michel (in sleeping cap and nightgown) and Jew Isidor (a hunchback with cloak, false nose and elongated fingernails, carrying a bunch of keys). Before the play began, the spectators were encouraged to show their feelings by booing and cheering.

Isidor's silhouette appeared first and was greeted with loud boos. He pranced about on his toes, raising his knees from time to time, as if contemplating a to dance. A choir of boys accompanied the pantomime with a rhyming chant:

> *With fuzzy hair and nose too long*
> *Through our fair land he crept along.*
> *And thought himself our Overlor'*
> *Isidor! Isidor!*

Fähnleinführer Hinrichs cupped his hands in front of his mouth to show that he, too, was booing. The Unterbannführer slapped his breeches again. Now the silhouette of Michel appeared, welcomed by wild cheering. Isidor, raising his arms in horror, waved his hands about as if to ward off an evil spirit. Michel bowed to the audience and the choir intoned:

> *Poor Michel had a rotten time*
> *Working away in Juda's slime.*
> *They set about him like a slave*
> *Called him Knave! Called him Knave!*

The boos became louder. Rolf shoved an elbow between Hannes' ribs. 'Remember old Levi? They're all the same.'

Behind the sheet Michel bent down submissively. Isidor stretched out his hands to mime a wicked fairytale magician. He hovered over Michel, mumbling silent curses.

He could not swallow the beastly pill,

the choir declaimed,

Of Jewish rule he'd had his fill.
He kicked the Yid to kingdom come
On the run! On the run!

Now Michel plucked a Jungvolk knife from under his nightgown and cut off the keys dangling from Isidor's waist. He followed this up with a severe kick, which sent the Jew sprawling. The boys began to stamp their feet rhythmically. Hinrichs and Kanzl demonstrated solidarity by joining in.

The chorus chanted the last verse:

Our house is free, our air is clean
It's homely now for you and me!
For Michel's master in his home,
He's sent the Yid to rove and roam.

The Jew cringed and grovelled, trying to get off the stage on his knees. Michel stood poised over him. After Michel had taken a final bow, the car lights were switched off. The play was over.

The next turn was a boy who imitated bird noises. He could do a nightingale, a crow, a canary and a seagull. He was followed by two boys who played folk-melodies on their mouth-organs. Fähnleinführer Hinrichs, catching Unterbannführer Kanzl in the act of looking at his wrist-watch, stroked his soft, blond hair. The final turn, he promised Kanzl, would be special: an all-Fähnlein effort. Kanzl folded his arms and nodded.

The platform was in darkness. Two boys started their drumrolls, a trumpet sounded a fanfare. Rolf and Hannes nudged each other and guffawed as Freitag ran on stage carrying a flaming torch. A line of Jungvolk members were revealed, their arms raised high.

'Bloody show-offs,' Rolf murmured.

One of the boys stepped forward and began to recite in a high ringing voice, while light from Freitag's torch flickered over his face.

'Light Conquers Darkness! To the nations of Aryan descent the sign of light is the swastika. Our Führer has given the swastika back its true meaning. The darkness that followed the last war has given way to the brilliant light of the swastika. Our Saviour! Our light!'

A second boy stepped forward from the edge of the platform and unfurled a swastika flag. He recited:

'You, fatherland's youth! You, comrades, who wear the brown shirt! Defend it! By force of arms, for your shirt is holy! Protect your flag, comrade! Protect it like a mother! The flag is our tomorrow! The flag is our honour! The flag is our courage! Let no-one mistake why we are alive! The Great War preserved us for the coming war!'

The boy was now joined by others. They all raised their arms in salute. Drums began to roll again, the trumpet sounded, voices rose up into the sky in perfect unison.

> *Ascend O fire and let your leaping flames*
> *Rise from the mountains of the Rhine.*
> *Rise Higher and Higher!*
> *See! Loyally we stand in the magic circle*
> *To watch you blaze forth in the fatherland's glory*
> *Sacred flame, call together our youth,*
> *That in the glow of fire*
> *Our courage may grow.*
> *Hear our petition,*
> *Father over life and death.*
> *Help us to win freedom.*
> *Be thou our shield!*

After a few moments of pious reflection, scattered applause broke out, then grew in volume to become a roar.

They rose. Fähnleinführer Hinrichs had mounted the platform clasping his belt. Behind him torch flames tore through the darkness.

Baldur von Schirach!

Hinrichs began with the name of the poet – who was also the Reich's Leader of Youth. This was his best-known work:

> *What is the greatest thing about him?*
> *He is not only Führer*
> *The nation's hero —*
> *But himself!*
> *Straight, steadfast, plain*
> *In whom rest the world's roots.*
> *His soul touches the stars*
> *Yet he remains a man —*
> *Like you and me!*

Kanzl now took up position next to the Fähnleinführer.

'Men of the Jungstamm,' he declared. 'With loyal hearts aglow we call to our beloved Führer: "Give us your orders! We are ready to obey, to do our duty, to follow!" Sieg Heil! Sieg Heil! Sieg Heil!'

'Sieg Heil!' echoed a hundred and sixty voices.

It was time for the final demonstration of loyalty: the Horst Wessel song.

Hannes sang, his eyes smarted. He tried vainly to recall the songs Georg had played in his room. How pale and petty they seemed! The voices thundering forth, celebrating German will, did not whine about class distinctions or social injustices. They did not beg for compassion. Neither did they ask you to make decisions or to revolt against authority! They ordered you to plunge into the great warm togetherness of Blood and Honour. No petty concerns about coffee or wheat! No parents or relations! No school! As you sang with the others, you were carried away to a great height and on into blinding light. Hannes sang on, locking out the last whispers of doubt . . .

*   *   *

In the tent, Lessing and Freitag hummed softly as they undressed.

'The great war preserved us for the coming war,' Lessing whispered. 'Good stuff. Wonder who thought of it?'

He blew his nose, then wrapped his blankets around him.

Hannes noticed that Rolf was making no preparations to go to bed. Though the Lights Out fanfare had sounded some time ago, he was carefully combing his hair, then brushing his cap carefully with his forearm.

'Off on a mission?' Hannes asked sarcastically.

'I'm not turning in just yet.'

'Where are you going then?'

'Out. Been asked to a party.'

'At this hour?'

'Keep your voice down. The others aren't in the know. Special farewell party for Unterbannführer Kanzl. By special invitation only.'

'Why did they ask you then?'

'Orderly,' Rolf said gravely. 'Going as an orderly.'

'Why you and not me?'

'Didn't volunteer to play the mouth-organ, did you? Now you're sorry you didn't volunteer. Only got yourself to blame if you get left out of things.'

'You didn't do anything in the show.'

'Ah,' Rolf said cryptically, 'that's different.'

Hannes found the idea of this clandestine party distressing. His mind was not only inflamed with envy, but by a disturbing memory that had to be warded off.

'Who else is going?'

'Just leaders. And orderlies. There's going to be lovely grub. Seen it. Smoked eels, shrimps in jelly . . .' He ran his tongue over his lips. 'Tinned cherries and all.'

'I wouldn't go if they begged me,' Hannes said. 'On their hands and knees.'

'Bet you wouldn't mind having shrimps in jelly . . .'

'I'll shrimp in jelly you in a minute,' Lessing barked at him. 'Bugger off and let the rest of us get some sleep.'

'I'll walk over with you,' Hannes said.

'No, you won't. Didn't you hear Lights Out?'

Rolf nipped out of the tent, busily whistling. What a friend, Hannes thought bitterly, starting to get undressed.

'Did you know there was a party?' he asked Freitag.

'You're well out of it.'

'Rolf says he's one of the orderlies.'

'Disorderlies, more likely.'

'They're having smoked eels and shrimps in jelly.'

Hannes hoped the repetition of the menu might elicit further information, but Freitag and Lessing were tittering under their blankets. Some dirty joke, Hannes guessed.

He felt too hot and muddled to sleep. Why did everybody make such a mystery over certain things? Images, startling in their violent newness, chased across his mind. He crawled between his blankets and gazed up at the roof of his tent. His mind started to rehearse secret rites in which Rolf might be involved. Was it anything like meetings of the Ku-Klux-Klan, he wondered, where one wore white nightshirts and hoods with slits in them? In the dark he became aware of the hairiness of the blanket, the hardness of the ground, a drowsy pain in his loins. He raised himself up again, peered across at Lessing and Freitag.

'What are you two whispering about?' he asked.

'Go to sleep, Nosey Parker!' Freitag raised his voice sufficiently for Hannes to hear snatches of what he was saying. The story concerned a Jungvolk member named Tillman, who had spent a week in a camp adjoining one occupied by the BDM, the national girls' organisation. One of the girls, Frauke, according to Tillman, had come home from camp all hot and bothered. A few weeks later Frauke had confessed to her father that she was expecting a baby.

'Only fourteen and a half, she was,' Freitag breathed, 'you can imagine what the old man felt about it. What he did, he locked her up in her room. Wouldn't let her go back to school or camp or anything. One night, Tillman climbed up to her room, helped her escape. Know what she did? Went straight to the police, reported her old man for calling the BDM names. Next day he got arrested, the old man. The girl hasn't seen him since.

Tillman says she's got the house to herself now, friends come up whenever they like, they have smashing pyjama parties and that . . .'

Freitag paused to nibble his thumbnail. When he resumed, his voice was too low for Hannes to hear more revelations. He turned over under his blanket, his mind now condemned to grapple with two quite dissimilar events. Rolf's farewell party with shrimps in jelly, and Frauke's disgusting pyjama parties. When he fell asleep, Rolf had not returned.

Next day Rolf took care to avoid Hannes. The camp was large enough for him to separate himself during the day's activities. It wasn't until evening, when they were crossing the Elbe again, that Hannes trapped him, as he leant across the rail of the ferry, head cradled in his arm. He looked pale. Hannes wondered whether he might be sea-sick.

The pause for compassion cost him dearly. Rolf looked up. A carefully planned speech, rich in innuendo and justified reproach, disintegrated in Hannes' mind. The best he could manage was a quaking grin, which permitted Rolf to swing from a position of vulnerable defence to headlong attack.

'Where you been hiding yourself all day?' Rolf now leant back against the rail, supporting his weight on his elbows. 'Didn't get your knife, did you?'

'No,' Hannes admitted. 'Next time, the Ram said.'

'Heard that one before.' Rolf scanned the horizon. 'Could have put in a good word for you.'

'Did you?'

'Maybe.'

The green and white ferry drew closer to the quayside. Hannes became aware of the familiar smell of brewing, of freshly caught fish and tar. The famous row of church steeples rose up darkly against a sky streaked with ribbons of pink and purple. Smoke oozed from the funnels of passing ships and hovered in the air like balloons.

Hamburg was a terrific place! He felt an expectant uplift, akin to the sensation he felt every time the lights dimmed in his favourite cinema, the Harvestehuder Lichtspiele on Eppendorfer Baum, just before the performance began.

'Tell you this,' Rolf said, 'they'll want to know a lot more about you before you get the knife. I'll probably be asked for a testimonial. Everything's changed now that Dorn's come in with us. Old Kanzl gave us some pretty good tips. How to deal with the Jewish conspiracy in Eppendorf, etcetera. There's spies everywhere, in the pay of Roosevelt, who's a Jew himself.'

Old Kanzl, was it now? Hannes knew he should be making use of this pause in Rolf's onslaught to launch his own well-prepared interrogation about the previous night's happenings, but his mind was wiped clean. Rolf was looking at him strangely.

'Shouldn't let on to Dorn you're so set against him, either. We're about to clean up for good and all. He's leading us. Old Kanzl says an Aryan is right in whatever he does *because* he is an Aryan. Makes sense to me. For a start, we'll expel from the depot anybody who uses foreign words. For anything that's worth saying, there's a good German word, says old Kanzl.'

'Depot is a foreign word,' Hannes said. 'And you seem to forget, we did old Levi's shop last week.'

'Shouldn't be too proud of your part in that, Hacker. Your trouble is you've got no public spirit. That's why you haven't won your knife. Probably never will now. Don't think I've forgotten that stamp business, 'cause I haven't . . .'

'Cut it out, Sandmann,' Hannes said, blindly thrusting on. 'I suppose what you were up to last night was public-spirited . . .'

The words were hardly out of his mouth before he realised that he had made a dreadful mistake. When Rolf was in one of his moods, you had to leave him alone, wait till the bile was squeezed out of his system. Rolf was looking at him boldly.

'Meaning what?'

'Freitag and Lessing said you went to that camp party as a disorderly.'

'A what?'

'Disorderly.'

Hannes sounded apologetic. Rolf drew himself up to the full size of his guilt.

'Say that again!'

'Didn't say anything. They said it.'

'All right, mate.' Rolf wagged his head with dreadful finality. 'Thought you was a friend. Now I know different. You've made your big mistake, Hacker. You're jealous because you weren't asked to the party, so now you want to take it out on me. For a start, I'll have to report you to old Hinrichs for slandering him and an Unterbannführer behind their backs.'

'I only repeated . . .'

'No use whining now, Hacker. You said these things, I didn't. Warned you before about being sly and telling tales. Can't afford to keep on people like you. Forget the knife. And if you know what's good for you you'll disappear from the depot pronto. Dorn hasn't forgotten what you did to poor old Schemel.'

Hannes knew there was a cool, logical response to Rolf's assault, arguments neatly filed away in his mind somewhere, but how could he find them now when a wheel of panic was spinning in his head?

'Forget it, can't you, Rolf?' he heard himself grovelling. 'Why go over all that again?'

'Never appreciated having a real pal like me, have you?' Rolf moved up to deliver the KO. 'Up to now I've been protecting you, Hacker. If you think that postcard is the only thing we got on you, think again. There's a few other things you're keeping quiet about, right? Like pouring away camp food while you stuff yourself with Sarotti chocolates. Like your old man getting arrested by the Gestapo. My dad told me about that.'

Hannes stood rooted to the spot, chilled by despair. I'll sort this out when I'm alone, he told himself over and over again. I'll think something out. But now he's got to leave me alone. I must be looking a fool, with not even a rail to lean against . . .

Rolf had started to whistle, staring at the setting sun which glazed ships and cranes and warehouses with a golden gloss. The ferry was making a turn, churning up water. Somebody blew a whistle, the boys scrambled down iron stairs to the deck below. Rolf's face was silhouetted against the violent reds and purples of the sky. The harbour was aflame with burning colours. The Jungzug was singing again:

When soldiers of the storm
March into battle
Their spirits soar —
And when Jewish blood spurts from the knife
We know that victory is ours!

Hannes recognised the song. There could be only one explanation for Rolf shouting these words at him now.

He *knew*.

The ferry thumped against the rotting wood of the landing stage; groups of boys clattered down the stairs to re-assemble. Hannes thought of a brown earth-worm, and the way it behaved when you cut it up into slices – an experiment Rolf had shown him long ago: each slice pathetically squirmed with new life, writhing in a ghastly multiplication of self.

I'm that earth-worm now, he thought: one little worm slice for Mama, one for Rosa, one for Hinrichs, one for Dorn and Rolf, one for Dr Gilbrecht and Papa, one for Erika, one for Georg . . .

One thing was crystal clear: his secret was no longer secret. Soon the whole of Eppendorf would hear about Hannes Hacker. Rolf knew him for what he was. He would find a way to destroy him once and for all.

CHAPTER THIRTEEN

During the next few days Hannes was at a loss to know what
to do with himself. He moped about the kitchen, listening to
the radio, poring over the sports pages for hour after hour.
He took old books and toys out of a suitcase under his bed,
methodically dusted and indexed them. He didn't tell his mother
where he was going when he slunk off to the tennis courts on
the Victoria Football Ground to earn a few Pfennigs as a ball
boy. When he asked his father if he could spend a day with
him at the department store, Papa told him not to be silly.

As a concession to what he called 'my interrogation',
Papa no longer tuned into German broadcasts from Moscow,
content to get his information from London and Hilversum.
Afterwards he declared that Soviet intervention in Spain on
the side of the Loyalists was now imminent. The ensuing chain
reaction was bound to bring about Hitler's downfall. A coalition
government of centre parties under Brüning would be swept
back into power.

Every evening Erika was out with Georg. She came home
late, kept out of Papa's way, never again mentioned her date
with Dorn. Hannes took good care not to remind her.

'You've been skulking around for days,' Mama complained
one morning through a cloud of steam. 'Have you quarrelled
with Rolf Sandmann?'

'You want to get rid of me?' he told her. 'Would I
be doing you a favour playing in the street with those
hooligans?'

He was at the bottom of a pit of indecision. Boredom
and inactivity, the uncertainty about what was happening at

the depot in his absence, mounting dread of the inevitable encounter with Rolf at camp, made him morose and tetchy.

On the third morning after the showdown on the ferry, he went out, telling his mother he was off to see Rosa. It was not until he was in the tram that he realised he had not changed his clothes. No matter. Where he was going one would look out of place in one's Sunday best. He stared out of the tram window, not really seeing the shops and passers-by; he practised thinking of nothing for as long as possible.

It was noon when he arrived at the gates of Georg's factory. Outside a rust-coloured building, men in blue overalls pushed trolleys laden with cardboard boxes which they stored in the back of vans. Hannes stared at the men as they went about their work; he envied them their anonymity.

A siren howled. More men wearing blue overalls poured from the building. Ignoring the watchman in his booth, munching sandwiches over a newspaper, Hannes dodged inconspicuously through the gates.

He found Georg sooner than expected. He was leaning against a bicycle shelter, hands pushed into overall pockets, his peaked cap worn sideways over one ear. He did not appear surprised to see Hannes hurrying towards him. He held out his hand and introduced him to his colleagues. He mentioned their names in full and pleased Hannes by calling him 'an old friend of mine'.

'Come to see me, lad?' Georg asked him in his lazy, comforting voice. 'Let's have a chat over a glass of beer then.'

The other men laughed, but Georg put an arm round Hannes' shoulder, as they sauntered through the gates.

'It's not about Erika,' Hannes was quick to reassure him. 'Don't you have to work?'

'Dinner-hour. Not that we're all that busy. Hear the Doctor raving on the wireless last night? Country "buzzing with burgeoning industry"? All that. Impressed our lads, he did. We're on short time again but they eat up anything old Clubfoot tells 'em. Wouldn't credit it, would you?'

They walked along a narrow cobbled street, down some steps to a small corner pub, dark and dank like a cellar. A tiled stove reached up to the ceiling, the stone floor was covered with sawdust. Groups of workmen sat round tables, drinking from tankards and smoking clay pipes. In the shafts of white sunlight, tobacco smoke whirled. A blowsy, henna-haired woman wearing a rubber apron served behind the bar.

'What will you have, Hannes?' Georg asked him, 'Lemonade or beer?'

'Beer.'

'One of yours?' the woman cackled as she drew the beer.

'My eldest,' Georg explained with a grin.

Hannes felt relaxed. You knew you were safe with Georg.

'For your eldest,' the henna woman said, setting a foaming pint in front of Georg and a glass of light ale before Hannes.

'Something I've got to talk to you about,' Hannes said at last.

'Speak up, then,' Georg encouraged him. 'You can still talk freely here. Old Flora's as red as her hairdo. Only never whisper. Lads in corner will think we're cooking up bloody revolution.'

'What it is, I'm not going back to school when the new term starts.'

'Discussed it with your father and mother?'

Hannes shook his head and sipped his beer.

'They wouldn't understand.'

'Why not tackle them?' Georg advised. 'You're only twelve, still got your mind to train, haven't you?'

'You didn't go to a secondary school.'

'I'm not proud of that.' Georg smiled wistfully. 'You get good reports, don't you? Kids at school like you, don't they?'

'I've got enemies.'

'Don't whisper, there's a good lad.'

'There's this Hoheluft gang . . .'

'Don't have to sing it either, lad.'

'I think they're on to me.'

'On to you?'

Hannes stared at his beer. 'What's wrong with me.'

'There's nothing wrong with you, lad.' Georg thumped the table but did not raise his voice. He gripped Hannes' wrist across the table. 'Nothing whatever. Don't ever think there is, either!'

He was like a rock, Georg.

'One of the lads in our gang at the depot. He's in my class as well. He could find out and broadcast it all over the school.'

'How can he find out?'

'Rolf Sandmann knows. He's in the gang. And he's leader of my Jungenschaft as well. And his dad is Blockwarden.'

'Those kids aren't as bright as you think. They got other things on their minds. Besides, your headmaster knows, doesn't he?'

'If it leaked out, he'd turf me out. Got no option. I'd rather leave before it comes to that.'

'Want a roll and some herring salad?'

Hannes shook his head. 'Having lunch at my grandmother's.'

Georg drained his tankard and got up, stifling a burp. 'Want to show you something first.'

'Very well then.'

Why did he sound so refined when he spoke to Georg? When one talked to Dr Gilbrecht one sounded like a slum kid, like Schmitt, who stank of mice. He drank up his beer. It tasted like old pennies.

'So long, Flora, love,' Georg shouted, and held the door open for Hannes. 'Makes a lovely herring salad, does old Flora.'

A tram rattled through grey suburban monotony, then swung westwards in the direction of the Alster.

'Going to Eppendorf?' Hannes wanted to know.

'Stop before,' Georg said. 'Grindel.'

They walked silently through quiet residential streets, lined with chestnut trees. The branches interlaced overhead, forming a leafy green tunnel. Georg knew all the answers. This trip had been a good idea.

They stopped in front of a grey building, set like an island in the middle of an asphalt yard. A tall hedge separated yard and street; through the open windows of the building they heard muted children's voices.

'See this?' Georg pointed to a wooden board inscribed with Hebrew letters. The board was peppered with tiny white marks, some letters had been defaced. 'Local lads come here for target practice,' Georg explained.

A bell rang out. Schoolboys spilled down the steps of the building, then walked quietly in the playground; a few wore embroidered silk skull caps.

'The Jews' school?' Hannes whispered.

There was no singing, no football, none of the running games played at his own school. They seemed an orderly lot, just strolling about in twos and threes, like prisoners exercising.

'They don't play games,' Hannes said.

'Don't, do they?'

They peered over the hedge. Boys were still coming down the steps and dispersing. One or two stopped to look at the ill-assorted pair who stood scrutinising their playground.

'Take a look over there,' Georg said.

At the far end of the playground, a group of SA men stood smoking and chatting.

'What are they there for?'

'Protection,' Georg mumbled.

'Those kids need protection?'

'Not kids, lad. *Public*!'

Georg turned to look at a small boy of eight or nine, scraping along on a scooter, yodelling a popular song. At the wooden gates, he took a catapult and some plum stones out of his pocket, and stood poised to take a pot-shot.

'Aim at the old bloke! He hits easy!' shouted an even smaller boy who had come panting up behind. He pointed at a grey-haired master, who was pacing up and down in the playground, one hand behind him, the other scratching his beard.

Before the bigger boy could act, Georg flung out an arm. The catapult landed on the ground. The boys scowled at Georg.

'What's up with you, mister?' the frustrated marksman asked. 'You a ruddy Yid yourself?'

'Filthy little perishers!' Georg roared at them. His face was flecked with purple patches. He reached out to 'smack the smaller boy's ear. 'Sod off, the both of you!'

The two boys looked astounded. Then they swung round

and fled down the street. Georg pretended to pursue them; they shrieked in terror. Georg now found himself confronted by a well-dressed woman, who carried a shopping net and numerous small paper parcels.

'I saw you,' she shouted, wagging a gloved finger at Georg. 'You ought to be thoroughly ashamed of yourself – hitting a small defenceless boy. If I could see a police-man, I'd report you. They're never there when you need them!'

Georg bent down to pick up the abandoned catapult, then popped it neatly into the woman's shopping net.

'Have a go yourself, dear,' he said with a bow. 'Old man with glasses and beard. He hits easy. Come on, lad.'

Georg put his arm round Hannes and guided him away.

'Ruffian! Jew-lover!' the elegant woman shouted after them. 'I'll have you reported!'

'That's how the land lies.' They turned the corner. 'If you left school, authorities would send you here. Reckon you're better off where you are.'

Hannes couldn't admit to Georg that the experience had excited rather than daunted him. They headed for the tram stop.

'I've seen local storm troopers get to work on those kids,' Georg said. 'School assembles, then they start "confiscating weapons". Lads are lined up against the wall, have to give up penknives, nails, bits of string.'

They waited for a tram at the corner of Rentzelstrasse. Suddenly, a new thought occurred to Hannes.

'You one, Georg? Secretly, I mean?'

'I'm not, but I sometimes wish I were!'

'Wish you were non-Aryan?' Hannes asked incredulously. 'Can't mean that.'

'Nowadays when I tell myself I'm German, I want to puke.'

'Can't say I'm glad I'm non-Aryan,' Hannes said. 'Anyway, my grandmother's expecting me . . .'

'Better not keep her waiting, then. I'll catch the next tram. Think it over. Talk it over with your dad. Right?'

'All right, Georg. So long.'

As Georg hurried across the road, Hannes remembered something.

'That boy with the catapult,' he wanted to tell him. 'I've done things worse than that.'

Georg scampered after his tram. Then he was standing on the platform, waving his cap at him. It's not right, Hannes thought. I ought to have a father like that.

Then he started to walk in the direction of the Haynstrasse.

'Collecting for *Strength through Joy* again?'

'Did pretty well, too.'

It was always easier and safer to lie than tell the truth. That's what life taught you: easier and safer to tell his father he had been playing at the depot when he'd been earning pocket money at the tennis courts; easier to tell his mother he was going to see Rosa when he went out to find Georg; easier to tell Bohrer he had been collecting for *Strength through Joy* than to confess that a Red had taken him to the Jews' school. Lie long and convincingly enough and you stayed safe.

'You're not in uniform,' Bohrer said.

'Changed before I came. That's why I'm late.'

Bohrer was sitting at the table in trousers and vest, cutting paper dolls out of his copy of *Der Stürmer*. He looked comfortably installed as his grandmother came into the room, a boiled chicken steaming on a tray.

'Chicken again, is it?' Closing his eyes, Bohrer tapped out a rhythm with his knife. 'Could get you five years in the old Konzertlager for that!' He chuckled, then set about carving the bird, tongue protruding between his teeth. 'Never mind. I won't let on.'

It didn't disconcert him that neither Hannes nor Rosa reacted. 'Got to admit, the both of you, I could make life pretty uncomfortable for you. Don't know why I go on spoiling you like this. We're tightening up, you know. Pretty soon now, the likes of you won't be allowed to work at all,

except in working gangs, know what I mean? Yellow stars,
the lot. Leg, sonny, or a bit of the breast?'

Hannes shrugged. Rosa was looking listless; smudges showed
under her eyes. When she caught him scrutinising her, Rosa
looked away.

'What happened to the red swan?' Hannes asked suddenly.

'It got broken,' Rosa said quickly. 'It was quite old, anyway.'

'Pretty thing,' Bohrer said. 'Shame really.'

'Help yourself to more rice, Hannes.'

'I've had all I want.'

Racing up the staircase half an hour earlier, he had felt
his head bursting with news to tell Rosa. Now he was
silent. There was a metallic taste in his mouth. He had a
headache.

His glance travelled from Bohrer, tucking in zestfully as
usual, to Rosa, who was playing with a dessert spoon. Later,
he promised himself, when they were alone, they would have
a good long talk. They would come back to him then, all the
things he wanted to tell her . . .

'It's hot,' he said. 'A pterodactyl would melt away.'

Only Rosa would understand the code. He looked at
her meaningfully. Bohrer, groaning with the effort, was
ripping a chicken wing. His grandmother's attention was
diverted.

'Terodactyl?' Bohrer said, 'That's a dinosaur, isn't it? Animals
don't melt. Anyway, those things haven't existed for ages,
have they?'

Silence. Hannes looked at Rosa again. She was piling up
empty plates.

'What you want to do on a day like this,' Bohrer licked his
finger-tips and wiped them on the tablecloth. 'Get on your
motor-bike, right out of the city, little place at the seaside,
clothes off, into the water, splash . . .'

'Who's coming this afternoon?' Hannes asked Rosa, ignoring
Bohrer. 'Anyone I know?'

'Nobody's coming,' Bohrer said before Rosa could reply.
'Your grandmother's got the afternoon off. We're all taking

the afternoon off. You two can have your little walk. Where is it you go . . . some jetty by the Isebek, is it . . .?'

Hannes looked at Rosa reproachfully. How could she have told him?

'Come on, Old Roses,' Bohrer said. 'The dessert! Want my swim. Getting a bit slow in our old age, aren't we?'

Later, watching the boats, listening to the music drifting over from the Uhlenhoster Fährhaus, Hannes asked Rosa if Bohrer always called her 'Old Roses' now.

'Sometimes,' she said with a distant smile, blowing out cigarillo smoke, 'it's Old Cow.'

Hannes shifted uneasily.

'Shouldn't allow it,' he said.

'What do you propose I do?'

He closed his eyes, then opened them again very slowly, hoping that yesterday's golden dream would overwhelm him. It was all still true, wasn't it? The curling cigarillo smoke, the boats hooting as they chugged past, rocking the jetty in their wake, the distant music, the water sucking against moss-tarred wood. Everything was still in place to work the old magic. Lilac bushes sprinkled faded blooms over the water, seagulls swooped onto the roofs of passing white boats as they sailed through willow curtains . . .

But the pterodactyl hovered on the window-sill, as it did in his dreams. The rest was a bag of tricks – the playing cards and silk handkerchiefs shabby old conjurers pulled out of their pockets at children's birthday parties.

He was no longer a kid, playing games with his granny by the Alster. He was Hannes Hacker, a paid-up member of the Jungvolk, who swore allegiance to his Führer at camp, who frightened kosher butchers in the Löwenstrasse and beat up cripples at the depot. He looked sideways at Rosa. Did she know him for what he had become?

All afternoon she had been glum and sarcastic. No point now telling her about what had happened at the depot. She had quite enough on her plate.

'Why did he let you go out this afternoon?' he asked.

'Special favour.' She took a deep breath. 'I've got to tell you something. He doesn't want us to come here again. We must stop plotting, he says.'

'Plotting?'

'We plot against him. So this, my Hannes, has to be the last time.'

She spoke tonelessly, with evident effort. She can't mean it, he thought. Perhaps she never really said it.

'I'm a bit old for all this anyway,' he said curtly.

'Too old?'

'Can't be sentimental to order, can you?'

Puffy white clouds had been drifting from the Alster towards its tributary, the Isebek. Now they cruised over the big orange house with its blue hydrangeas. Hannes noticed that the shutters were down; nobody sat on the balconies. The fortunates who lived here must be on holiday. Or they had all been sent to a concentration camp, the *Konzertlager*, as Bohrer liked to call it.

I'll never live there now, he thought. Never.

Rosa turned to face him.

'If I don't do as I'm told he'll report my clients, he says. For patronising a Jewish business.'

Yes, yes. Why did she have to go on? Was she enjoying telling him all this? Trampling on their Friday ceremony! He longed to be far away from the jetty, from Rosa. He wanted to be alone, sort out his feelings, find a reason for their atrophy.

'We'll try and fit in our talks between clients,' she said with sudden desperate enthusiasm.

'Yes,' he said. 'Let's do that.'

They went on talking, but for Hannes it had become an effort. Time crawled. There was nothing left to say. She tried the old allusions, made him jump up to signal to the boats as they drew near. It was quite pointless. Kids' Stuff. After one more long pause in their conversation, he asked her casually if she would like to see him leave Eppendorf to go to the Talmud-Tora school.

'I shouldn't advise it,' she said. 'Imagine what your father would feel about that.'

Now clouds hung low, hiding the turrets and steeples of the orange house from view. He glanced down his old clothes, at his dusty boots. I've become a street-corner yob, he reproached himself.

'It's going to rain,' he said. 'Better be going.'

'What's the matter, Hannes?' she asked him.

'Nothing's the matter,' he said roughly. 'Just don't talk to me all the time as if I were a little boy.'

'It wasn't very good today,' she stated when they arrived back at the Haynstrasse.

He shrugged. 'Never mind.'

They said goodbye. He considered kissing her on the cheek, she looked so sad and lost. Then he decided against it.

Next morning he told his mother he was going to the tennis courts, then he took a tram to the Jewish school. He stood by the gates for a while, feeling a forbidden excitement. Presently, a bell rang, the boys came streaming down the steps for their mid-morning break. They promenaded, as they had done the day before, watched by the group of SA men, who stood smoking in their corner. The old teacher with a beard, and a younger colleague, who wore a black hat, were marching up and down, reading from the same book. Hannes was thinking it would be easy to walk through the gates, go up to them, ask to be admitted. Then he realised somebody was speaking to him.

'What's your name?' the boy asked.

It was one of *them*, no doubt about that. He had lanky dark hair and thoughtful eyes and wore a silk cap on the back of his head. He was carefully dressed.

'Hacker.' Hannes composed himself. 'Hannes Hacker. What's yours?'

'Weissfeldt,' the boy said. His mouth was turned down with chronic scepticism. 'David.'

A motor-cycle rattled past, they had to wait for the noise to

subside before they could continue. The brief respite convinced
Hannes that David Weissfeldt would be his friend for life, that
he could turn the key to all his needs. They could see it
through together. He would draw on David's strength, wisdom,
experience. David would condone the things he had done at
the depot, appreciate the lost magic of the jetty, understand
his conflicts because their experiences would be identical. In
David Weissfeldt's grey eyes he saw reflections of his own
search for someone wanting to share an unbearable burden.
How could he have believed for so long that Rolf Sandmann
could play that part? Rolf was stupid, shallow and cruel, he
understood nothing of the shadowy private worlds of people
like himself and David.

'Noticed you yesterday, you and your father,' David Weissfeldt
said when the motor-cycle had passed. 'First class thing to
do.'

He spoke calmly, with that casual sophistication, that austere
maturity that confirmed what Hannes had instinctively known
about David Weissfeldt from the start.

'That wasn't my father,' Hannes said. 'Just a friend.'

David looked first right, then left, before he lowered his
head as if examining something on the ground.

'*Sholem Aleichem*,' he murmured.

'What?' Hannes asked anxiously. 'What did you . . .?'

'Sorry,' David said. 'Better run along . . .'

Something stirred in Hannes' memory, something Rosa
had taught him years ago. A wide smile spread over his
face.

'*Aleichem Sholem*,' he cried.

'Thought as much,' David Weissfeldt said. 'Welcome to our
prison. Joining us?'

'Trying to.'

'Come round to my side of the gate.'

'Thanks,' Hannes said.

'I'm terribly short-sighted, I'm afraid,' David Weissfeldt
said when Hannes stood next to him. 'Do you mind?' He
carefully took a pair of glasses from his breast-pocket and
put them on.

'Lucky man,' he said quietly, when he had completed his scrutiny. 'They'd never throw stones at you.'

'Why haven't you shut down for the holidays?'

'We get time off for Yom Kippur and Rosha Shana,' David said. 'Surely it's the same where you come from?'

Hannes frowned briefly. 'Yes, of course.'

'How old are you?' the other boy asked him.

'Thirteen next Christmas,' Hannes said brightly.

'Christmas?'

David Weissfeldt raised an eyebrow. He seemed to think Hannes had made a joke. 'Having your Bar Mitzvah in Hamburg?'

'Er – I'm not sure yet.'

'Where do you come from then?' David asked, smiling encouragingly. 'Not far, judging by your accent.'

'I don't come from anywhere. Born and bred in Hamburg.'

'You go to an elementary school then?'

'No, proper secondary school. Like this one.'

'Like this one?'

It was a bit of an ordeal, this interrogation, but David Weissfeldt obviously had to guard against spies. Anyway, he had nothing to hide here! Hannes almost gave a shout of joy. *Nothing to hide*! Wasn't that the real meaning of friendship?

'Eppendorfer Realgymnasium,' he proclaimed.

'Really?' The smile around David Weissfeldt's lips dissolved. 'That's impossible, surely.'

'You mean because of . . . of what we are?' Hannes grinned confidently. 'There are ways round that.'

'Are there?'

'They don't know,' Hannes told David eagerly. 'I've fooled them!'

'But that's absurd,' Weissfeldt ripped off his glasses in that very grown-up way of his and began polishing them with a handkerchief. 'They don't let you take *Shabbes* off for a start, do they?'

'They don't, but . . .'

'And when you're changing, can't fool them, can you?'

Hannes frowned. 'I don't get you.'

David put his glasses on again.

'How can you explain to the bastards that you're circumcised?'

'But I'm not!' Hannes exclaimed, shocked.

'Ah, well,' David Weissfeldt said. It was almost a sigh. 'Ah well,' he said again, this time with finality.

'If they found out I wasn't one hundred per cent,' Hannes assured him, 'they'd certainly turf me out!'

'Yes,' David Weissfeldt said languidly. 'Dare say they would.'

'So there it is,' Hannes tried to emulate the other's languor. 'Think they'll let me transfer here?'

David scratched his chin pensively.

'Not sure if that would be really suitable . . .'

'Not *suitable*? How do you mean?'

'I'd better go now. Thanks again for the – gesture, yesterday. Couple of our people noticed it. We appreciate things like that.'

'Wait a minute, David . . .' Hannes followed the boy deeper into the playground. 'Couldn't we meet somewhere? My grandmother lives in Eppendorf. Her name's . . .'

He stopped, confused. David Weissfeldt was already waving from a distance.

'I expect we'll run into each other some time.' Then he stopped as if something had suddenly occurred to him. 'Don't suppose you go to our local *shul*, do you?'

'What?'

'Synagogue.' David Weissfeldt seemed anxious not to embarrass Hannes any further. 'Not to worry,' he said apologetically. 'That bell means us, I'm afraid. So glad to have met you. Goodbye.'

Hannes was too late to grasp his hand. David had run off to catch up with his friends, who were walking up the steps.

Hannes looked after him, too stunned to move. He remained standing still until the playground was empty. Only the SA men who had arrived on top of the steps were looking down at him, cigarettes in their fists.

I don't belong here either, Hannes thought. Must have been

crazy to imagine it. There he stood, without the slightest excuse, unprotected, in the playground of the Jews' school!

He turned, broke into a run. Never again . . .

CHAPTER FOURTEEN

Two o'clock. Another torpid afternoon; Papa and Erika were at work. Mama was out shopping. Hannes was quite alone when the bell rang. They had chosen the right moment.

There were six of them at the door: Rolf, Dorn's disciple Karl-Heinz, Werner Schemel and three members of Dorn's Hoheluft gang. Hannes recognised Kurt Friess, the well-spoken boy who had loftily challenged Rolf's authority only two weeks ago.

Hannes stared at them as in a trance. The only hint of menace was the shifty grin on Werner Schemel's face – enough to tell Hannes they had not come to ask him down to the depot to play games.

'What's up with you?' Rolf asked. 'Why are you hiding? You missed camp.'

'Had 'flu. I'm better now.'

'Ask us in,' Schemel said impatiently. 'Go on, Hacker.'

'What's it you want?' Hannes asked stiffly.

This was it. This was the base of the pyramid of all his fears, fantasy translated into fact. They brushed past him, and marched into his room.

'Had the 'flu, did you?' Rolf asked sardonically. He sat on the bed, flipping through Hannes' copy of Edgar Wallace's *The Four Just Men*, which lay open, propped against the pillow. Hannes stood by the door. On Werner Schemel's face the smirk remained intact. Hannes shifted his weight from one foot to the other and folded his arms.

'Any objections?'

'Come on, Rolfie,' Schemel hopped about, smashing his left

fist into his right hand. 'Let's get started.'

'Why don't you go down,' Rolf asked, 'keep Lore Meinke company? She's missed you. Me and Werner and the rest of us, we'll look after this place for a bit.'

Hannes forced a smile. That enemy, lounging on his bed, fingering pages of his Edgar Wallace, could he ever have been a friend? Where had he made the first mistake? What had pushed him down this steep slide?

'You going?' Rolf asked him.

'I live here, don't I?'

'He don't half look scared, Rolfie!' Schemel crowed. There was no mystery why *he* was there. He had come to settle personal accounts.

'Stay if you want then, Hacker,' Rolf said. 'We've got our orders. We shall carry them out regardless. Take it or leave it.'

'What orders?'

'You'll see in a minute what orders.'

Rolf put two fingers in his mouth and whistled. Having received their signal, Rolf's minions set about plundering the book-shelves. They dragged down novels and biographies by Stefan Zweig and Emil Ludwig that had survived many moves, his father's yellowing reference books, the Brockhaus Encyclopaedia, the collected plays of Goethe and Schiller, an illustrated edition of Maupassant's short stories (out of bounds to Hannes for reasons never explained), a tattered atlas. They piled the books up on the floor in tall stacks, then bundled them out into the corridor. Rolf pulled out a suitcase that protruded from under the bed and spilled out the contents.

Hannes looked on in a kind of stupor as old treasures – Grimm's Fairy Tales, volumes of Karl May, Conan Doyle, Jack London – were hauled off with the rest of the books. He did not try to intervene. There were six of them, all thirsting for a fight. While supervising the work of the others, Rolf occasionally glanced at him, hoping for some act of provocation.

'Confiscated,' he explained. 'Part of our anti-subversion drive. Random raids. Hard luck we hit on you. Not my fault.' When Hannes remained silent, he went on, more aggressively: 'You'd know a bit more about our activities if you didn't hide yourself away all the time. My dad's OK'd this operation. He was in charge of the book-burning exercise on the Kaiser-Friedrich-Ufer. Jewish pornography, Communist propaganda, that's what we're looking for.'

'Won't find any here,' Hannes said.

'Warned you about being secretive, didn't I? The Jew stamp, all that? Those dirty lies you told about old Kanzl on the ferry.'

Empty words! Rolf showing off in front of his Hoheluft louts.

'My father will deal with this when he gets home,' Hannes said quietly. 'Burglary is against the law.'

'This ain't no burglary,' Karl-Heinz exclaimed, 'who needs your bleeding books?'

'If the books are in order they'll be returned,' Freezy followed up. 'If they're not, they'll be burned. That's not against the law, is it?'

Hannes' mind became a jumble of authors' names, titles, regulations, rules. Among his father's books, some *might* have been banned; who could know for sure? Was there a law in force against foreign authors? For all he knew, Conan Doyle's real name was Cohen. And how could one be sure there were no old envelopes tucked away between the pages of some books? (Why was everybody so careless?) Some books had belonged to Mama. Could they be inscribed with her maiden name? Rosenteich. *Rosenteich*! All hope was snuffed out. If the louts didn't know already, they'd be sure to find out now.

'Get a move on, clear them books!' Rolf commanded.

Werner Schemel, in charge of operations at the shelves, had discovered an old family album and was leafing through its pages.

'We want this as well, Rolfie?'

'The lot,' Rolf told him. 'Don't read the bleedin' stuff here. Don't want to stick in this dump all day.'

'Yes, sir!'

Werner Schemel was carried away by an ecstasy of official-dom. Rolf Sandmann had finally recognised his true worth.

'You wait,' Hannes said, wagging his head. 'You just wait till my father finds out.'

They did not wait. The shelves were bare, leaving only narrow stripes of dust. The boys thundered down the steps, carting away their loot. Hannes heard a few loud thuds, then Rolf cursing, finally the bellowing and laughing dying away in the courtyard.

When Hannes heard Erika's key turn in the lock, he rushed out of the kitchen and drew her into their bedroom.

'Don't tell 'em,' he begged. 'They don't know. I haven't told them. They haven't seen it yet.'

'But that's ridiculous.' Erika stared despondently at the empty shelves. 'They're bound to find out.'

'The books might be brought back tonight. They say they're only confiscating them . . .'

'Confiscating? Grubby little gangsters, that's all they are! That's what comes from associating with a bunch of . . .'

'They're cleaning up Eppendorf!'

The vertical lines between Erika's eyebrows deepened.

'Did you say that cretin Werner Schemel was one of them?'

'He's not their leader, though.' Hannes watched her pin her beret to her hair. 'Where you off to now?'

'You're coming with me,' Erika said. 'I've done that old bitch enough favours in my time.'

'Who? Where are we going?'

Frau Schemel opened her front door, but only by a few inches; the chain remained tautly drawn between door and frame. She was a stringy, tight-lipped woman, a red nose projecting from a suspicious, foxy face. Her hair was pinned up into an untidy bun.

'I'm just busy with our supper, Erika.'

'This won't take long, Frau Schemel.'

With undisguised reluctance Frau Schemel withdrew the

chain but kept her visitors firmly on their side of the threshold. From a dark interior came the smell of lentil soup.

'It's your Werner, Frau Schemel,' Erika began. 'While we were out this afternoon, he and his friends broke into our flat and made off with all our books.'

'Books? I know nothing about books . . .'

'Hannes is my witness.'

'Doesn't sound like my Werner,' Frau Schemel said benignly, adopting a bogus accent, which she usually reserved for party officials.

'It may not sound like your Werner,' Erika retorted. 'It was him, all the same.'

'You really must be mistaken. I saw my Werner in the tram-yard. He was playing there all afternoon. Saw him with my own eyes.'

'He broke into our flat!'

'I'm not having you shout at me!' Frau Schemel slipped back into the more congenial North Hamburg accent. 'Not in my own four walls, I'm not.'

'I've only come because I need your help to get our books back, Frau Schemel. When you were housebound with bronchitis and needed somebody to run your errands . . .'

'No good trying to excuse your rudeness by digging up the past,' Frau Schemel told Erika. 'Accusing a disabled boy of being a common burglar . . .'

Erika sighed: 'Can't you understand what I'm trying to tell you? Werner has got himself involved with a gang of thugs . . .'

Naked fear stirred in Frau Schemel's eyes.

'Thugs?' she echoed dully. She tried to shut the door. 'Can't give you any more time, Erika Hacker,' she cried. Her nose, Hannes thought, was growing fleshier and redder by the minute. 'Thugs, indeed! If you have any complaints, see the Blockwarden, Herr Sandmann. What's it got to do with me? Thugs indeed!'

'Please, Frau Schemel . . .' Erika entreated. The woman was drawing the chain across her door.

'If my Werner did as you infer,' she proclaimed, artificial

accent fully rehabilitated, 'he must have had his reasons. Innocent people don't get carted off by the police at seven o'clock in the morning for nothing, do they?'

Then she slammed the door in their faces.

'It's beyond belief! I'm told nothing! The two of you rush out . . .' Papa was beside himself. Hannes decided to sweat it out. He gazed inertly at a slice of cheese on his plate, fascinated by its gloss and symmetry. 'What reason did they give? Why didn't you call the police? And what are you grinning at? Do you find this amusing? My library has been burgled! Your friends are involved . . .'

'It can't be his fault . . .' Mama interjected.

'That's right, take his side! Why can't he speak up for himself? Who let them in? Why did they pick on this place? Why don't you answer me, boy?'

'Don't know what you want me to say,' Hannes said. 'I told you what happened.'

He kept his gaze directed on his slice of cheese. Why did his father always turn on him instead of protecting him from people like Rolf and Bohrer and Dorn and Hinrichs and Waldmeister? A proper father would. Hannes felt himself growing tinier and tinier. Now he was a maggot about to creep into the cheese.

'I've had enough,' his father cried. 'You admit your little hooligans to these premises, then you can't even be bothered to answer my questions. Bad enough having you run about the streets with your Jungvolk tykes at all hours of the night, doing God knows what . . .'

'Please don't shout, Ludwig! The neighbours can hear every word . . .'

'I've told him, Meta,' Erika said, 'I've told him time and again. That Rolf Sandmann and his chums, they're nothing but a gang of little thugs . . .'

Hannes was right inside the cheese. They couldn't see him, soon he wouldn't be able to hear them.

'I'm going to find those books,' his father said, kicking back his chair. Two patches of red coloured his cheeks. 'I'm going out this minute, and you're coming with me!'

'Give them till tomorrow, Ludwig . . .'

'This minute!'

Hannes felt his arm roughly gripped, but managed to scramble loose. When his father tried to pull him up again, he clutched the legs of the table with his hands. His father wrenched them away, and slapped his face hard. The blow landed just above Hannes' ear. A stinging pain sent a red curtain shimmering down over his eyes. He lifted his plate and sent it crashing against the stove. Hoping to deaden the angry throbbing in his head, the sense of bottomless humiliation, he picked up every cup, saucer and plate within reach and hurled them against the stove.

'Go on, have me arrested; see if I care!' He could hear his mother moaning about thin walls. His father swayed above him, breathing alcoholic fumes. 'I'll smash this whole place up! You just don't care anymore! Not about me, not about Rosa, none of you . . .'

He stopped; the flood of rage was draining away as abruptly as it had come. Trembling with contrition, he gazed at the shattered crockery.

His mother was about to get up.

'No, you don't, Meta.' Erika stopped her. 'Go on, Hannes, you sweep up this mess.'

Hannes got the dustpan and brush out of the cupboard and knelt down, grateful something occupied his hands. When he looked up, he found his mother in tears. A wave of love and regret, as intense as the recent torrent of anger, swept over him. He brushed the broken plates and cups into the pan and threw them into the cardboard box under the sink.

'Now he's sorry,' he heard Papa mutter, dregs of exasperation in his voice. 'Sorry for himself, Erika added.'

'I don't know what comes over him,' his mother said dismally.

'I'll get those books back, Mama,' Hannes said quietly.

'Why couldn't you have said that before,' Papa asked, 'instead of acting like a madman?'

'Hadn't even finished reading *The Four Just Men*,' Hannes said. 'Now I'll never know who the man behind the green mask was.'

'That's very important,' Erika said. 'God, you make me sick sometimes, Hannes.'

'Leave him alone,' his mother told them. 'He's all right now.'

Later his mother went out, Hannes didn't ask where. He lay exhausted on his bed, waiting for it to grow dark outside. When he heard his father's steps coming down the corridor, he surmised he was off to Sandmann's. Instead, the door opened; his father came in and stood over him.

'That was an unfortunate spectacle you made of yourself,' he said, fingering his moustache, eyes roving about the room. 'Made your mother cry,' he added.

He looked for somewhere to sit, seemed to settle for the bed, then changed his mind, leant awkwardly against the table.

I see, Hannes thought, Erika's sent him in to have a Heart-to-Heart.

'Why do you act like this? Aren't times hard enough? Haven't I got enough problems without you adding to them? Don't I try to do the best for you children?'

'I know, Papa,' Hannes said. 'I have apologised.'

'That's better.'

His father ran his tongue over dry lips and twirled the belt of his grubby bathrobe. There was nothing restful about him, nothing comforting. Even when he tried to be paternal, he hovered in the far distance, lifeless and blurred. A snowman, Hannes thought, a melting snowman.

'I really think,' Papa said, biting on his empty cigarette holder, 'you might go and have a word with those friends of yours.'

'They're not my friends any more.'

'Well, the Sandmann boy then. You two are very chummy, aren't you . . .?'

'Why don't you go yourself?'

'Why don't I go where?'

'To Sandmann's. You said you wanted to find your books. Well, *you* talk to Rolf Sandmann . . .'

'You expect me to do that? Draw attention to myself? It's useless trying to talk to you like a grown-up human being . . .'

'I only thought . . .'

He had begun to feel sorry for his father, but he hovered too far away to hear, too far to be touched. He had not the faintest notion what was happening in the streets of Hamburg. Hannes remained still, gazing up at the ceiling. The street lamps washed it with a shimmer of light.

'You only thought . . . Have you any idea how long I have to work in that stifling store to earn what you've just smashed in a fit of hysterics? Are you always going to be like that?'

He didn't expect an answer. It was his parting shot. Hannes heard the front door close, eager steps fumbling down the staircase. He, too, wanted to be as far away from the family as possible. Hannes knew exactly how he felt.

It was dark when his mother came into the room. When she switched on the light he saw she had tied a scarf around her neck. She wore her shabby summer coat; it was much too short, the lining showed under the hem. She came across to the bed, handed him a brown paper parcel.

'For me?' he asked in disbelief.

His mother nodded. She sat down on the bed to watch him unwrap it. He noticed from the wrapping that she had been all the way to Tronbart's, the big booksellers on Eppendorfer Baum. They often stayed open late. Mama had brought him a new copy of *The Four Just Men*.

'Mama!' he exclaimed. 'Mama, we can't afford it!'

Helplessness and shame welled up in him, reawakening the pity he had felt for his father. He wanted to love his mother; he found he could only despise himself.

'I know you're unhappy, Hannes,' she said. Then she began to cry again. 'I know how hard it is for you . . .'

'Sorry I'm such a rotten son,' he said. 'I'm going to be different from now on . . .'

'I'm not such a very good mother . . .'

'Yes, you are,' he said, 'you're the best mother in the world. This isn't *your* fault . . .'

He looked at the colourful book jacket. *'It's impossible not to be thrilled by Edgar Wallace . . .'* What a waste, he thought, all that money, all that effort, and for what? He had already read the book – all but ten pages of it. He had even taken a peep at the end. He knew the identity of the man behind the green mask. Why did she have to believe everything he said in a fit of temper? Besides, the gang wouldn't keep those books forever. He flung his arms around his mother, hugged her, felt her tears on his cheeks. Briefly he permitted himself to weep with her.

They came for Erika at dawn. The men went straight into their bedroom and stood there while Erika got dressed. They were not the men that had come before, they wanted neither coffee nor conversation.

'I shall lodge a protest about this with your superior,' his father mumbled hoarsely, turning up the collar of his bathrobe. 'I was given an unequivocal assurance we would not be inconvenienced again. That was a mere ten days ago. I cleared up this matter . . .'

The men did not answer him. They kept their eyes fixed on Erika, who buttoned her dress with trembling hands. They had faces you would not remember, faces that appeared at your door at five o'clock in the morning and were never seen again.

Hannes wondered if the other men had been given the sack for being too friendly. He thought he understood what was happening: Frau Schemel had reported Erika. Or had Dorn decided to get even with Erika for standing him up? Either way, all this was his fault. In the dim morning light, the shadows moved nimbly. Nothing more was said. Hannes felt quite numb. Maybe it was happening, maybe he was dreaming it. How could one be sure?

Erika fumbled through the contents of her handbag, before the men took possession of it. Then she embraced her mother, who stood huddled in her threadbare summer coat. While his father pointlessly renewed his protests, the men urged Erika out of the front door.

Hannes went back to bed and turned his face towards the wall. He could not face his parents in the kitchen. By now they would have realised that everything was his fault. They would never forgive him. As for Erika, if they ever allowed her to come home, she would never speak to him again. He couldn't even ask her to forgive him.

Under the bed clothes, he curled himself into a ball, going over and over his anxieties, until Mama came in and called him into the kitchen for breakfast.

CHAPTER FIFTEEN

'Thought you was dead, Hannes.'

He heard the bouncing of a tennis ball, then became aware of the familiar rancid smell that reminded him of white mice. It was the 'Hannes' that made him stop. Had Schmitt lain in ambush for him, he would have called out 'Hacker.'

Turning as casually as he could, he came face to face with Rolf Sandmann. He stood with his arm around Schmitt, grinning the frozen smile of the boy from the Jungvolk posters.

'Don't he look posh?' Schmitt asked. A grimy toe gaped through a hole in his right gym shoe.

'Off to the flicks?' Rolf joined in.

A tram rumbled out of the yard and drew to a halt in front of them.

'I was just off . . .' Hannes began.

'Thought you'd come down to see old Dorn,' Rolf said.

'It's Friday,' Hannes said, a tremor of confusion in his voice. 'You know . . . my relations . . .'

Waiting passengers boarded the tram. The conductor had his hand on the bell-wire.

'Dorn wants to see you,' Rolf said. 'You're not in trouble, don't worry.'

The conductor rang his bell, the tram moved away. Hannes felt his shoes glued to the asphalt.

'Not still sick, are you?' Schmitt asked.

'I'm all right now.' Hannes turned to Rolf. 'What about my books then?'

'Books?' Rolf shrugged. 'Take them any time you like.'

'Why didn't you bring them back?'

'Nothing personal.' Rolf sounded petulant, as if he had been unjustly accused. The books were waiting for him at 'Headquarters', he told Hannes. They had been examined and found fit to read.

'Come on, then' he added. 'Let's go get them.'

Rolf and Schmitt crossed the road, walked in the direction of the Hoheluftchaussee. Hannes trotted behind. Relief at the sudden restoration of Rolf's grace had magically dissolved all dread. What remained was the niggling thought that he was expected for lunch in the Haynstrasse.

'You can collect your knife this week-end, by the way. Fähnlein's assembling for a big rally.'

The news overwhelmed Hannes. He jumped high in the air; he'd scored Eimsbüttel's winning goal.

'Told you,' he yelled, slapping Rolf's back. 'Told you I'd get it!'

'No need to crow,' Rolf said. 'Haven't got it yet. Smashing about the points, though, isn't it?'

'Yeah. Great.' In the course of Georg's nightly visits to ask about news concerning Erika, he had shown Hannes the latest sports pages. Germany's position at the top of the Olympic table was now beyond challenge. Rolf's 'points' referred to German victory over the USA.

'Knew we'd do it,' Rolf said. 'Those Hottentots can't beat us!'

'No,' Hannes agreed. 'They can't.'

'Headquarters' was the abandoned building-shed in the Bismarckstrasse where Dorn had wanted to meet Erika. When Hannes entered, he felt like a new boy at school. Dorn sat on an upturned crate, a copy of *Der Stürmer* on his knee.

'Come for your books?' he asked Hannes without looking up.

'No hurry,' Hannes told him with determined nonchalance. 'Any time.'

'This isn't a bloody library. Don't want your stuff cluttering up my place. Move it!'

Hannes turned to Schmitt and Rolf. 'Give me a hand with this lot?'

'Schmitt'll help,' Rolf said. 'I've got to talk to Dorn.'

The books lay about in untidy heaps. They had clearly not been touched. Nobody had had the patience to look for forbidden authors or incriminating envelopes. Just another game, Hannes thought. He felt a sudden heady contempt for Dorn. He lost interest too quickly, lacked real cunning. He merely played at leadership. If only they'd let *him* lead, he could show them a thing or two . . .

'By the way,' Dorn asked, showing his yellow teeth as if he wished to make a gift of them. 'When do I get to meet that sister of yours? Thought you was fixing up a date?'

'Soon as she gets back,' Hannes assured him. 'She's gone to the seaside.'

That was the story the family had devised to explain Erika's absence. Papa was certain Erika would be coming home 'tomorrow'. Three 'tomorrows' had already passed, but he reminded his family that he had personal experience of 'their' interrogation techniques.

'Old Koch gone off with her?' Dorn enquired.

'What do you take her for?'

The others laughed. Hannes fell in with their laughter. They knew nothing. They had bluffed as usual. The possibility that Erika's arrest was not entirely his fault so elated him that he forgot about his Haynstrasse visit.

'What's the programme today, Dorn?' Schmitt asked.

Dorn took out his knife and flicked it to the ground, where it stuck, blade quivering.

'For a start, clear out that rubbish, Hacker. That's an order.'

'What are you waiting for?' Rolf added.

Schmitt helped Hannes carry the books home. They stacked them outside his front door. Then Hannes searched for his old copy of *The Four Just Men*.

'That's for you, Schmitt. Don't tell Rolf I've given it to you.'

Hannes' mother was too angry with him for having let Rosa down to comment about the return of their library.

'Don't you realise she'll be out of her mind with worry?'

she scolded him. 'You'd better think up a good excuse
this time.'

'Too late now,' Hannes told her. 'Anyway, I'm expected at
the shed.'

'What shed?'

'New headquarters. Made it up with Rolf. They're giving
me the knife next week-end.'

'But Rosa's waiting for you, Hannes. I don't understand you
any more . . .'

'Can't help that,' he told his mother curtly.

What was the point of going to the Haynstrasse when Bohrer
would be supervising them the whole time, not even letting
them go to the jetty? The last time had been hopeless. What
mattered was getting back to the shed quickly.

'You wanted me to make it up with Rolf, didn't you? he
asked. 'Don't know what's up with you these days, Mama.
Everything I do is wrong.'

'You might at least have telephoned Rosa.'

'Didn't have any change on me.'

She glared at him. She knew he was lying.

'Off you go then,' she said. 'I'll phone Rosa myself. But
don't think I'm giving you lunch . . .'

'I can get my own.'

He cut himself a slice of bread, wolfed it down with slices
of sausage and a glass of water. No time to lose.

He had been wise to hurry back to the shed. The gang was
assembled. Dorn was eating plums. Rolf was reading *Der
Stürmer*, Schmitt picked a new sore on his chin. A couple
of Dorn's henchmen held cigarettes hidden in their fists and
grinned up guiltily. Kurt Friess was there, too, and some of
the other book-raiders.

'What's this, then?' Dorn asked, putting down his bag of
plums. He pulled a crumpled handkerchief from his pocket
and, as Hannes approached, extracted a slimy object from
the folds of his handkerchief.

'Don't know – a balloon, I suppose,' Hannes said.

He was rewarded with a round of jeers.

'A balloon!' Dorn sniggered, squeezing the handkerchief back into his pocket. 'Ask that Red friend of yours, that Koch, if he fetches his balloon along when he gets goin' with your sister, why don't you?'

The thrills which Hannes had anticipated did not materialise. Time was killed at the shed the same way they killed it at the depot: shouting, pummelling younger boys, games which ran down before they had properly begun. There was only one change. Dorn had usurped Rolf's position. As the afternoon wore on, Hannes thought again about the layer-cake that was his life; the fresh, creamy slice of Olympic summer had crumbled away pointlessly.

'What about some action, then?'

Hannes read simmering resentment in Schemel's eyes. Among those assembled in the shed, only Werner Schemel still constituted a threat. The cripple had never forgiven him for that beating. It would have been forgotten long ago if Dorn or Rolf had been responsible. They were leaders, entitled to dish out indiscriminate violence. It had not been Hannes' place to do him injury.

'Let's get cracking, Dorn,' Schmitt said. 'We'll be back at school soon. Thought we was cleaning up Eppendorf?'

'We'll clean it up, don't you worry.' Dorn grimly lit a cigarette to denote serious thinking. 'You kids still got a lot to learn.'

Hannes watched, fascinated. Dorn casually held the lighted match until the flame died. He looked quite debonair at times – like Harry Piel or Mathias Wiemann, the film stars.

'Some of you may think this area is fairly clean,' Crisply, Dorn tossed the burnt match aside. 'Well, it ain't. Not by a long chalk. I was talking to some of the SA boys the other night. Place is crawling with undercover Commies, Jews, even Cosmos.'

'What's Cosmos?' Schmitt wanted to know.

'Men with filthy habits,' Dorn informed him. 'Old Schindinger from the SA knows all about them. Cosmos are disgusting, endangering the health of the nation, he says. They got to go.'

With a cutting gesture and a truncated whistle, Dorn indicated what lay in store for the Cosmos.

'Any Cosmos in Falkenried?' Schemel asked.

Dorn shook his head.

'They're mostly plutocrats. They live on the banks of the Alster. We'll concentrate on undercover Reds and Yids in Eppendorf.'

'I bet Bentini's one of them,' Schmitt said. 'Him and that greasy delicatessen shop of his in Lehmweg.'

'Bentini's Italian, you nit,' Rolf told him.

'There's Italian Jews,' Schemel ventured.

'Old Bentini's not one of them,' Rolf said. 'He gets drunk at our pub most nights. Party member.'

'Who else is there?' Schemel wondered impatiently.

The atmosphere was becoming alive with danger. Prolonged inactivity was sharpening their keenness to find new Siegfried Levis. Hannes examined the soles of his shoes. It might have been wiser to go to Rosa's after all.

'Let's get the Yids,' Schmitt said.

'None left around here,' Hannes said, a little too quickly.

'How would you know?' Rolf asked. 'You don't know everybody. Even my dad doesn't, and he's Blockwarden.'

Dorn took a deep drag at his cigarette.

'If anybody has any information, knows anything, suspicions, even involving people in this shed, it's their duty to report details to me.'

'They're all safely tucked away on the other side of Eppendorf, the rich swine,' Karl-Heinz said.

'What about you, Leo?' Dorn suddenly glared at Schemel. 'You clean?'

'One hundred per cent Aryan.' Schemel saluted clumsily. 'Rolfie knows all about me.'

'Do I?' Rolf asked, grinning.

'Yeah,' Schmitt shrieked. 'What do we know about you?'

'Don't start on me again,' Schemel wailed. 'You know I'm clean. Everybody knows me. And my name ain't Leo, neither.'

'Looks like a Yid, walks like a Yid,' Karl-Heinz said.

'What did you say your name was, Leo?' Dorn narrowed his eyes. 'Schlemiel, was it?'

'Why always pick on me?' Schemel protested in desperation. 'Why not him?'

He pointed at Hannes. 'He could be one. Look at him, sly bugger.'

'Well, Hacker,' Dorn showed his teeth. 'What about it?'

'I go to an Eppendorfer Realgymnasium?' Hannes said.

'What's that got to do with it?'

He knew he had to think of something quickly. Somebody in the shed was for it. It was as inevitable as the way those pinball machines worked. You shot out a ball, it fell into a hole. Even if it came back the first time, you pitched it back until it plunged into one of the holes. Then the lights started popping.

'Why don't you ask *him*?' he exclaimed. The door to the shed opened, Jürgen Kloth came sauntering in. He looked tanned after his fortnight at the seaside; he was even more smartly dressed than usual. He wore a spotless white shirt and a crisp blue bow-tie.

'Yeah,' Rolf cried. 'Good idea. What about old Asthma?'

Hannes had merely meant to suggest that they ask Kloth to confirm that they both went to the Eppendorfer Realgymnasium, where Jews were not tolerated, but Rolf's aggressive reaction had opened up an entirely unexpected way out of his predicament. A pin-ball machine could tilt.

Schmitt jumped up, furiously tugging at Kloth's neat bow-tie. The bow collapsed. Schmitt yelled in triumph.

'What was that in aid of?' Kloth frowned.

'Ain't in the Jungvolk,' Karl-Heinz prompted Dorn.

'You all know bloody well why,' Kloth said.

'He's got asthma,' Schmitt and Schemel chorused joyfully, collapsing on the floor with laughter.

'How do we know he has?' Dorn grimaced shrewdly. 'Anyone seen a medical certificate?'

True, they only had Kloth's word for it. Hannes took a deep breath. Danger had been momentarily averted.

'Ask my parents,' Kloth cried. 'Ask anybody . . .'

'Stinking rich, like all the Yids,' Schmitt squealed. 'Living over their luxury café on Eppendorfer Baum!'

'Quiet,' Dorn said. 'Let's not get over-excited. Now then, Kloth, what does your old man do?'

'You know all about me, Dorn.' Kloth's voice quaked. 'We've got this cake-shop . . .'

Serve him right, Hannes told himself. Jürgen Kloth should have stayed in Travemünde. Him and his bloody puppet theatre, coming back, looking like a shop dummy, sucking up to Dorn and Rolf. If Jürgen Kloth never went back to school, if he also stayed away from the shed, there would be so much less to worry about.

'This cake-shop,' Dorn enquired. 'Is it a certified Aryan establishment? Has it got a "No Jews" sign in the window?'

He stubbed out his cigarette and folded his arms. Nobody moved. Excitement had arrived at last.

'My dad's been a member of the NSDAP. since before 1933,' Kloth cried. 'We been National Socialists longer than any of you lot. Two months ago we chucked out two Jewish waitresses . . .'

'Sounds to me you learned that off by heart.'

Dorn grinned, his yellow teeth shimmered. Hannes experienced a shudder of delight. He'd come face to face with one of the ghost train monsters.

'What about your mother?' Dorn asked. 'She clean?'

Kloth bit his lip. So there was something he was hiding!

'She's Belgian, if you must know,' Kloth confessed.

'Belgian, is it?' Rolf exclaimed. 'Why haven't we been told about this before? You're as bad as old Hacker. Secretive.'

'Didn't think it was important . . . She's Aryan, though.'

'One hundred per cent?'

'You bet.'

Dorn now moved closer to Kloth.

'We got no proof about this asthma of yours. Or your Belgian mum, for that matter. They're alibis. Typical Jewish trait, that . . .'

'Excuses!' Werner Schemel contributed. 'Won't join the Jungvolk. He's not even disabled like me!'

'Why don't you ask Hacker here?' Kloth protested. 'We're in the same form at school.'

Dorn turned towards Hacker.

'True?'

'What?'

'Tell him, I don't have to do PT, Hacker!' Kloth defeaded in desperation.

'Right,' Hannes said. 'He's excused PT.'

Dorn whispered something into the ear of his lieutenant, Karl-Heinz. Then he crossed to the door of the shed and opened it.

'Well, son, here's your chance to prove what you say.'

'Prove what?'

'That you got asthma.'

'How?'

'Run from here to the depot.'

'That's much too far, Dorn.' Kloth had begun to sweat. 'I'm not allowed to run that far!'

'How far is far, Kloth?'

'It's half a mile, I bet.'

'Rubbish. If you was in the Jungvolk, Kloth, you'd have learnt about measuring distance by now. Off you go, mate – from here all the way down Lehmweg, that's barely 400 metres.'

'I can't, Dorn! I'll get an attack! Hacker!' Again he turned to Hannes for help. 'For God's sake . . .'

Dorn reached out, pulling Kloth into the street by the scruff of his neck. Then he gave a sign. Together, the little group crossed the busy Hoheluftbrücke. Jürgen Kloth was pushed to the front.

'Tell 'em I can't do it, Hannes,' Kloth begged again. 'Tell 'em I can't.'

Hannes blinked up at the sun. If Kloth didn't run, they'd think of something worse. Remain silent, and they'd forget about you.

'We'll come with you, Kloth,' Dorn said. 'See you don't get hurt.'

The day was merging into warm, mellow dusk. Some shop-windows along Lehmweg already shimmered with light.

'You don't understand,' Kloth whined. 'I just can't run that far. I can't run at all. Hacker knows . . .'

'On your marks,' Dorn ordered, as Kloth cowered down in the gutter. Hannes, his muscles tense with excitement, caught a glimpse of Kloth's eyes as they ogled Dorn beseechingly.

'Get set . . . GO,' they cried in unison.

Kloth raised himself and started to jog down Lehmweg. The others trotted on the pavement beside him.

'Come along now,' Dorn encouraged Kloth, 'You can make it a bit faster, can't you?'

'Pick up those feet,' Rolf said.

Men on their way home from work stepped back to let the gang pass. A woman leant out of her window to complain to a neighbour that sport was the only thing kids thought about nowadays.

'You're doing well, Kloth,' Dorn shouted. 'Too bloody well.'

'Won't call him Asthma after this,' Rolf panted. 'Don't deserve it.'

Hannes ran close behind Rolf. It wasn't unlike that time they had stormed up that hill in camp. No need now to bother with dummy grenades.

'Would have been more fun to see old Schemel try this,' Rolf spluttered. 'Old Kloth's not a Yid, anyway.'

'I know he isn't,' Hannes said.

'Can't be too sure, though.'

Less than two hundred yards from the depot, Kloth collapsed. He lay gasping in the gutter; his pursuers stood over him, unsure what to do next.

'He's got it all right,' Schmitt said.

'Looks terrible, don't he?' Schemel asked.

Kloth's shoulders twitched. With every breath his throat emitted a rasping sound. Dorn tipped the body over with his foot. Hannes shrank from the sight. Kloth's face was blue, his eyes bulged, not only with terror and pain; Hannes thought he also saw in them a glint of pride, almost of gratitude. They had allowed him to prove himself.

'So he's got asthma,' Friess argued coolly. 'He can still be a Yid.'

Rolf nodded. 'Freezy's right.'

'You, Leo!' Dorn ordered. 'Take a closer look at him! Unbutton his flies!'

'Do *what*?' Schemel asked. Had he heard properly?

Friess came to the rescue with icy logic.

'Dorn wants you to have a look – see if he's got a circumcised cock.'

'No — ' Werner Schemel could not believe his ears. 'That's disgusting. I'll do anything you want. But I won't do that. It's dirty.'

'I'll have a go, Dorn,' Friess said coolly.

He bent down, did what was necessary with detached efficiency. Then, not without pride, he offered Dorn his diagnosis.

'Not a real Jew,' he reported. 'All he's got is asthma.'

'What's all the commotion?'

A burly, sweating policeman shouldered his way through the group around the supine Kloth. 'What's the matter with this lad?'

'Friend of ours,' Dorn told him in a clipped accent and stood to attention. 'Asthma attack. Doing all we can, officer. Need a doctor.'

The policeman looked at Dorn dubiously, then bent down for a closer examination.

'I'll telephone for an ambulance,' Schmitt cried, and made off across the road.

'Wait for me,' Hannes called after him. 'I'll come with you.'

'It's really all Hacker's fault,' Rolf Sandmann summed up the situation. There was some sadness in his voice. 'He and Kloth go to the same school, don't they? He could have saved us all this trouble.'

The following afternoon Hannes marched with Rolf and their JV unit to join the rally on the Heiligengeistfeld. He held his head erect, his shoulders were drawn back firmly, his eyes scanned the horizon. He had become Rolf Sandmann's equal. That morning, he and three others had paid their fee of 35 Pfennigs and been presented with a shining new knife inscribed

BLOOD AND HONOUR

There had been no difficulty in passing the oral examination; he'd learnt the answers by heart. Questioning him, Fähnleinführer Hinrichs winked at him; evidently he regarded the test a mere formality. He began with Hannes' sporting achievements.

'75 metres?'

'11 *komma* 3 seconds.'

'Good. Long jump?'

'3 metres 80.'

'Good enough.'

Hinrichs passed on to the historical part of the exam.

'Führer's birthday?'

'April the twentieth, sir.'

'Correct. Was Wilhelm II a good Emperor or a bad one?

'Good one, sir.'

'Correct. Why?'

'He was brave in battle and dedicated to the greater glory of the fatherland, sir.'

'Correct. Why did we lose the war?'

'We were stabbed in the back, sir, while our troops were victorious in battle.'

'Stabbed by whom?'

'By agents of Bolshevism and International Jewry.'

'And . . .?'

'Er – oh, yes, by Social pacifists, sir.'

'Correct. Why must members of the Jungvolk and the Hitler Youth have nothing to do with the offspring of Jewish parents?'

'Because they are sworn to work for the destruction of the fatherland.'

'And?'

'And because they pollute German women and girls.'

Hinrichs closed his book. The final part of the test *he* knew by heart.

'How do you recognise an area Jungvolk leader, Hacker?'

'White cord; three gold oak leaves; black chinstrap; maroon armband; tunic inscription in silver.'

'You've done it, Hacker. Congratulations!'

Afterwards, the Fähnlein assembled to hear a lecture on political economy, given by Hubertus Wolfratshausen, a sober looking Professor of Political Science, wearing party insignia in his buttonhole and duelling scars on his cheeks.

He began by handing round a fifty million-mark banknote. Thirteen years ago, the Professor pointed out, that could not have bought a loaf of bread. The Murder of the Mark, as he called it, was committed by weak-kneed administrators of the Weimar Republic and former enemies of the fatherland, secretly collaborating through an infamous network of Jewish and Free-masonry cells. National Socialism had resurrected the Mark, offered work and bread to all, and dealt suitably with Jewish speculators who had exploited both the Capitalist and Bolshevik systems to further their plans for world domination.

'Our glorious young nation,' the Fähnlein was told, 'plundered during fourteen years of shame and humiliation, is now back on its feet, thanks to the vision of one man of genius. Hunger, unemployment, foreign exploitation, private profiteering have all been abolished, political strife smashed. New arterial highways, our rehabilitated armed forces, revived heavy industries, would guarantee not only the fatherland's economic present, but also its military future.

'National Socialism,' Professor Wolfratshausen concluded, 'will never again permit the waste so characteristic of countries whose systems depend for survival on waste. Take Canada and America, where, during peaks of mass unemployment, thousands of tons of wheat go up in smoke, so that prices can be pegged at an artificially high level. Take South America, where, year after year, coffee is dumped into the sea to safeguard the profits of international coffee speculators . . .'

*   *   *

Marching at Rolf's side, Hannes grinned as he recalled that
last part of the lecture. What would Georg say now? The way
that Communist singer had carried on, you'd think the German
government was *in favour* of burning wheat and drowning
coffee . . .!

'What are you grinning at?' Rolf asked.

'Thinking.'

'Thinking,' Rolf mimicked him. 'Needn't think you're the
cat's pyjamas just because they've given you the knife. We
had to earn ours. Now it's just a formality. They've relaxed
the rules, anybody can get that knife now.'

The glow Hannes had felt during the day grew dim. How
could he have been so naïve as to believe Rolf would regard
him as an equal now?

In Rolf's scheme of things, there was no such thing as
fairness. A rival's achievements were not honoured. What
Rolf called friends were, in reality, a lower species – vassals
like Schemel and Schmitt, whom he could bully or patronise,
or pre-destined leaders he could idolise – like Fähnleinführer
Hinrichs or Dorn. There was no other category.

As he got used to the rhythmic thud of marching feet all
around him, Hannes became aware of a nagging pain in his
belly. Those green apples he had eaten after the lecture?
They had looked so shiny and crunchy on the barrow. Instead
of going home for his midday meal he had bought a bag of them,
squatting down on the Eppendorfer Baum bridge, quartering
each green apple with his new knife . . .

'So don't let me hear you swank about your bloody knife,'
Rolf was saying. 'The way you always crow about everything,
Hacker, that's one of your worst features. So you got your
knife. Dorn couldn't care less. Matter of fact, you're in serious
trouble with Dorn.'

'That's what you think.'

'That's what I know. Kloth's old man went to the police.
Old Jürgen might be laid up in hospital for weeks.'

'What's that got to do with me?'

'No good playing the innocent,' Rolf instinctively hit a faster
stride. 'And keep in step, will you? Typical – swanks about

the knife and doesn't even know how to march. Can't deny you started all that stuff with Jürgen, can you . . .? About him being a Yid and everything. We got witnesses, Dorn and me. Everybody in the shed knows you had it in for Kloth. Pounced on him the moment he came through the door, back from holiday. Forgotten how you bashed old Schemel . . .?'

'Bastard,' Hannes murmured.

'Swear at me again, Hacker, I'll report you to Hinrichs. Have to. They can revoke your knife any time. Bet they will, too, when they find out about Jürgen . . .'

Out of the corner of one eye, Hannes saw Rolf's flushed cheeks; his eyes sparkled.

'Traitor,' Hannes muttered. 'Do what you like.'

'Try and wriggle out of it,' Rolf said. 'We'll have a song now.' He raised his arm. "German Eagle",' he shouted. 'One, two, three and . . .'

Hannes groaned. Those bloody apples, churning his insides. He could hardly lift his feet. How he longed to be lying down on Rosa's chaise-longue, the soft rug covering him, keeping him warm.

It has been reported to me,' Dr Gilbrecht's voice boomed, *'that during your school holidays you staged an attack on a fellow pupil, whom you accused of being Jewish, that you subsequently induced in this boy an asthma attack. You will go into the playground, stand with your back against the wall. I will personally execute you.*'

The pain was hammering away in his stomach. They were all bawling 'German Eagle' now. Rolf looked challengingly in his direction. If one could only quietly die, he thought. Just for a bit. The grey cube couldn't be much worse than this.

Under the blaze of a thousand flaming torches, battalions of Jungvolk, Hitler Youth, SA and SS packed the Adolf Hitler Platz. The Rathaus was hung with illuminated banners, 'ONE PEOPLE, ONE NATION, ONE LEADER!' Under a night sky, sprayed with stars, Hannes stood and watched shadows moving like dancers in yellow rectangles of light beyond the town hall's balconies.

Hannes tried shifting his weight from one foot to the other. A stone seemed to fill his belly; irritation had turned into a dull, monotonous ache. Perspiration glazed his forehead; by now he was too weary to wipe his face. Erika was right. No kind old man with a white beard looked after you from his seat in the clouds. To protect you, there was only your mother, but if she happened to be Jewish, you could forget that, fight your battles on your own. His hand groped for his knife. They would never have given it to him if they hadn't thought he was tough.

A ripple moved the crowd. Behind the lighted windows, the shadows became more distinct. Loud voices shrieked out fragmented orders. The boys in the row in front stood on their toes, someone behind him pressed hot hands on his shoulders to get a better view. The two giants beside him, who held torches aloft, changing arms every three minutes, became animated. Flames painted deep hollows on their faces as they joined the swelling chorus:

WE WANT TO SEE OUR FÜHRER – WE WANT TO SEE OUR FÜHRER – WE WANT TO SEE OUR FÜHRER.

Hannes took a deep breath. The ache had begun to drill into his bowels. With his awareness of pain heightened, he thought he could imagine hearing Rolf Sandmann's voice thanking his Leader for winning the Olympic Games for Germany.

The shadows behind the balcony windows merged and blocked out the light. A hatless, solitary figure in a grey uniform stepped out and raised his arm in acknowledgement of the tumult below. A roar like an aeroplane engine swept up from the ranks below. Flaming torches were raised high. Hannes was reminded of *Triumph of the Will*. Then the face had been huge, filling the screen. Now there was just this white blob in the darkness. Hannes heard himself bellow as loud as he could, drowning his pain in an ocean of sound. He poured all his strength into that shout, hoping for exhaustion, then oblivion.

The man on the balcony was no longer receiving cheers; his

piercing voice was stabbing, jabbing at the quivering, burning flesh below him:

'*And we all know – Germany lies before us! Germany marches within us! Germany comes marching behind us! The fatherland has now regained its honour! Returned to its beliefs! Overcome economic hardship! Signalled cultural progress! This I can say to you tonight in all good conscience. As God is my witness!*'

When it was all over – the delirium, the noise, the release – the Rathaus lights still blazed; the shadows had moved elsewhere. The last fanfares were heard, the Volk was dismissed. In the crowded Mönckebergstrasse leading off the square, the Fähnlein reassembled.

Hannes found that his pain had eased slightly. Rolf was leaning against a wall, his face suffused with elation. He was impatient to do battle for Him, to climb into that glorious Eternity of Victory, with Valhalla awaiting those who followed His command.

Among the men and women who now thronged towards the tram stops, Hannes noticed groups of tourists, people he had often seen sitting in the Alster cafés, their eyes hidden behind sunglasses, eating expensive ices with whipped cream.

'Richter! Fröhlich!' Fähnleinführer Hinrichs commanded. 'Are you all blind? Can't you see those ladies require assistance? On the double!'

Hannes watched the two Fähnlein members scurry across the road. Two elderly ladies in long tweed coats were struggling through the crowd, carrying suitcases. The Führer's visit had probably been the final adventure of their trip abroad. Had they not been told roads to the station were closed to traffic?

Richer and Fröhlich picked up the suitcases, explained to the ladies in sign language that they would escort them to the station. The ladies began searching their handbags for change. The boys gestured that no tip was required.

Both ladies appeared to be rather deaf. Instead of speaking, they shouted at one another.

'You must admit, dear,' one of them cried in English. 'They're perfect little gentlemen.'

'I've always said,' the other one yelled back, 'that's the kind of discipline we've lost in England . . .'

Fähnleinführer Hinrichs saluted as they passed by. Hannes had never seen him so pleased with himself.

Hannes hoped to find his parents asleep, but when he let himself in, his belly full of marbles, he noticed a strip of light under the kitchen door. He recognised Erika's voice. Flinging his cap into his room, he rushed into the kitchen.

The reunion had not been joyful. Mama was leaning across the table, rubbing Erika's hands to comfort her. Papa stood behind Erika's chair, head lowered, hands buried deep in his bathrobe pockets. Erika looked up to greet Hannes. Her eyes were swollen with crying.

'Did they hurt you, Erika?' he asked breathlessly. 'They didn't torture you, did they?'

'Must you ask stupid and tactless questions the moment you come home? Go and change your clothes. I'm not having you parading in that uniform around my house.'

Erika held out her hand to Hannes, then kissed him on both cheeks. Astonished and embarrassed, he rested in her arms for a moment. It was all right. She didn't blame him for her arrest.

'What did they do to you?'

'Nothing really. Just asked questions.'

'What did they want to know then?'

Erika burst into tears, as if she had been holding them back for too long.

'They've got him,' Mama whispered to him. 'Arrested.'

Hannes' mind filled with an image of Georg on that tram platform, cheerfully waving at him.

'They'll . . . they'll send him home again soon,' he said quickly, 'they did you and Papa.'

Erika pawed her handbag. She pulled out a squashed cigarette. Hannes watched her light it. She looked five years older than the last time he had seen her. She was turning into Mama! Soon it would no longer be possible to distinguish between them. The idea stirred panic in his heart.

'This is different.' Erika sucked at her cigarette and stared at her matchbox. 'They're charging him. Stirring up political unrest or something. It means Fuhlsbüttel. Maybe even Dachau. Seven years . . . Oh God . . .' She bit her knuckles. 'I'll be old when he comes out . . . I keep thinking, I told them something . . . they kept at me . . .'

'Drink some milk, Erika. I'll give you one of my tablets I take for my migraine. Try not to think about it. You're home now. Get a good night's sleep . . .'

'Try not to read too much into this, my girl.' Papa spoke with an edge to his voice, afraid of being interrupted or ignored. 'You're not a child. Try and face the situation calmly. This man isn't Jewish; you tell me he's never been a member of the KPD. He starts with a clean sheet. They've got more to do than clog up their prisons with plumbers or whatever he is. I do understand these people's mentality . . .'

'Oh yes,' Erika said, turning away from him to blow her nose. 'You understand.'

'Those Seven Years of yours! They won't last another *two*! Don't give in to an anxiety neurosis! The world doesn't begin and end at Eppendorfer Weg. Pressure will be exerted from abroad. The League of Nations is keeping aces up its sleeves. Do you imagine men like Litvinoff and Duff Cooper are just exercising their lungs when they . . .?'

'A fat lot of help Litvinoff and Duff Cooper are to my Georg! Everybody who still bothers to think is being pushed behind barbed wire. Children are taught to denounce their parents. What are your wonderful foreign politicians doing about that? Grouse-shooting with Herr Göring when last heard of . . .'

'That man has filled you up with half-baked left-wing ideas. Now you think you're politically educated. I wrote left-wing leaders before you were born!'

'He won't tell them anything,' Hannes reassured Erika.

'He doesn't *know* anything!' Erika pushed her fingers through long, untidy hair. 'You've got to send Hannes away, Meta. Out of this bloody country. Either they'll put him away, like Georg, or he'll end up as one of *them*. Look at him!'

'What's the matter with me?'

His hand moved towards his knife.

'Write to Palestine,' Erika yelled at her mother. 'Write to Uncle Peter and Auntie Ida. They'll take him. They've got to. If you won't do anything about this, I will.'

'Palestine's all desert,' Hannes said.

'They've done a lot of building and planting there . . .'

'Palestine is hardly suitable . . .'

'You only need an affidavit, Papa. You need a lot more for other places. No-one wants poor Jews.'

'Palestine!' The idea seemed to embarrass Papa. 'England, perhaps, until all this blows over . . .'

Hannes' head was swimming. He was chasing through the desert on horseback, pursuing Bedouins riding on camels. When his father spoke the word 'Palestine', he remembered the playground of the Jewish school, David Weissfeldt retreating from him with distaste. Now his mind filled with images of leafy parks, green lawns, old castles presided over by butlers, elderly Lords in deep armchairs, faithful golden retrievers by their side, staring into roaring fires . . .

'England!' he cried. 'I'll go there any time!'

Illustrations from *Little Lord Fauntleroy* dissolved into stately Rolls-Royce cars, fog-bound football stadiums, the battling giants of Arsenal and Aston Villa, reported by the *Kicker* week after week – Drake, Bastin, James. . .!

'Whom do we know in England?' Erika asked. 'Not a soul. No, it has to be Palestine, whether you like it or not, Papa. If you hate the idea, I'll write to Uncle Peter myself.'

There was a fierce, blotched look about her face. Mama placed a calming hand on hers.

'I can't help thinking, my girl, this is all a bit premature.'

'Premature?' Erika turned on her father. 'Premature?'

'Dearest, don't get excited.'

'What are you waiting for, Papa? That they send me to Waltershof to do forced labour – like poor old Dr Schirm? That they force you to divorce mother? That would suit you, wouldn't it? You could leave Tietz and go back to the Anzeiger, scribbling stuff about lovers on the banks of the Alster . . .'

She looked up. Her father was morosely gazing out of the window. In its reflection, his mouth looked drawn, his eyes damp.

'I didn't mean it,' Erika said. She put her hand on the sleeve of the unloved, unloving stranger by the window. 'I really didn't, Papa.'

When Hannes got up next morning, Erika was still snoring. He guessed she'd taken one of Mama's sleeping pills. The sun, filtering through the window, washed patches of her face with light. Her skin looked greasy. Even in sleep she frowned, lips drawn into thin, parallel lines. If Dorn could see her now, he wouldn't want to take her out.

In the kitchen he found Mama at the table, bent over a bowl, mixing butter and sugar with a large wooden spoon.

'You're taking this cake to Rosa's,' she said. 'She'll want to hear that Erika's back.'

'It's not Friday,' Hannes protested.

He recoiled from having to explain to Rosa why he had let her down last time. He had looked forward to spending the day using his knife. Some of the kids in the neighbourhood were bound to be impressed, even if Rolf wasn't. He saw himself astride Dorn's crate in the shed, the blade glinting under his fingers as he whittled away at a piece of wood, or, better still, slicing a cigarette, then sharing it with the Hoheluft gang, watching them choke . . .

'You didn't go last Friday.'

'Why don't you go yourself for a change?'

He bit into the buttered roll she had put on a plate for him. The belly-ache was still grumbling away in his insides. Going to the lavatory hadn't helped. And all the time he felt hungry. Greedily munching his roll, he had hiccups before he had finished.

'I've got too much to do,' Mama said. 'And it's you Rosa wants to see.'

'Don't think it means all that much to her now.' To stop the hiccups he held his breath for as long as he could.

'I'll go as a favour to you, Mama. I'll play Little Red Riding Hood for you. Can I lick the bowl?'

'When I've finished.'

He watched his mother energetically beating the egg whites.

'Erika stayed up to write to Uncle Peter last night,' she said. 'Papa's gone out to post the letter.'

'Does that mean I'm going to Palestine?'

'If Uncle Peter agrees to have you.'

'When do I go?'

'As soon as the papers come through. It takes time.'

'Don't I have to go back to school then?'

His mother looked up from her work.

'You don't mind going?'

'Why should I mind?'

'We might all be separated for a long time.'

'You can all come later on, can't you?'

His mother brushed loose strands of hair from her face. A few specks of flour stuck to her chin.

'Your father won't go to Palestine.'

'No, I suppose not. Still, I'm coming back, aren't I?'

'Papa still insists it'll all blow over,' Mama said, hiding her eyes from him.

He was not listening, galloping across the desert, a romantic silhouette against an orange sunset. Don't care if I never come back, he thought. Got my knife. They're waiting for me at the building shed in the Bismarckstrasse. And then I'll conquer the desert . . .

CHAPTER SIXTEEN

With the cake wrapped in brown paper and his swimming togs tucked under his arm, Hannes set off to walk to the Haynstrasse. He tried to avoid both depot and building shed. They would only want to know where he was going and why, and what was in his parcel. Soon now, all the worrying, the hoarding of guilty secrets, would be behind him. He would sail to a new life in the desert, like the adventurers in Karl May's tales. Waldmeister would no longer drone into his ears about Siegfried and the other heroes; Kloth's old man could report him to Dr Gilbrecht; Rolf Sandmann could go to hell. They would never find out he'd gone to Palestine. He would be far beyond their reach. The future was flight and adventure. He would be lonely for a time, but being left alone was what he looked forward to most of all.

It was a sparkling morning. He was whistling to himself when he caught sight of Lore Meinke outside the famous perfume shop on Eppendorfer Landstrasse. She was bouncing a coloured ball against the wall, catching it deftly on the rebound or returning it with her fists, a flat hand, or even her head. Preoccupied with counting and bouncing, she did not notice Hannes until she dropped the ball. He trapped it under his sole.

'My ball, please.' She smiled shyly. He lifted the ball with his toes. She caught it and pressed it to her chest. She wore a green taffeta dress with a clean white collar. Her fringe was as straight as if cut with the help of a ruler. She really was the neatest, the most attractive girl in the whole of Eppendorf.

'What's that under your arm?' she asked him.

'Old magazines.'

'Don't look like old magazines.'

She blinked against the sun.

'You waiting for old Rolf?'

'No.' She shook her head. 'For my aunt. You?'

'I'm going swimming. Thought you might have a date with Rolf. 'Emperor', remember?'

She bounced her ball. 'We don't play that any more.'

'Bet you'd still put the same number if we did.'

'Might,' she said, scratching her knee. 'Might not.'

She was not only pretty, he reflected, she was highly sophisticated. With most girls you couldn't talk like this. They just stood around and giggled. Lore was like Erika. She knew. *Things.*

'Come over to the tram stop a minute. Want to show you something.'

'What for? My auntie's only doing some shopping.'

'Been to Dorn's building shed lately, you know, Bismarck-strasse?'

'Don't like it there,' she said, falling into step with him.

'Don't you like Dorn?'

'Hate him,' she pouted. 'That time he asked me all those questions. Don't you remember?'

'I don't like him either.'

They were conspirators now, exchanging secrets. His heart thumped as he led the way. There was a shelter at the corner, with a white bench, for people who didn't want to wait in the rain. The toilets were next door. There was always a horrid smell there; Hannes had been told old men waited there to give sweets to kids. *Perverts*, Schmitt called them. And Schmitt knew what he was talking about.

'What did you want to show me?' Lore asked.

He produced his knife, removed the blade from its sheath. You weren't supposed to carry it when you were out of uniform, but he was glad he had it on him now.

'Come a bit closer,' he said. 'I'll show you.'

He pulled out one of his hairs and sliced it.

'Rolfie's had one of those for ages,' she said.

'Not like this one. It's the latest model.'

She was close enough for him to count the freckles on her nose. Rolf claimed he had kissed her. On the mouth. She had liked it. Rolf was a liar.

'Take a look at the inscription,' he said.

'I've got to get going,' she said. 'My aunt is short-sighted. She can't see me here.'

'Don't you like it here?'

'Not much.'

He closed his eyes and groped for her hand. She did not withdraw it. He took a deep breath; he did not know what to do next; he let her moist hand fall on her lap.

'What was that in aid of?' she asked.

'Ah,' he said, blinking against the light. Like Rolf would have done.

'You got a dirty mind,' she said. 'I'm surprised at you.' She leant against the wall, ball squeezed under her arm. She examined her fingernails, spoke very calmly. She wasn't nearly as scared as he was.

'Mum says I have one,' she said.

'What? A dirty mind?' Hannes was deeply shocked.

'Everybody has. Bet you have one as well.'

'You mean secrets and things?'

'Sort of secrets.'

'I got lots of secrets,' he boasted. 'More than anyone in Eppendorf.'

'That's what Rolf says.'

'What does he say?'

'That you got secrets.'

'He doesn't know. He couldn't even guess. Nor could you.'

'Bet I could.'

'Bet you couldn't.'

'Is it about Angora?'

She was scrutinising her fingernails, occasionally wetting one between her lips.

'Not interested in her,' he told her contemptuously.

'She is in you, though.'

'I don't care.'

'Not interested in girls, Hannes?'

'Some.'

With a girl like Lore it was hard to keep off the subject of love.

'Go on then,' he reminded her. 'You haven't guessed any of my secrets.'

'I guessed about Angora.'

'You got it wrong. One more guess. Or you'll have to pay me a forfeit.'

'I bet my aunt's looking for me.'

'You can't guess. You owe me a forfeit.'

'I'm not playing.' She dropped her ball, he rushed forward to catch it. Her skin was so smooth, she smelled of soap. He thought of the heat under the pink sunshade. For the first time he noticed the blonde down on her cheeks.

'My auntie's really waiting,' she said. 'Go on, then, you promised – *what* secrets?'

'I'm going away,' he told her.

She seemed disappointed. 'Are you? Where?'

'To England. I'm going to live with a Lord in a park with a dog.'

'What sort of dog?'

'Golden retriever.'

He accompanied her back to the perfume shop. They crossed the road, she started bouncing her ball. Had she lost interest?

'I've got tons more secrets,' he said quickly. 'Exciting ones. I'll tell you for a forfeit.'

'Don't like kissing games.'

She crinkled her nose. He felt ashamed of himself. All he wanted was to kiss her. He would have to make it up to her.

'I'll tell you anyway,' he said. 'My No.1 secret. If you still want to know.'

'All right. Tell me.'

'You won't ever tell a living soul?'

'I won't tell.'

'Swear.'

'Cross my heart and hope to die.'

'I'm . . .' He swallowed . . . 'I'm an Indian.'

'You're not,' she said. 'They look quite different.'

'That's why I'm going to England.'

'They got no Indians in England.'

'I'm only half, really. Half Red Indian.'

'Red Indians don't live in England, either.'

'They do, some of them.'

'Anyway, got to go now,' she said. 'My aunt's just coming out of the shop.'

She hurried away without glancing back, still carrying the ball under her arm. Rolf had told him lies about Lore. He was prepared to bet she'd never kissed anybody on the mouth. She'd slap Rolf's face if he as much as tried.

Still, he and Lore shared secrets now. Perhaps she could even be trusted to know the whole truth. He might write to her. From Palestine. Maybe she wasn't even one hundred per cent Aryan. They would keep each other's secrets. They were as good as engaged. She would come out to the desert, together they would shelter from the heat under a pink shade . . .

Hannes broke into a joyful run.

Rosa did not reply to *La Donn' è Mobile*. The window remained closed. He rang the front-door bell and waited. He rang a second, a third time, surmised she was out; he pressed the bell button of the basement flat. After a few moments, Herr Tetzlaff appeared to ask him what he wanted.

Herr Tetzlaff was grey, sickly-looking, in his sixties; he wore a crooked pince-nez and two days' growth of stubble. His breath smelled of alcohol. Hannes knew from Rosa that, before he had started to drink, Herr Tetzlaff had been a mathematics professor. His wife had left him years ago, now he was just the janitor in the block of flats where he once had a luxurious flat. A *Nebbich*, Rosa called him. For a while he had given algebra lessons to backward boys. Now he served the Party as Blockwarden and spied on everybody. Before Bohrer had appeared on the scene, Rosa had often sent Hannes 'down' with gifts of beer and cigars, knowing that Tetzlaff had the power to have her evicted whenever he wished.

'What is it?' Although it was a fine, warm day, Tetzlaff pressed the lapels of his shabby grey jacket against his throat. 'What did you ring my bell for?'

'My grandmother's gone shopping or something. Could you let me in with your keys?'

Tetzlaff grumbled that he had other things to do besides letting kids into other people's flats, but he admitted Hannes and called the lift. One had to be careful with these Jungvolk types. A bunch of keys bulged in Tetzlaff's pocket, dragging down his trousers, revealing grubby underwear.

Hannes went straight into Rosa's sitting-room and lay down on the chaise-longue. His belly-ache had come back, he had a craving for food to ease the pain. He got up, opened the mahogany sideboard, where Rosa kept surprise bars of chocolate for him. He found nothing except old tablecloths and napkins. He was about to go into the kitchen to scavenge there, when the telephone rang in the consulting-room.

An elderly voice said she was glad to find somebody in, she had tried all morning. She asked for an appointment. Hannes scribbled the name down in Rosa's book; he felt efficient. He found some boring biscuits in the kitchen, then went back to the sitting room, where he stretched himself out on the chaise-longue.

The flat was eerily silent. He could hear himself crunching biscuits. From time to time muted sounds drifted up from the street: a lorry growling over asphalt, a pneumatic drill, a tram clanking in the distance. He felt bored. He finished the biscuits, noticed the grandfather clock had stopped. That would explain the silence. He climbed on a chair, wound up the clock, moved the hands to indicate twelve o'clock. High time Rosa was back from her shopping. And where was Bohrer? As he moved the chair back against the wall, he felt hungry again. It occured to him that a slice of Mama's cake would not be sorely missed. Rosa wouldn't hold it against him. Give her another five minutes. If she hadn't come then, he would eat a slice.

She didn't come. He unwrapped the cake, used his new knife to cut it. After he had eaten one slice he cut himself another, then a third. He lay back on the chaise-longue, munching cake and listening to the grandfather clock. The pain couldn't have been caused by those apples – it was going on for too long. He got up, wrapped the cake so as not to be tempted again. Then he left the room to go to the lavatory.

He opened the door and bumped his head against something large and hard. He recoiled. It wasn't until after he had switched on the light that he saw Rosa's dangling legs, toes pointing at the tiled floor. He staggered back into the corridor, then ran out of the front door. Why did she have her shoes on, he kept asking himself? He slithered down the staircase. Why hadn't they fallen off?

He kept his thumb jammed on the basement bell-push until Tetzlaff appeared.

'Upstairs,' Hannes said, 'I think my grandmother's hanged herself.'

Tetzlaff stared at him, blinked, his watery eyes swimming with disbelief. Then he pushed past Hannes. It took too long to wait for the lift. He started to climb the staircase, wheezing with every step.

'In the lavatory,' Hannes said.

He waited by the door. Tetzlaff went inside. Mustn't forget the cake in the sitting-room, he thought.

'You all right, boy?' Tetzlaff came running out of the lavatory. 'Glass of water, anything? Go and sit down, I'll see to this. Go on . . . in there . . .'

Instead, Hannes went into the consulting-room, just to make sure everything was in order there. The jars and bottles and tubes all stood in their proper places. A clean sheet had been stretched across the table. He went over to the wall calendar. It showed the previous day's date. He tore off the top page, stuffed it into his pocket.

'Better go home, boy. Go home!' Tetzlaff stood at the door; he looked very pale. 'You'd better tell your people. Somebody had better come . . . do the necessary. Want to use the 'phone?'

'Where's Bohrer?' Hannes asked.

Tetzlaff was about to reply, changed his mind, muttered under his breath. Hannes followed him into his grandmother's bedroom.

'Not in here,' Hannes told Tetzlaff, who was opening the wardrobe doors. 'It's her bedroom.'

'His stuff's gone,' Tetzlaff announced, out of breath. 'Hopped it.'

'Hopped it?'

Tetzlaff turned back the eiderdown of Rosa's bed. 'Left his pyjamas, though.'

He's getting it all mixed up, Hannes thought. It's *her* room. Tetzlaff picked up an envelope from the bedside table and handed it to him. 'Meta' was written on it in Rosa's neat handwriting. Hannes folded the envelope, put it into his pocket, close to the knife. So she hadn't written to him. Not even that . . .

Looking up, he found Tetzlaff staring at him over his crooked pince-nez. Hannes turned away, picked up his rolled-up towel and swimming trunks from the sitting room, slammed the front door behind him.

It was warm outside. Why had he felt so cold in the flat? Wilting pink petals from the wild rose bushes had collected all along the edge of the gravel path. He felt goosepimples starting up on his arms. Mustn't be late for his swim. He walked along Loehrsweg in the direction of Schröders Park.

At the corner of Woldsenweg an ice-cream vendor had stopped his cart. Could it be Panse, Eimsbüttel's famous centre-forward, who was reputed to earn his living selling ice-cream in Eppendorf? On a little blackboard the vendor (who turned out to be a stranger) had chalked up available flavours: strawberry, raspberry, vanilla, lemon. The smallest cone cost 5 Pfennigs. Bloody hell, there were no coins in his pocket. Rosa had always told him – one had to have 20 Pfennigs on one, just in case one needed to take the Underground home. Quickly, he tried to think about something else. The ice-cream vendor took no notice of him, he was concentrating on reading his *Anzeiger*, which he held folded; Hannes could just about see

the sports page with a photograph of the Olympic Football Final:
Italy v. Austria. ITALY'S TWO GOLDEN GOALS was the headline.

He walked on; it was a really hot August afternoon, quite
unusually hot for Hamburg. He wanted to take his Jungvolk
cap off, but remembered just in time that it was not allowed.
The pain in his belly was back again. I should have gone straight
home, he told himself.

It was far too late for that now. He could never go home
again. He started to run; they were expecting him at the
swimming baths in Kellinghusenstrasse.

He'd always liked Schröders Park. Rosa used to look after
him, all those years ago, when he played in the sandpit. Later,
that was out; Rosa had observed some kids pissing into the
sand. When it rained, they sheltered under the so-called
Hottentot huts with their thatched roofs. You could pull off
straw in passing. That was not allowed, either. What was
permitted, and then only sometimes in winter, was to glide
over the frozen pond. You could also ride down the hill on a
sledge after a snowfall.

But it was summer; the meadow at the end of the park
was crowded with children playing. This time the young
Kindergarten teacher was sitting out in the open with her
charges, rehearsing a poem.

Swimming things clamped under his arm, Hannes was about
to walk past this small fry when he heard what the teacher
was rehearsing for them in a sing-song voice:

A Murderer the Jew has always been
Says our Good Lord Jesus Christ.

The book lay open on the pretty teacher's lap. She wore
a clean, cream-coloured apron with red and purple rabbits
skilfully stitched on to it. Wanting to make sure their voices
didn't overlap when it came to the refrain, she began to conduct
the children:

So never trust the fox in forest green
Or any Jew wherever seen.

She held up her well-worn copy of 'Bauer's Bilderbuch' so that the children could see the pictures for themselves.

Hannes watched. The young teacher had freckles like Lore Meinke and the same Hamburg accent.

> *They love their Führer true*
> *They fear the Lord in heaven blue*
> *The Jews they must despise*
> *They don't belong, they have to go . . .*

He climbed the stone steps of the municipal swimming baths, where he went with his class on Wednesday afternoons during term time, walked through the entrance marked 'Men'. He showed his identity card to the lady at the door but tried to dodge the supervising pool attendants. He had always hated them, even when he was a little boy, when Rosa had taken him for his weekly swimming lessons. The big men clattered over wet red tiles in clumsy great clogs, booming out orders, you never knew why or at whom. When you wanted your locker opened, they glowered at you.

Hannes got undressed, skipped down the stairs, found a free shower, groped for the hot-water tap. By mistake he switched on the cold. In the instant the icy jets hit his face, he remembered that he had forgotten the cake on Rosa's table. There it would stay, going stale and crumbly, just the kind of fatal mistake the mystery murderer made in an Edgar Wallace novel. He quickly turned off the tap; a spasm of pain throbbed along his thighs, moving upwards, along his sides and arms. He shivered, his knees buckled, as his mind opened to an image he'd tried to shut out.

It wasn't true, it couldn't be.

'Stop that!' somebody shouted.

Hannes realised he had been yelling at the top of his voice. He stumbled to the edge of the pool, teeth chattering. The pain had surged up to his chest, now it was in his throat, his sight became blurred.

As he climbed the rungs to the highest springboard, he could smell chloride, hear a blur of voices below. He held fast to the rails to prevent himself from slipping, then began to walk to the end of the springboard. He stopped, looked down. It's not true, he told himself once more, it's that dream again, the one about the ghost-train. Hadn't she told him she'd wait? Hadn't she said it again and again – all she still wanted was to know what would become of him . . .?

A promise!

'I want to wake up now.' His voice seemed to belong to somebody else. '*I want to wake up! She's betrayed me . . .*' As that final thought hit him, he rocked on his heels, stumbled, fell forward into space.

The searing pain he felt as he crashed, belly first, into the water shut out everything else. He tried to crawl towards the side of the pool – like a dog. His muscles refused to obey. He tried to call for help, sour water splashed into his mouth.

'Don't want to, don't want to,' he kept thinking as he went under. Huge hands now pulled at him, nails clawed and scratched, fingers clutched him by the throat, pulling him further into the depths. He felt his limp body dragged over the marbled edge of the pool. Someone had thrown a towel over his shoulders, anonymous hands were rubbing his back. Water burned like acid in his nose and throat, he had to breathe through his mouth, he could hear his own chattering teeth. When he finally opened his eyes he glanced down along his legs, saw his toes pointing towards the water's surface. Now he knew for certain he was not dreaming. None of it had been a dream. Not any of it. He started to scream until, finally, someone held a towel over his gaping mouth.

POSTSCRIPT

verdrängen [fɛr'drɛŋən], *reg.v.t.* drive out *or* away, dislodge, displace, supersede, supplant, oust, push *or* thrust aside, expel, crowd out; (*Psych. etc.*) suppress, repress; *verdrängte Bevölkerung*, displaced population. **Verdrängung**, *f.* removal, ousting, dispossession, displacement (*also Naut.*); (*Psych.*) suppression, repression.

The German verb *verdrängen* is evidently untranslatable – at least into English. A pity, since post-war Germany has twice been assailed by *Verdrängung* on a massive scale.

Generations of Germans have been accused of *Verdrängung* – of *thrusting away*, of *pushing out of the mind* undeniable truths associated with guilt, with responsibility for evil. The use of words like *Holocaust* and *Stasi* are classic instances of *Verdrängung*. They provide a wall behind which one can conceal complicated or uncomfortable emotions. Six million murdered Jews, nearly half a century of dictatorship, are reduced to statistics or words that do not inflict pain.

Shelves of books have been written about the German people's apparent inability to ponder the roles they played in their country's tragic twentieth-century history, their refusal to acknowledge, come to terms with, *mourn* the systematic killing of millions of *fellow citizens* whom they neither feared nor hated. That these mass murders were committed during an aggressive war fought simultaneously on several fronts is too horrific an idea to be faced squarely. It has to be kept at bay, balanced with or set against the crimes of other nations, in some way rationalised or even denied. It certainly cannot be allowed to clog the business of living.

Verdrängung has now been going on in Germany for so long, it lies so deeply embedded in the nation's conscience, that the majority of 're-united' German people now fervently wish to 'draw a final line' under events 'that happened so long ago'. They also long to be told by obscure politicians or 'historians', whom they don't even respect, that the Holocaust was 'propaganda', that Auschwitz never happened at all. If such fantasies could be proved (and they can, of course, never be proved) what a great liberation of stricken consciences that would cause, what a bright signal to start all over again with a clean sheet . . .

It is not, however, other people's *Verdrängung* with which this addendum is concerned, a postscript to a novel (my second) that I wrote during the years 1957–8.

It is my own.

The World that Summer was written as a fictionalised memoir of my childhood in Hitler's Germany. I did not want my memories to fade, wanted to bear witness to what it was like to live as a non-Aryan boy in a Nazi state. I also wanted to describe daily life in the city of Hamburg under Hitler, and evoke the fascination of Fascism that held millions spellbound. Finally, and most importantly, I felt impelled to depict the most cherished relationship of my early years, the love for my Jewish grandmother. It was a *forbidden* love: a 'normal' German boy could not have a Jewish grandmother, let alone admit his love for her if he wanted to survive.

Leaving aside the conventional disguises of all autobiographical fiction there is one indisputable truth I share with my novel's hero, Hannes Hacker: a loving relationship with a grandmother whose existence had to be denied, a love – and I didn't 'know' this when I wrote the book – that was to become the emotional *Leitmotif* of my life. But . . .

I did not tell the truth.

In the novel's final chapter, Hannes Hacker visits his

grandmother's flat, as he does every Friday. There, in the lavatory, he finds her hanging by the neck. The stories of Hannes Hacker and Robert Muller have many parallels. In this instance I *automatically* veered away from the truth – a typical instance of *Verdrängung*. In 1957, twelve years after the end of the war, I simply could not *face* the awfulness of what really happened to my grandmother. The basic facts are simply told: I escaped from Hamburg on a so-called *Kindertransport* in 1938 when I was thirteen. My parents followed a few months later, just before the war started. What I have needed to *thrust away* ever since is that I started a new life and left my grandmother to her fate . . .

After the war I knew of course that my grandmother, like so many of my relatives, had 'perished in the Holocaust'. I allowed myself to be fobbed off with a convenient story, concocted by well-meaning relatives in a neutral country, that the Nazis had *evacuated* my grandmother from Hamburg, that they had sent her on a ship destined for Riga and that the ship was sunk by an allied submarine.

It wasn't until I was sixty-four – my grandmother's age when she disappeared – that I finally felt the need to search out the facts of my grandmother's death. I found old letters, visited archives and libraries, talked to authorities in Hamburg who collected known facts behind the mass deportations. These 'evacuations', I discovered, were organised by local bureaucrats even *before* the famous 'Final Solution' was decreed by their masters.

For half a century, neither federal nor local government made genuine efforts to investigate this mass murder of fellow citizens. There were 'files', of course, but I found them incomplete: the secret of my grandmother's murder died with her; in the great and prosperous Federal Republic it was nobody's responsibility. The dutiful city fathers of Hamburg (who for several decades nurtured the myth that Hamburg remained actively anti-Nazi during the Hitler years) understandably felt no compulsion to incriminate their fathers and grandfathers. I was to find out that their predecessors had not sought to procure a quick death for their Jews.

In order to free homes and flats for more deserving citizens, Hamburg's non-Aryans were herded into so-called 'Jew houses'. They were then harassed and hunted by hundreds of bureaucratic *edicts* invented by administrators who, to the end of their days, claimed that they were only doing their duty.

Some of these edicts were merely grotesque. Others show a desktop sadism that beggars belief. These edicts came hard and fast. Non-Aryans were forbidden to keep pets. They had their radios confiscated. They had their telephones cut off. They were forbidden to move to another street or town. They were certainly not allowed to emigrate. They could buy curtailed rations only at specific times, in particular shops. They were not allowed to go out after eight o'clock at night. They were forbidden to visit cafés, cinemas, theatres, sports grounds. They had to 'sell off', (i.e. *consent* to have stolen from them) all their valuables. From the age of six, they were forced to wear the yellow star. They were refused soap rations, forbidden to use public transport, not allowed to enter public libraries. And all this time the victims of this teutonic torture, people like my grandmother, continued to tell themselves: *Things could not get worse because, at heart, the Germans liked the Jews. As much as the Jews liked the Germans* . . .

I still ask myself: were these bureaucrats not busy enough with fighting their war on several fronts, with cleaning up the streets after the bombardments, with endless wartime shortages? Evidently not. Petty-minded restrictions continued to be devised until, in the end, people like my grandmother, the Jews of Hamburg, of Germany, had been robbed of everything except their lives.

The day came – as it had to – when my grandmother received a curt letter requiring her to report for 'evacuation to the East'. Seven hundred and twenty-seven other non-Aryans (including the city's Chief Rabbi) reported to board this particular train – the fourth of seventeen such cattle-truck transports destined for Riga. (Other trains had destinations like Minsk, Auschwitz, Theresienstadt). The unspecified 'orders from on high' must have provided an extraordinarily heavy work-load for Hamburg's dedicated railway staff during that winter of 1941–42.

What happened to my grandmother in Riga? I still don't know and have become reconciled to the fact that I shall never know. Nobody knows. Nobody has bothered to find out. Nobody is *zuständig*, another word for which there is no counterpart in English. Try: *proper, appropriate, authorised, responsible, competent*. I can only guess. Possibly my grandmother was sent to a nearby concentration camp. Or marched off in the snow to the local ghetto whose inhabitants (with irrefutable logic) had been murdered to make room for the new arrivals. Possibly she was herded into an icy forest outside Riga and shot. Or she never left the station since it had been found more convenient to shoot thousands of new arrivals on the spot and to bury them under the rails.

I never found out exactly how my grandmother died because there is no grave, no stone, no record, no file. She certainly did not (like her fictional counterpart) end her own life before the ultimate horror began.

The World that Summer was first published in an earlier version in 1959. It has been dramatised and made into a film. For republication in English and German I have edited my prose style but have not changed the structure or the characters. It's the story I wrote all those years ago – the story of a time remembered by most Germans as the idyllic, sunny Olympic summer of 1936. This time, however, I did not want that story to be read without the addition of my own confession – the truth behind the fiction.

ROBERT MULLER
May 1994